BLACK
SOL

Praise for *Black Sol*

'Mihir is intense! Mihir is brutal! Mihir is focused! Mihir is unforgiving! Mihir is an avenger! Mihir is a gentleman! He is my type of guy.'

—**P. Bilimoria, media professional**

'Hard-hitting facts about the current times ... the writer has woven a spell that leaves us yearning for more. His style of storytelling is spellbinding and crisp!'

—**Lt Col. Vikrant Adhikari, Indian Army**

'Captivating, fast-paced depiction of the dark world of human trafficking, efficiently tackled by a competent army man.'

—**Dr P. Warty, oncologist**

'*Black Sol* was a day's read for me. Unputdownable! Exciting edge-of-the-seat plot! I loved the detailing of the locations, clearly something that's etched and very well researched. The nuggets of information are very cool. It's an out-and-out thriller. Also, I'm a sucker for places, and went hunting for those places on Google Maps and Google Earth. I suppose place names have been altered a bit, except key cities (please do let me know, it's eating me up!). I've grown up in the Northeast, and the description of the terrain and weather, how it feels to live in that climate, it's real.'

—**Lt Sandhya Suri, author, Indian Navy veteran**

BLACK SOL

VENGEANCE IN THE HEART OF DECEIT

SACHIN WARTY

HARPER
FICTION

An Imprint of HarperCollins *Publishers*

First published in India by Harper Fiction 2024
An imprint of HarperCollins *Publishers*
4th Floor, Tower A, Building No. 10, DLF Cyber City,
DLF Phase II, Gurugram, Haryana—122002
www.harpercollins.co.in

2 4 6 8 10 9 7 5 3 1

Copyright © Sachin Warty 2024

P-ISBN: 978-93-5699-660-1
E-ISBN: 978-93-5699-904-6

This is a work of fiction and all characters and incidents described in this book are the product of the author's imagination. Any resemblance to actual persons, living or dead, is entirely coincidental.

Sachin Warty asserts the moral right
to be identified as the author of this work.

All rights reserved. No part of this publication may be reproduced, stored in a retrieval system, or transmitted, in any form or by any means, electronic, mechanical, photocopying, recording or otherwise, without the prior permission of the publishers.

Typeset in 11/14 Minion Pro at
Manipal Technologies Limited, Manipal

Printed and bound at
Thomson Press (India) Ltd

To Radhika, Atharv and Bhrugu,
my whole world.

Prologue

12 January 2018

Sneha, a young woman, was travelling alone in a prepaid taxi from Terminal 3 of the Indira Gandhi International Airport, New Delhi. She wished her brother was there to pick her up, as promised; she would have felt safer with him around. They were orphaned early in life and he had always been there to look after Sneha, to care for her.

But not today. As usual, his leave had been cancelled at the last moment. What could have been a long-overdue reunion for the siblings was now a lonely weekend for her.

It was nearly 2 a.m., foggy and very cold. Their apartment was still another thirty minutes away. Sneha was tired from her long flight, half-asleep, curled up in a corner of the rear seat. Somewhere along a dark, isolated stretch of a partially constructed road, the cab slowed, then pulled up to the left and stopped. An instant later, the door was yanked open.

Sneha was dragged out by two assailants and tossed into a small ditch next to the road. Despite being disoriented and shocked by her rude awakening, she tried to escape. But she was dragged back by her legs and pinned down by the two men. The third man, her cab driver, ripped her skirt and panties off; another tore her jacket and bra off her body. She lay naked and shivering on the cold, wet earth. Helpless, frightened and mortified, Sneha screamed. Her desperate cries for help petered out into the black night. No one could hear her, no one would come to rescue her.

Leering, the cab driver spread Sneha's legs, his hands reaching for the zipper of his trousers. They took turns, repeatedly. After they had finished, they sat around her violated and bleeding form, laughing and abusing her. Later, all three got up and took turns to kick Sneha in the face, again, and again, and again.

∼

A few weeks later, a shadowy figure stood on the outskirts of a small, dusty village in a dull corner of Gurugram, bordering Delhi. It was hard to believe that such a place could exist so close to the national capital and its relentless, non-stop pace. The quietude of the village was in sharp contrast to the modern, noisy and flashy culture Delhi had come to reflect in recent times.

The village had the usual mix of pucca and kutcha houses. Its population was no more than 5,000. It was a hamlet, where social distinctions were clearly visible in the layout and relative prosperity of the localities. The so-called prosperous side was made almost entirely of bricks and mortar; the clean roads had covered drains and streetlights. A few hundred metres away, packed cheek by jowl, were a few score kutcha houses made of clay and mud—the poor section. The sad hovels were separated by narrow, filthy by lanes, with almost no drainage systems. It was pitch dark in this part of the village.

The figure looked at his watch. Midnight. It was bitterly cold. He was all alone, with just a sliver of a moon amid wispy clouds for company. The street was deserted and the villagers were in deep slumber. Except for the barking of the odd stray dog, the settlement was quiet. He was dressed in all-black, merging into the surrounding darkness.

The figure approached the main road that ran through the centre of the village. It was well-lit and, hence, not the ideal way to approach his target, but it was the only one available. The house he intended to visit was the tenth in a row of seventeen, all of them packed tightly together. A large courtyard was enclosed by a high wall. In one corner was a shed for cows and buffaloes. There was just one door giving access to the courtyard and the house beyond on the opposite end. The dwelling would normally have a large veranda and four to five rooms, with a kitchen. The toilet was separate from the main house, in one corner of the courtyard.

Walking towards the first electricity pole, he searched on all sides and found what he was looking for. At about 6 feet from the ground, fixed on a concrete pole, was a rectangular box, the size of a small shoe carton, with a lever about 6 inches in length on one side. He pulled the lever down gently. The entire street went dark. He waited for five minutes. Nobody reacted.

He now walked slowly towards the tenth house and its occupants. It had not been easy finding those responsible, but he was a man driven by vengeance, refusing to give up till he had what he wanted. His informant had told him that all three targets were living in the same house—forty-five-year-old father, twenty-year-old son and the father's nineteen-year-old nephew. There was one woman—perhaps the mother of the twenty-year-old—who would be spared. Not the others. Those three deserved to die, painfully.

The shadowy figure had prepared carefully for this night—days upon days of reconnaissance and discreet watch over the targets, till he knew them better than even their mothers. His buddies had volunteered to help, but he had refused. It was his score to settle and his alone.

Finally, he was ready. His moral conscience was buried deep beneath seething anger. Tonight's plan would free his soul from the endless, guilt-ridden torment it had lived through over the past few weeks. Soon, it would all be over.

The man approached the house and stood still, listening to sounds emanating from within on the off chance that the occupants might be awake. Not likely, but he was cautious. Five minutes later, he scaled the low wall noiselessly and landed on his feet in a crouch, silent as a ghost. Using the cover of the cattle shed, he approached the veranda. The cows stared at him and continued to chew their cud.

He took the first door on the left, where he knew the older man would be. If he was with his wife, it could get messy. But he was past caring. He tried the doorknob. Locked from the inside. No surprises there. He walked to the centre door and tried the knob. It turned. Careless fuckers, he thought. But then, they had no reason to be careful. He stepped inside, silent as a ghost. Standing very still, he slowly scanned the layout of the room. He identified two figures sleeping on a bed just wide enough to accommodate them. The room stank of stale air.

Knocking them unconscious in their sleep, he bound and gagged them, heaved them onto his shoulders with ease, as if they weighed nothing, and dropped them in the centre of the courtyard. The man then retraced his steps into the room. He had noticed a small door in one corner, probably leading to the main room on the left where his last target slept. He turned the knob. Locked. Only one option left. Using his strength, he ripped the knob and its entire mechanism from the door. On the other side, the sudden noise woke up both occupants. As they looked around, dazed and confused in the darkness, a huge figure materialized in front of them. He slapped the woman with just enough force to knock her unconscious. He then dragged the man by his neck and threw him in the courtyard next to the unconscious pair.

The older guy looked up at him, eyes wide with panic. The eyes that stared back at him looked like two burning embers of coal. The father tried to shout, but no sound came from his throat. Naked terror had taken control of his mind. Sweating profusely, despite the cold, he watched helplessly as his attacker reached behind him and took out a khukri, his weapon of choice. The older man wet his pajamas.

The hooded man gagged all three men. No point in waking up the neighbours with their agonizing shrieks of pain thanks to what he was going to inflict upon the prone figures. With a look of raging anger and hatred, he got down to the task at hand. He began with the eldest. The other two, who had woken up by now, watched in horror as the hooded figure sliced the older man's ears off, then gouged out his eyes and threw them at his feet. The older man tried to shriek, the pain intolerable, but he gagged on his spit as the dark fluid from his punctured eyes ran down his face. The intruder then tore open the man's shirt to systematically work his way down.

The other two watched in horror at the sight unfolding. Aware that a similar fate awaited them, they made desperate attempts to untie themselves. The intruder continued his work. It was going to be a long night. He did not bother to look at the gory mess he was making.

In the village, no one had even stirred.

1

Delta Company Operating Base, Unit 263, Northeast corner of India

21 December 2020
1.45 a.m.

The Company Operating Base (COB in army jargon) was located about 500 metres north of an isolated junction of two roads, called the North Karimpuhl Bypass Road and Bisota Road. North Karimpuhl was the nearest town of any significance, about 3 kilometres from Bisota, the location of the COB. It was a dark night, with a slight breeze. The base was silent. All activities had wound down and the soldiers had retired for the night, except for the guards on the perimeter towers. All lights had been switched off. In one hut, however, a night lamp continued to burn. The throw of its light was reined in by carefully drawn curtains.

Chris was very careful; he did not want to draw any unnecessary attention towards his hut. Seated at his study table, he sipped warm brandy in a goblet, continuously twirling the fluid. He was apprehensive at the thought of what he might uncover in a few hours and the brandy calmed his nerves. He waited patiently.

Exactly fifteen minutes later, Chris got up, switched off the lamp and left the hut quietly. He was dressed in black, invisible to all, except a trained eye. The stars and the half-moon were hidden by dark clouds; fog was beginning to build up as if seeping out of the porous, wet earth. Visibility was down to a few feet. It was perfect for his task, he thought, with a faint smile on his lips. This was one meeting he wanted to keep to himself. After that, he would be ready.

Moving along the wall of his hut and staying within its shadow, Chris moved quickly to the next one, tucked away in the south-west corner of the camp. It was 25 feet from the fence and empty at this time of the night. Crouching down on his haunches, he crawled to the fence, next to a small gap, which could barely fit a man. At the fence, lying still, he waited, listening intently for any sound out of the ordinary. Hearing nothing, he crossed over.

Chris then sprang up and began moving quickly, eager to keep his rendezvous as planned. Twenty-nine years old, standing at 5 feet and 10 inches, and weighing 75 kilos, he was lean, athletic and in peak physical condition. In combat gear, with a 5.56-mm INSAS rifle, he could finish his battle physical endurance test of 5 kilometres in under twenty-one minutes, averaging four minutes and twelve seconds to a kilometre—much faster than the required time of twenty-five minutes. Tonight, he was more comfortably dressed and armed with only a Fairbairn-Sykes fighting knife, a family heirloom carried by his grandfather in World War II, and then his father in the 1965 and 1971 India–Pakistan wars. It would be easy to cover the 8 kilometres to his rendezvous point north-west of the camp—thirty-two minutes one way, Sixty-four minutes total for the return trip. Fifteen minutes at the most with his contact. That would make it seventy-nine minutes. Chris could be back in his hut by 3.55 a.m. and first light on 21 December would be at 5.58 a.m. Plenty of time.

Moving south-west, he came across Bisota Road. Chris turned right and started jogging on the black tar surface, using it as a navigation aid. It was a narrow, one-way road built on an embankment—a common feature in the region where heavy rains were the norm and where roads are elevated to keep them free from floods during monsoons. After a kilometre, he crossed the Jama Masjid, a poor, small-scale replica of the original one in Delhi. About 200 metres later, the road turned sharply to the south-west. Chris left the comfort of the road and moved in a westerly direction, cross-country, towards the town of Bilbor, more than a kilometre away.

The place itself was divided into two parts—the eastern bigger than the western—separated by a seasonal river about 300-metres wide. At this time of the year, the riverbed was partially dry and could be crossed on foot at some places. Years of experience in counterinsurgency in Jammu and Kashmir and the Northeast had taught him one valuable lesson—avoid human habitation like the plague.

Villages and towns tend to be quiet at night. But they are also unintentionally equipped with one of the most ancient and effective early warning systems of the world—street dogs. They could sniff out an outsider a few hundred metres away. It normally began with the barking of one dog and, within seconds, there would be a continuous chorus as the other canines reciprocated the call. It was a foolproof system of warning that could destroy the most elaborate of plans. Let sleeping dogs lie, he thought, and turned left to give the town a wide berth, leaving it well to the north of his path.

It was exactly this logic that had prompted the source to pick an isolated spot for their meeting. He also happened to be a resident of Bilbor and left the town at about the same time that Chris was crawling out of the gap in the wire fence. Walking south, he left the last hutments behind him and chose a small culvert on the kutcha road as a navigation aid, and turned west into the fields. An unseasonal downpour the previous night had left the fields with 6 inches of standing water.

He negotiated the fields by walking on a small, raised portion created by the farmers that not only separated the fields, but kept the water level even.

By now, fog had enveloped the whole countryside. He could barely see anything ahead of him. It was troublesome, but worked to his advantage. Walking another 2 kilometres, he saw the distinct outline of tall trees. They spread in a north-to-south direction for about 300 metres. He picked a spot next to a distinct, dead tree, easily recognizable as all the others were lush, thick with leaves. The man had a strange sense of empathy towards this tree. Its death, in sharp contrast to so much life around it, was not very different from his life. He reached the spot and waited. With a few minutes to prepare, he glanced nervously over his shoulder every few seconds, as if expecting someone to materialize out of the shadows. Despite the cold, he was sweating, from a sense of dread that chills one to the bones when chances of survival are slim. Tonight, he was petrified. They would kill his family if he did not do exactly as they told him to. He had no choice.

Unknown to Chris and the source, a young, diminutive man from the hills in the north, dressed in black overalls, a balaclava covering his head, leaving only his eyes exposed, quietly left a settlement a couple of kilometres west of the rendezvous point and made his way on a small track heading east towards a junction of roads called Joodipath. He moved north on this road for about 500 metres, before turning east towards a riverbed. He crossed the stream at its widest, shallowest point and climbed up an embankment where he had a clear view of the dead tree about 100 metres ahead of him to the east.

The little man lay down on the ground and took out a pair of night-vision goggles from his knapsack. The device had a catadioptric telescope which gave him a wider, aberration-free field of view. As he switched it on, the landscape in front of him developed an eerie, green hue. It took a few seconds before his eyes adjusted to the vision through the scope. He could now clearly discern the terrain in front of him, especially the dead tree, his primary focal point.

Reaching behind him with his right hand, he retrieved a semi-automatic pistol. Equipped with a polymer grip, it was a snug weapon that operated on the principle of short recoil and was designed with a non-rotating barrel lock. It used a subsonic round that created less noise and came with a magazine of 20 rounds. He screwed on a suppressor. The weapon had been the young man's companion for many years and was his trusted instrument of choice. He settled down and waited.

Chris was now half a kilometre from the point where he was to meet the source. He could faintly make out the line of trees against the dark sky, exactly towards the west. Being cautious, he decided not to approach the meeting point from the most obvious direction. Turning north, Chris walked for about 300 metres before turning west. The dead tree was now clearly visible, diagonally across from him. Chris continued walking in a westward direction till he was positioned exactly north of the tree line, with the dead tree in it. Nimble-footed and using the thicket to conceal his approach, he began to move towards his destination, which was now about 100 metres ahead of him.

Chris's movements were picked up by the prone figure through his night-vision device. The officer's movement impressed him as he moved furtively through the undergrowth. The soldier was good, extremely good. Had it not been for the night-vision goggles in his hands, it would have been nearly impossible to detect the officer's movement. The prone figure unstrapped the night-vision device, got up quietly from his position on the embankment and began to move silently towards the dead tree.

At the same instant that the hooded figure got up to move, Chris, as if alerted, suddenly stopped about 50 metres short of the meeting point. He had sensed movement in the tall grass towards his right. He listened hard, holding his breath, instinctively closing his hand around the knife. Five minutes passed, then ten. He heard nothing. He waited for another two, before moving again, this time more tentatively. He was certain he had picked up movement. How was it possible that somebody would be at the exact same place and time that he was scheduled to meet his source? Too much of a coincidence. And Chris did not believe in coincidences. He was now a few feet away from his source and could easily see the villager's silhouette. Chris listened intently, keeping his gaze turned slightly away, not looking directly at the place where he had suspected the movement, trying to catch any patterns out of the ordinary. Hearing and seeing nothing, he half rose from his crouch and resumed his movement to his meeting point, just a few metres away. The source never saw or sensed Chris's arrival and was startled as he turned around to face him.

The man from the foothills knew that his field craft was as good as his adversary, Chris's, if not better. He was surprised when Chris picked up on his movement. For a moment, there was panic. He thought that he had blown it and lay very still in the thick underbrush. A few tense minutes passed before he saw Chris resume his movement. He relaxed and smiled to himself. The soldier should have listened to his instincts.

A few feet later, he hunkered down behind a tree just a few feet shy of where both men, his targets, were standing close to each other, deep in conversation. Their voices were so hushed, the conversation did not even carry a few feet to where he was hiding. The assassin got up slowly from his crouched position, raised himself on his left knee and planted his foot firmly for stability, his right leg relaxed. Placing his left elbow on his raised leg, he cupped his hand in the shape of a makeshift cradle and placed his right hand, the one holding the weapon, into the hollow of the cradle. The weapon was now aimed at Chris's midsection. Even under normal circumstances and in broad daylight, it would have been a difficult shot; the target was oblique to the line of fire. He could not afford to miss. If the officer got away alive, the whole plot could unravel. The consequences could be quite unpleasant.

A short barrel makes a pistol inaccurate. The position of the target also increases the degree of difficulty. To obviate the problem, the man fired two rounds in quick succession, a double tap, towards the dark silhouette that was Chris. The suppressor muffled the sound of the shot. The bullet travelled the 20 feet between the assassin and Chris at 900 feet per second. The time taken by the bullet to travel to its intended target would be twenty milliseconds. At the instant that the pistol was fired, Chris turned towards the direction from where the rounds had been fired, warned as if by instinct. The first bullet missed its mark by less than 3 millimetres, and merely grazed Chris's jacket as it went through the gap between his abdomen and left arm. He was not so lucky with the second one, which followed a millisecond later. Since the killer was at a lower level than Chris, the bullet entered his right side in an upward trajectory between the bottom two false ribs. It ruptured the liver and then the heart in the right ventricle and exited through the left, puncturing the left lung and deflecting off the left collarbone before exiting the body.

Chris went down senseless—breathing, but barely alive. He knew he would be dead in a minute. Just then, as if on some morbid cue, the moon slid out from behind the clouds, bathing the earth with its white luminescence. The killer got up from his crouched position, walked the short distance to the prone figure of the dying soldier and looked down at him through remorseless eyes. He lowered his weapon and aimed carefully, his stance casual, legs spread apart, his left thumb loosely tucked inside his belt. Through his shocked, dying eyes, a moment before the third round shattered his head, Chris saw a strange earring hanging from his killer's left earlobe, resembling a hideous skull. The moonlight shone eerily on it, accentuating its ugliness.

The assassin then turned towards the source and raised his weapon, aiming it between the terrified eyes of the villager from Bilbor and fired. Then, sitting down on his haunches, he went through both the dead men's pockets, retrieving a small diary from the source and quickly glanced through its contents. He put it away in his jacket. The killer rummaged some more, this time through Chris's clothes, and came across a knife. It was nearly 12-inches long, with a 7-inch blade. The moment he touched it, he knew it was a masterpiece. In mint condition, beautifully crafted and precise in its make, the knife fit snugly into the palm of his hand. Engraved just below the hilt, on the blade, was 'Major Steven Zachariah 1942'. A soldier's family. As a professional in the business of killing, this was a trophy that the assassin would keep for himself. The dead officer lying on the wet earth in front of him would not mind for he had no need for it now.

A minute later, his job finished, he keyed in a coded message to a predesignated recipient. It was received and deleted almost immediately at both ends, leaving no trace of the communication. With no further instructions, the killer disappeared into the night without a trace.

2

He walked in a daze to the gruesome site. It had been more than four days. It was a cold, grey morning, foggy and wet. The earth beneath his feet was hard, but he felt nothing; his mind was numbed by shock. Dreading what he would now see, he walked down the short slope to the nullah hidden by dense undergrowth. The stink of the stagnating sewer hit his nostrils. And then, he saw her as she lay, head and torso beneath the water, belly and legs bloodied and mutilated. He felt light-headed, part of something surreal. He tried to run, but his feet refused to move. His breath, short and raspy in the cold air, felt as if it was being sucked out from his body.

With a start, Mihir Pratap Singh sat up in bed; his muscled torso bathed in sweat, heart beating rapidly, eyes flitting from corner to corner. His mind quickly absorbed the familiar surroundings—he was home. He calmed down.

It had been almost three years since that terrible night, but the nightmares continued to haunt him, etched in his tormented mind. His guilt made him remember, which only magnified the pain. He looked at the bedside clock; it was three in the morning. He rose and walked slowly to the glass door overlooking the bedroom balcony and stared at the vast countryside beyond. The night sky was thick with rain clouds; streaks of lightning illuminating the horizon. It would rain soon.

Naked and half-awake, Mihir turned and walked around the dark apartment, the cold weather kept at bay by central heating. He looked around, eyes searching the flat. His subconscious mind still hoped to find Sneha—her eyes full of laughter, her warm embrace still fresh in his mind. Maybe she would materialize from one of the many dark shadows that now engulfed the emptiness of his home.

But the apartment remained silent, hollow. Crestfallen and angry at himself, Mihir walked over to the bathroom and showered in ice-cold water, punishing himself awake. Donning track pants and a jogging top, he closed the front door and sprinted eleven storeys up to the roof of the apartment block, barely out of breath.

Sneha was still on his mind when Mihir stepped on to the roof. Placing himself at its centre, eyes closed, hands folded in prayer, he began a series of fluid, graceful movements, which seemed like a combination of gymnastics and dance, but were actually an intense physical regimen from an ancient Indian martial art, considered by some experts as the oldest in the world.

Mihir's muscled 6-foot, 3-inch frame looked ominous in the dark night. Each movement was filled with pent-up anger and regret. There was a dull ache somewhere in the corner of his heart.

The regimen continued at an intense pace for two hours. The workout exhausted him, finally relaxing his tense muscles and calming him down. The vestiges of his nightmare retreated to the recesses of his mind—at least for now.

At first light, as Mihir was descending the stairs to his apartment on the sixth floor, the squall finally hit Gurugram with a loud crack of thunder and blinding lightning. He showered again and got ready for work. It would be a bleak day, matching the sombreness of his mood.

DLF Cyber City in Gurugram, located in sectors 24 and 25A, is an Information Technology Enabled Services Special Economic Zone (ITES SEZ). Spread over nearly 15 hectares of prime land, it is one of the leading business hubs in the National Capital Region. It houses some of the world's top multinationals and is virtually the centre of gravity of the capital's IT business. Situated within Cyber City, catering to the people working there, is Cyber Hub, a vast, swanky courtyard of cafes, restaurants, pubs and even an amphitheatre. In one such café sat Rehaan Khan, casually observing his thirty-one-year-old colleague and former special forces senior, over a cup of cinnamon cappuccino.

Shortly after Mihir was forced to leave the army, his closest friend, Captain Rehaan Khan, had followed in his company commander's footsteps. Together, they had established a security firm—not the run-of-the-mill kind that dotted the urban landscape, and provided security guards to housing societies and offices, but a very specialized one. The firm hired only a handful, but the very best. Service in India's special forces was a prerequisite. Each member was a battle-hardened veteran of years spent in anti-terror and counterinsurgency operations in the Kashmir Valley and the Northeast.

Mihir and Rehaan's company operated under the radar. It was officially listed as a security consultancy, but there were no advertisements, no hoardings; only word of mouth. It had a select clientele.

'Bad night? Nightmares?' asked Rehaan, guessing the reason behind his senior's sense of unease.

'They never seem to leave,' a red-eyed Mihir replied, picking up his cup of black coffee.

'You've had your vengeance. That was nearly three years ago.'

'Justice was served, as it should have been on such vermin.'

'You can't keep blaming yourself for what happened to her.'

'I wasn't there when she needed me the most. Raped and mutilated. I can't get that image out of my mind. I still hear her in my nightmares. How she must have pleaded with her rapists. Her shrieks and cries that night, begging for mercy, for her life. How her frail body must have tried to ward off her attackers,' hissed Mihir angrily, through clenched teeth.

'I wonder if this was what we risk our lives for,' he added, as an afterthought.

Rehaan acknowledged the moot point that soldiers always worried about their families back home, especially those living in remote small towns and villages, where the administration and the law existed only in name, making their families vulnerable to criminals and predators such as land sharks. The disconnect between those on the streets and those in uniform was disconcerting. Except for platitudes by leaders on television about the courage of soldiers defending the nation's borders, there was little empathy for those in service of the nation. The soldiers were often shocked by the shabby treatment meted out to them by some people. It was this attitude that made you wonder if it was all even worth it.

~

While Mihir sat with his friend in Gurugram, 2,300 kilometres away, a quiet, uneventful night had turned into a frenzied morning when the men realized that their commander, Chris, was missing. His continued absence led them to organize a search around the premises, which drew a blank. A sense of concern crept in as the men realized something was not right. Standard operating procedure kicked in and the HQ was informed. Within minutes, quick-reaction teams were dispatched and a tracker squad was requisitioned from the neighbouring dog unit. Lieutenant Colonel Sumer Singh, a tough, no-nonsense guy and the unit second-in-command, took charge of the search operation. He was determined to find the missing officer.

At around the same time in Kochi, Kerala, Genevieve Zachariah, oblivious to the tragedy unfolding far away in the east, was getting ready for another long, exhausting day at her office. Gene, as she was called, was not only the director of a finance company but also the owner of a fashion modelling agency. Life had been maddeningly busy and she hadn't spoken to Chris in the last two days. They did WhatsApp each other, though. In fact, she had received a message the previous night, in which he had promised to come home to celebrate Christmas—their first together in nearly two years. She glowed just thinking about the prospect.

At midday, Gene's phone buzzed—a number she did not recognize was calling. At first, she did not pick up, apprehensive of unknown callers. But this caller seemed persistent. She finally answered out of exasperation.

'Hello! Is that Mrs Zachariah?' asked Lt Col Sumer Singh.

'Yes,' she replied.

As she listened, her world crashed around her.

~

It was early in the evening when Mihir, back in his apartment after a busy day at work, received the call from Genevieve, his old friend's wife. Through her sobs, he heard the news in silence. He sat thinking for a long time after he hung up the phone. Around midnight, he got up, packed an overnight bag and left for the airport.

The funeral was held two days later in an old church in Kochi. The place was full of friends and family. There was also an officer from Chris's old unit, which happened to be Mihir's old one too.

Standing in the second pew, Mihir watched as people went to the coffin to pay their last respects. Grief-stricken, broken and helpless, Gene was standing in the front row with Chris's parents, her own parents and other relatives. No parent wishes to outlive their children.

As Mihir expressed his condolences to Genevieve, the officer walked up and shook his hand.

'Hello Mihir, long time,' he said solemnly.

'Karan.'

'This is quite a shock. When was the last time you spoke to Chris?'

'I don't remember ... Maybe a couple of months ago. Any idea what happened?'

'I spoke with the unit. We only know that he was shot twice while meeting a source.'

'And the source?' Mihir asked.

'Found dead within a few feet of Chris. Also shot,' Karan said.

'And where exactly was this?'

'That is the intriguing part. He had gone out of the base alone. Nobody knew where he was until a search party with tracker dogs located both bodies a few miles from the unit base,' Karan explained.

'What the hell was he doing there alone?'

'Beats me. You know the standard procedure. A court of inquiry has been ordered. Well, I will let you know if something comes up.' He shook Mihir's hand before leaving.

It was late afternoon by the time the ceremony got over. Mihir followed the family as the coffin was loaded on to the hearse for Chris's final journey, under an overcast sky. Beyond the compound of the church, the narrow road was full of cars, with their headlights on, negotiating the evening traffic. Office workers returning home to their families. Life seemed to carry on with an almost unemotional relish. But for Chris's family, life would never be the same again.

Standing on the steps, bracing against the wind and the oncoming rain, Mihir contemplated his next move. He felt a hand on his arm. It was Gene. It was one of those moments when one allows silence to do the talking. No words were going to comfort her. After a few quiet seconds, she thanked Mihir for attending the funeral. He merely nodded. In a weak voice, she told him she was planning a gathering of close friends and relatives for Chris next week, and asked him to attend if possible. He just nodded and looked away, avoiding her searching gaze. She kept her hand on his arm looking at him, seeking comfort. He had none to offer.

Mihir was angry. He had lost a good friend. He wanted to leave, get out and go to someplace normal, where people laughed and drank, enjoyed music and had fun. Life was too short. Death was an unpleasant interruption to life and its pleasures, and it seemed to be doing so in his life with sickening regularity. He patted Gene's hand and prepared to leave. She nodded and walked down the steps of the church.

At the bottom, she suddenly turned around, looking up at him with tearful eyes. 'I have done nothing to deserve this,' she said, almost choking on her words.

Mihir was saddened to see her like this. Life had dealt her a crippling blow. She would miss Chris. He would miss Chris. He was a memory now. It was all so sudden.

3

Bondhuroh is a mid-sized town located on the banks of the Barak, serving river-bound transport. It earned the sobriquet 'Bon Mot'—island of peace—when militancy and secessionist movements were rampant in the Northeast, years ago.

British records dating back two centuries made a reference to the town as a significant trading post for local goods. With a population just under 3,00,000, Bondhuroh has a healthy sex ratio of 988 females to 1,000 males—a happy place where women are on an equal footing with men. It also has over 90 per cent literacy, much higher than the national average. High literacy levels spawn a thirst to know more, especially beyond the confines of a small town. Thanks to the internet, time, distance and awareness are no barriers today, as youth from remote towns land up at cities to realize their ambitions.

Looking towards such a future with a great deal of hope was sixteen-year-old Maymunah Basumatary. She was the eldest of four children, with two brothers and a sister, all between the ages of five and eleven. Her father, Ranjan, worked as a daily contractual labourer in the Bondhuroh municipal office. Her loving mother, Santati, was also a devoted wife. Maymunah loved her family to a fault. They had just about enough money to get by, but never enough to spend on luxuries. Sometimes, late into the night, she could hear her father and mother whispering, rueing their inability to do better for their children. Money always seemed to be the problem. She would often cry herself to sleep, each time silently making a promise that she would make things alright for them.

At school, Maymunah was an average student, but was stunningly pretty, despite a stature of just 5 feet and 2 inches. Like all girls her age, she was becoming aware of her beauty and the effect it had on the boys in her class—they lined up to be friends with her.

But Maymunah was attracted to one particular boy, Kankan, two classes her senior. Over time, they had struck up a close friendship.

Kankan was tall and rakishly handsome, with tousled hair. He also seemed more sensitive and mature than others his age. They would walk back home from school, talking about their shared interests in books and music. One day, he gathered his courage and kissed her. She melted into his embrace and kissed him back. She was in love.

One evening, after classes, he took her to a café. It was mid-January, the best time of the year, a few months before the sultry summer arrived. The day had been particularly glorious, with warm sunshine and clear skies. The café was awash with the last rays of the setting sun. Exams were around the corner, but Maymunah and Kankan were also excited about their upcoming summer vacations.

'What do you plan to do after the exams are over?' Kankan asked.

'I haven't thought about it. Maybe, I'll go visit my relatives in the village. And you?' Maymunah wondered.

'Try my luck in various competitive exams and see where it goes.'

They sat silently for some time, comfortable in each other's company. Finally, he broached the subject.

'In a couple of years, you will be entering college. Have you thought about your future?' he asked, guardedly.

She looked at him quizzically, raising her eyebrows.

'Like what? It is still some time away, you know.'

'You are very pretty, Maymunah. You could try your hand at acting or modelling,' he explained.

'Who would look at a small-town girl like me? We are very poor,' she rued. 'One needs money and contacts to get a break. My family has none. And if I get famous, how will you deal with my large male fan following? You will be jealous like hell,' she teased him with a smile.

He watched her intently for some time before speaking. 'You have always wanted to do something for your family. Promise me that you will keep an open mind about this. Maybe I can help you.'

'Yeah, yeah, I will. Look, can we go now? I have to be home before dark or my mother will start worrying,' she said impatiently, getting up and leaving the café. Kankan watched her go.

Unknown to Maymunah, a woman dressed casually in jeans and a tank top watched her and listened to the conversation carefully. Her name was Silki and, as if to justify it, her hair was shoulder-length, silky smooth and worn straight. Silki was in her mid-thirties, but looked much younger.

A minute after the girl left, Silki got up from her chair and walked over to where Kankan was seated.

'Nice. I like your choice; very pretty,' she said.

Kankan whirled around at the sound of her voice, startled. 'You should be more careful, you know,' he retorted.

'Relax, will you? She never saw me. What do you think?' Silki asked.

'Maybe she is ready. A little nudge is all that is needed,' he said.

'I think so too. You have done well. And, as always, you need to be rewarded,' said Silki, slowly sliding her hand down to his thigh, looking at him with a smile.

Maymunah walked back home, thinking about her conversation with Kankan. As the family sat down for their frugal evening meal, she nearly opened her mouth to speak to her father about what her boyfriend had mentioned in the café. But then, she paused and decided to broach the subject some other time. For now, it was important to concentrate on her exams.

In a small hotel room in a narrow by lane, Silki watched Kankan sleeping peacefully on the bed beside her. Just a while ago, the room was filled with sounds from their wild, passionate session. She reached down and fondled him. It was amazing how quickly he could be aroused again. Kankan opened his eyes, smiled sleepily, turned and lay on top of her. Sliding inside, he moved slowly and gently. Kankan watched as Silki closed her eyes and moaned with pleasure, the first waves of sheer ecstasy hitting her once again.

4

It was well past midnight when Mihir drove his black SUV to Terminal 3 of the Indira Gandhi International Airport in Delhi. It was a cold, moonless night and the fog had begun to descend like an opaque blanket. Soon, visibility would be down to a few feet. He hoped his flight would not be delayed or cancelled. He climbed on to the national highway at IFFCO Chowk, which had heavy traffic even at this time of the night. Trucks and heavy-load carriers were moving in an endless line on the left-most lane, leaving the two centre lanes for smaller vehicles. The road intersected the flight path of aircraft landing and taking off from the airport—so, for someone seated in an aircraft a thousand feet above, the taillights of cars and trucks on the road below would look like a river turned red, flowing endlessly in and out of the city. Mihir wondered if Delhi ever slept.

Leaving Ambience Mall behind, Mihir drove past the vast expanse of an old, defunct toll plaza, once the site of perpetual traffic jams. Short of Mahipalpur, he left the highway for a slip road that took him to the approach road for IGI. He crossed the two security checkpoints, the first just off the highway and the second much closer to the arrival and departure bays, where closed-circuit TV cameras recorded every vehicle entering and leaving the airport. Mihir drove to the departure bay, where he was met by a chauffeur from his company. He would wait till the boss was airborne before driving off in his SUV.

Mihir's flight was scheduled for 5.30 a.m. and took off just as dawn was breaking over the horizon. The aircraft, an Airbus A321, would take approximately two hours and fifty minutes to reach Guwahati. Time for him to think. Mihir always chose an aisle seat—this time, it was in the middle of the aircraft, next to the emergency exits. This allowed him to stretch his legs out comfortably. Twenty minutes later, the aircraft levelled off at 35,000 feet and set course for the east. He watched through his window as the early morning sun painted the Himalayas a gentle orange hue.

Mihir's mind went back to the conversation he had had with Genevieve. He gathered from her distraught account that Chris had been out for a counterinsurgency operation. The incident took place early in the morning. Apparently, Chris was alone when he was shot. He should have been accompanied by at least one quick-reaction team in case he was headed for a specific operation based on firm intel. He had paid for it with his life and he had died on the spot.

Nobody went out alone on an operation; it was against standard operating procedures. Why did Chris violate them? What was he doing alone? Mihir could not fathom the answers to these questions. They seemed irrational from a professional standpoint. But he had also known Chris for many years. He may have been a tad impulsive at times, but he was not careless.

His mind drifted to the memory of the first time he had met Chris—it was immediately after Chris was commissioned into the same battalion in which Mihir was a company commander. He had mentored Chris in his early years as a soldier, a couple of years prior to Mihir's selection and permanent secondment to the parachute special forces (Para SF).

Chris was a gregarious youngster who loved music and dance. His carefree demeanour belied a tough attitude when it came to his work. Mihir had tried later, unsuccessfully, to win Chris over to the Para SF, but Chris was too involved with the battalion and the men he commanded to volunteer for anything else.

They had stayed in touch, occasionally meeting at battalion reunions, until disaster struck Mihir's personal life, when his sister, Sneha, was raped and murdered. Looking at her violated and mutilated body lying at the edge of a dirty sewage stream, he changed. The old Mihir died with his innocent sister; the transformed Mihir was bitter, angry that he had failed to protect his young sibling. Guilt consumed his soul.

The cops expressed helplessness in tracking down the culprits. The heinous crime got a brief mention in the local newspapers and TV channels, but only for a few days. Life moved on.

Returning to the unit four weeks later, scarred and hollowed out emotionally, Mihir decided to resign and leave the army. When his unsympathetic commanding officer refused to entertain the resignation, Mihir lost it. The pent-up anger and frustration burst. He retaliated.

What followed was unfortunate, but it happened. It took three soldiers to restrain him; his victim had to spend two weeks in the hospital before being discharged. Mihir was court-martialled and dismissed from service. Only his numerous gallantry awards in the line of duty and in the face of the enemy earned him some reprieve.

Mihir took the fall badly; it added to the trauma over his sister. He experienced first-hand the insensitivity of the system he had been a part of. His hopes of empathy vanished when his punishment was announced. Drinking binges took him to the brink of alcoholism. He drank to forget, but the hurt only returned with greater force. He barely slept or ate, and became a ghost of his former self. His sister's memory haunted him every second; guilt overpowered him. Mihir shut himself in physically and mentally, refusing to engage with the world for weeks.

Avenging his sister did help, but it did not bring her back to life. Mihir lost friends; colleagues deserted him. The few that remained tried to encourage him to get his life back together. Chris was one of them—he never gave up on Mihir.

Gene also took to the task. The couple were caring but firm with him and brought him back from the brink. In Gene, he saw the sister he had lost so tragically. Gene and Chris were so happy together, so in love; they were like sunshine in Mihir's dark, depressing life.

Chris's current tenure with the unit was to end in a few months and he was due out on a staff appointment. That would never happen now. Mihir had lost two people he loved the most—first his sister and now Chris. He did not know what prompted him to get on to the aircraft and head east, but he owed it to Chris. Somehow, he could not just let go without visiting the spot where Chris had breathed his last.

His train of thought was interrupted by the stewardess offering him breakfast. The hot coffee provided a welcome break from his dark thoughts. Once the attendants had cleared the plates and the cabin lights had been dimmed, with still an hour to go to Guwahati, Mihir closed his eyes and drifted off into fitful slumber.

5

He could have been easily recognized by his face had he chosen to expose it, for it was a face like no other. But he kept it hidden for a good reason. His face was hideous, with a complete absence of distinctive features. It was as if it had been blasted by intense heat, leaving nothing but a knotty, pale, almost igneous rock–like skin cloaking the bone beneath. Then there were two deep-set eyes, without eyebrows or eyelashes, fixed in an unblinking stare.

The locals called him the 'Monster' and stayed away.

Physically, he could not close his eyes. He could barely sleep. His breath came out in a raspy rhythm due to the absence of the principal organ of the olfactory system, the nose. His ears were a mess of tissue and cartilage that barely kept the external acoustic canal open. His pate was bald—the absence of hair only enhancing his unsightliness. The Monster hated his face.

There was one more thing about him that few people knew—he was afflicted by satyriasis. He felt the initial pangs of the obsession at age twelve when he was castigated for masturbating in front of his siblings. The elders brushed it off as a harmless prank. But it only grew worse as he got older. Every two or three weeks, he would dither between manic euphoria and a sense of depression. On many occasions, the Monster had contemplated suicide.

His insane sexual desire found a release in the company of prostitutes, excessive masturbation and a pornography addiction. He found new and innovative methods to satiate his urge—the more bestial he was, the more satisfied.

Seated on a low plastic chair, the Monster was contemplating the fate of his next victim. She lay sprawled naked on the cold, hard floor in front of him. She was innocent, a victim of her circumstances and, surprisingly, he felt sorry for her. Her predicament was not unlike his own a few years ago.

The Monster thought he was an innocent bystander to an encounter between insurgents and security agencies in a small, remote village in the northeast corner of the country. The action ended with the elimination of two of the cadres, while a third, the most important one, got away. The agencies also suffered—three dead, including their commander.

The security agencies would not let it rest. Returning late that night, they barged into each poor dwelling and searched for the missing insurgent. All males above the age of sixteen were rounded up and forcibly marched to an unknown destination. The Monster did not know how long they marched—maybe three or four days. His family desperately searched for him, but he was nowhere to be found.

Hours became days and days stretched into weeks. He did not know why he had been rounded up. He had done no wrong. Till then, the Monster had never thought much about the existence of God, but now he wished from the bottom of his heart that He existed. He prayed desperately for release from the agony.

Starved, ragged and scarred, he was left for dead in a remote forest. He lay unconscious for two days until he was rescued—not by God, but by the insurgents who were the reason for his pain and suffering. They took him under their care and nursed him back to health. But the Monster could never recover completely; the physical and mental scars he carried would now torture him for the rest of his life. When he went to meet his family after more than a year, he had become a soldier of the underground.

The Monster burned with rancour at life's injustice and harshness. It fuelled his hatred for the perpetrators and he vowed revenge. His comrades found him driven, possessed with a manic energy that belied all sanity. He was feared by the authorities. His brutality exceeded all bounds of decency. He did not spare even the families of his enemies, murdering and raping regardless of age.

The security agencies were now determined to eliminate the Monster. The cat-and-mouse game continued for two years before he was finally cornered in a bamboo hut in a hamlet. The officers burnt the hut down; he lost three comrades in the fire. Everything in the hut turned to ashes, except him. Badly burnt, the Monster managed to crawl out.

His surviving buddies took him to a hideout across the forest into another land. Over several months, he was once again nursed back to health. But the fire had turned him into a hideous apparition. The Monster was maimed for life and could be nothing but a burden to his comrades. He decided to quit the insurgency and went back into a society he had left years earlier, armed with a new identity. The Monster knew he would be safe. The agencies thought he was dead. And who would recognize him now anyway? To avoid attention, whenever he stepped out, he always wore a full-face pollution mask and dark glasses.

~

In the present, the Monster gazed into the terrified eyes of the poor girl. She was so beautiful and vulnerable. Her naked, shivering body, her light-brown nipples erect in the cold, stirred in him an all-too-familiar feeling. He unzipped his fly, walked over to her and pushed himself roughly inside her mouth. She gagged and tried hard to breathe, unable to scream or cry for help. After he had finished, he turned her around and massaged himself back into an erection. As the Monster entered her from behind, she screamed in pain. Listening to her cries, whimpering and begging for mercy, he felt even more excited and started ramming into her harder. At the precise moment he was about to come, he slit her throat with a sharp razor.

The Monster watched with lust-crazed eyes as blood sprouted from her in a fountain. The girl grasped for air. Her desperate attempts to breathe made blood froth from her throat, producing a sick, gurgling sound, which he relished with his own moans. She went limp as life seeped out of her. Exactly then, he ejaculated inside her.

The Monster collapsed on the floor and wept, as if the burden of what had just transpired a moment ago was too much for him to bear. Behind him, the door of the shed opened and two men walked in, with the sliver of light laying bare the scene of doom inside. They picked up the dead girl, wrapped her up in a gunny bag and proceeded to dispose of her body. She would never be found.

Sometime later, when the shed was quiet again, the Monster got up and walked out slowly, eyes cast down. Numerous pairs of petrified eyes watched him from behind the bars of a cage as this insane episode unfolded in front of them.

6

The Lokpriya Gopinath Bordoloi International Airport in Guwahati was very crowded when Mihir landed before mid-morning. The airport was in the midst of a major expansion. In his earlier tenures in the Northeast, Mihir had always felt that Guwahati was punching way below its weight. This was a forgotten and neglected corner of India.

But perceptions were changing now, and this region was being looked at as the gateway to the ASEAN nations and South-East Asia. Consequently, the central and state governments were paying a lot of attention towards developing infrastructure at a rapid pace. So, Guwahati airport was transforming into an international airport from a domestic one.

Mihir walked down the arrival lounge towards the baggage carousel. Though he had not checked in any luggage, he waited there for Genevieve. Her flight from Kochi had already landed and she would be coming down to collect her stuff. Despite his objections, Gene had insisted on coming along to Chris's unit.

He saw her five minutes later, walking down the stairs next to the escalators. She was 5 feet and 8 inches, and her smooth walk showed off a well-toned body and a modelling career cut short by her marriage to Chris. Her dark glasses hid her light-brown eyes and accentuated her sharp features. A Mediterranean skin tone, highlighted by a thick shock of curly hair worn till the shoulders, completed the picture of stunning beauty. Even in grief, Gene looked beautiful. Mihir waved to draw her attention. She walked over and hugged him, thankful for his understanding. Mihir held her for a brief moment—his embrace an assurance that all would be okay.

They exited the airport and got into a prearranged taxi, courtesy of Rehaan, who had organized the logistics. They took the southern exit out of the city to avoid its congested interiors. This state road would connect them to National Highway 27, which would take them through Nellie, Nagaon and across the Brahmaputra to the town of Tezpur, covering a distance of more than 200 kilometres. As he looked out of the window, Mihir marvelled at the sheer natural beauty of the Northeast, as yet unsullied by the haphazard growth seen in other parts of India. This part of the country was like a breath of fresh air.

They reached Tezpur by late afternoon and the sun was already low on the horizon. Though India has a single time zone, Tezpur seems almost two hours ahead of western India, so it would get dark by around 4.45 p.m. They turned north at the main intersection, called Mission Chariali. Chariali, in Assamese, means the place where four roads intersect, while the 'Mission' in the name is probably thanks to the Christian missionary hospital next to it.

Past Mission Chariali, they took the northerly road to Balipara. There, they checked into a hotel on the outskirts of the town and decided to continue their journey the next day.

After freshening up, they met in Mihir's room at 8 p.m. and ordered room service. They ate quietly for some time before Mihir spoke.

'I just saw a hint of a smile. What is it?' he asked.

'Oh! Nothing really. Just some fond memories.'

'With Chris?'

'Yes … the first time I met him. It was a chance meeting in a lakeside restaurant on the outskirts of Shillong. I remember it as clearly as if it were yesterday. The sun was setting, its last rays reflecting off the water, this golden shimmer … I walked in with my friends just as the lights came on in the restaurant. There he was, seated in the veranda overlooking the lake, in his uniform. So handsome. I had always been a sucker for uniforms.'

'And he also saw you?' asked Mihir, urging her on.

'He must have felt me staring. He turned around, and well, caught me in the act. He stood up, smiled and bowed, offering me a chair. I stood still, wide-eyed, embarrassed. But after that brief minute, I was a goner,' Gene remembered with a smile.

'And he had no clue about your credentials? What was it I remember reading? Youngest model ever to open her own modelling and advertising agency? And that was before your relationship with Chris.'

'Yes, talk about a slap to one's ego. He had no clue who I was.' Gene laughed and continued, 'I was all of twenty-three. A successful career, and a handsome officer and a gentleman for a lover. It couldn't have been more heady than that. He almost saved me.' She spoke wistfully, looking down at the carpet, as a forlorn expression came across her delicate features.

'Saved you? How?'

When she didn't answer, Mihir continued, gently holding her hand and trying to reassure her. 'You shouldn't have come here, Gene. There is still time, turn back.'

'How could I not? I had to see for myself where he spent his last living moments,' she replied, eyes moist.

'It will only cause you more pain, imagining what he must have gone through while he was drawing his last breath.'

'I want to feel that agony. It's as if the pain brings me closer to him every time I go over his last living moments. I can't seem to let go. I am afraid I may lose him forever.'

Gene looked away, her voice breaking, her eyes brimming with tears. 'And the worst part? Knowing deep down that I can never see him again … ever.'

'I know how you feel. The pain never goes away. It gnaws at your soul. It's a pain that one feels acutely, with the guilt of not being there when you were needed the most,' Mihir said, emptily.

'Can you do something for me?' Gene asked as she got up to leave for her room, searching his face for answers.

'Yes?'

'Avenge him,' she said in a tormented voice, and then closed the door behind her. Her demeanour was laced with a coldness Mihir had never seen before.

~

Late in the night, when the hotel was deathly quiet, the clock in Mihir's mind woke him up at precisely 1 a.m. Even in the army and in countless anti-terror operations, he had never needed a watch or a clock—his instincts never let him down. Donning a black cardigan over his dark jeans, Mihir quietly opened the door, just enough to observe that the main light in the passageway had been switched off. A dull illumination was now provided by low night lights, 6 inches above the granite floor at regular intervals.

The corridor was covered by a CCTV camera. He had observed the exact location and spread when they were being escorted to their rooms by the bellboy. All was quiet in the corridor now; the guests long since having retired to their rooms. Mihir closed the door, walked across his room and stood by the rear window. He parted the drapes slightly to scan the view outside.

His window overlooked the side of the hotel where the service vehicles came to unload their deliveries. The parking lot was deserted and the service door was locked from the outside. Clearly, no deliveries were expected that night. The distance from Mihir's window on the first floor to the concrete fence was about 30 feet, mostly covered by the service parking lot. It was partially lit by weak fluorescent lights, leaving the portion next to the wall of the hotel in virtual darkness.

Mihir noiselessly slid the window open, with enough space to wiggle out of the room. He stepped on to a narrow parapet, about 8 inches in width, that skirted the wall just below the window. Sliding along the wall, he came to the corner of the building where two walls intersected at right angles. Corners like these are used by architects to seamlessly tuck in drainage pipes from the roof and bathrooms. Mihir found one just broad enough for his large hands. He used a classic grip and noiselessly slid down the pipe in less than three seconds, landing on a concrete skirting next to a flower bed, ensuring that no footprints were left on the soft earth. Taking care not to disturb the manicured plants and flower bed, he carefully stepped over them and walked along the wall of the hotel, remaining in the shadows.

From where Mihir was standing, he could clearly see the entrance to the hotel lobby and the drive from the main gate, which was at a distance of about 50 metres. It was empty and no one seemed to be watching. Not convinced, Mihir crept towards the wall and, in one quick movement, jumped over it. He landed on the other side, taking care to remain on his haunches for a couple of minutes. Assured that his movements had not been discovered, he moved along the wall till he was level with the main road.

From his concealed position next to the wall, he could see the main gate to the hotel and a stretch of nearly 100 metres on either side of the national highway. This was a quiet stretch, in complete darkness—the black tar road merging with the moonless night. Except for the faint wash provided by neon signs of cheap hotels along the road, there was no other illumination.

Mihir knew they would be somewhere close by. He had noticed the tail the moment they had left the airport. The colour, make and model of the car were all nondescript, chosen to blend in with the other vehicles on the road. He had noticed two occupants. The driver seemed young, in his twenties. The passenger looked to be in his early forties. They had followed at a discreet distance, ensuring there were always two to three cars between them.

Mihir guessed they were foot soldiers—their lack of imagination exposed them. Not changing the car for over 200 kilometres was a fatal mistake. Whoever wanted the tail to be discreet had failed. Or maybe the tail was meant to be discovered? A way of sending a subliminal message, a warning that Mihir's movements would now be monitored. But warning for what? To stay away, maybe. But stay away from what or whom?

It was natural for the foot soldiers to have taken a break too, but checking into the same hotel as them would have been a dead giveaway, definitely not subtle. They would most probably check into a cheap hotel nearby—close enough to keep their subjects under constant watch and also follow at a moment's notice. Mihir's guess was that the hotel would be about 200 metres from his own.

From his position, he could discern two hotels that fit the description exactly. One was just ahead his own and the second was 100 metres down, towards their destination. Mihir knew what he would do had he been in their place. He would pick the second one, because that was the direction his targets would most likely take the next morning. After having noticed Mihir and Gene turn into their hotel, they would have continued to drive in the same direction, maintaining the façade of discretion, which would have taken them to the next hotel.

Mihir crossed the road in a crouch and, keeping himself concealed in the shadows of trees that lined the road, approached the hotel. It was more like a bamboo shack. There were three small huts, also made of the same material, which were most probably the guest accommodation. There was only one car parked in the small space in front of the hotel—the same one that had been trailing them. Unexceptional and white. The occupants were most probably sleeping in one of the huts.

Mihir approached the car carefully and took a peek inside. Nothing much, just the usual stuff: A used bottle of water in the centre console bracket, a map on the dashboard, a few Assamese music CDs on the rear seat. The occupants were locals. He came back to the tail end of the car and noted the registration number.

Back in his hotel room, Mihir sent the details of the car to Rehaan. He was confident of an answer by midday. He then took a long, hot shower, which loosened his stiff muscles, lay down in his bed, closed his eyes and awaited the arrival of dawn.

While Mihir was relaxing, a medium-sized figure dressed in dark clothes walked quietly past his room and gently knocked on a door at the end of the corridor. It was swiftly opened to let the figure in. After precisely fifteen minutes, the figure left again, taking care not to alert any of the staff on duty. His presence for those few minutes would never be caught on camera. It was as if he was never there.

7

The silent vibrations of Samanta Borphuken's cell phone drew his attention to the number flashing on his screen. The thirty-five-year-old owner of BPN Logistics hadn't saved the number, but recognized it well enough to feel a chill down his spine every time he was contacted.

The caller had visited Borphuken in his office a few months ago. He was a diminutive man, no more than 5 feet and 4 inches, and Borphuken had noticed the strange earring hanging from his left ear—a fat skull in shiny white metal. But it was not even the skull that attracted his attention. The man had the deadest eyes Borphuken had ever seen.

Borphuken had not recalled an appointment with any client that late in the evening. He was due home in thirty minutes. Despite his busy schedule, he prided himself in being a family man. Most of his time was taken up in running a thriving business. In addition, Borphuken had become a member of a political party, which had made serious inroads in this region, and hoped to fight the election on their ticket in two years.

'What can I do for you, Mr …?' Borphuken had asked, looking expectantly at his unannounced visitor.

'Never mind my name. Can we sit down? This may take a while,' the small man replied.

'Then I suppose we could schedule this meeting for tomorrow, 10 a.m.? I have to get back home.' Borphuken, had walked towards the door.

Before he could reach it, the man with the earring locked the door. 'Please sit down. It will take as long as it takes.'

Borphuken prided himself on being a man of considerable clout in the region. He was the one who leaned on others and bent them to his will. He wasn't used to being spoken to in this tone. Cursing under his breath, he tried to slip by, but the visitor had nonchalantly placed his right palm on Borphuken's chest and pushed him. The businessman careened backwards into a chair; the suddenness had left him stunned. He remained in the chair, suddenly fearful, not attempting any resistance.

'Now that we understand each other perfectly well, I want you to listen carefully to what I have to offer,' said the man coldly as he sat down on the edge of the desk, looking down at Borphuken.

'I'm listening,' Borphuken had muttered, ashen-faced.

After the visitor had departed, Borphuken left for home, an hour late. He noticed several missed calls from his wife. As he parked his car, his wife and daughter came running up to him. Pandemonium had broken loose. His servants were out searching for his nine-year-old son, who had been missing for an hour now. His wife was hysterical and was sure something terrible had happened to the boy.

Barely able to keep calm, Borphuken told them not to panic and joined the search. When the family almost gave up and were about to call the police, the boy walked in through the front door. Apparently, a stranger had picked him up and taken him for a ride in his car, given him an ice cream and dropped him back. As the family celebrated in relief, Borphuken's cell phone rang.

'Nice kid. Well-behaved. And a very pretty wife too. Keep them safe. Do as we say and no harm shall come to them,' said the man, before hanging up.

Borphuken knew what he had to do then. He had quietly picked up the phone and passed precise instructions to his subordinates in his company—he did what the unknown visitor had told him to do.

It was the same number flashing on his screen now. Borphuken picked it up and, with a feeling of dread, listened carefully to the instructions he was to follow.

~

The road from Bondhuroh to Guwahati via Shillong is nearly 300-kilometres long. It is a combination of National Highways 6, 37 and 27. Even though the terrain is hilly and the road narrows in several places, traffic is heavy with large cargo carriers, container vehicles and trucks taking up a majority of road space.

The route is prone to landslides during the monsoons, leading to frequent delays for travellers. Even so, it is ideal for trade and the movement of goods between the states of Tripura, Mizoram and southern Manipur via Guwahati. From Guwahati, the cargo is then transported by the national highway network, or by air or rail, across the Siliguri Corridor to the rest of the country.

Scores of transport companies jostle on this road for space. Borphuken's BPN Logistics, one of the largest operators of inland container vehicles in the region, operated on this route. The company owned a fleet of around 200 trucks of various sizes. Some of them were fitted with containers which were ordinarily 20-feet long, 8-feet wide and 8.5-feet high. In the logistics business, this cubic capacity is called one TEU, or 20-foot equivalent unit. These are standard intermodal containers, easily transported and interchanged between different modes of transportation without having to unload and reconfigure the load each time. The space inside is large and cavernous, allowing for all kinds of cargo. Some containers are temperature sensitive, mostly for food and pharmaceutical products like vaccines. These modified containers are called refrigerated containers, or reefers, and can keep items fresh over many days.

The Northeast is rich in natural resources. With wet weather almost year-round, and fed by an array of rivers and water bodies which bring rich alluvial soil from the upper reaches of the Himalayas, the agricultural products grown in the area are all organic. The produce is packed in reefers and transported to intermodal cold-chain logistic hubs, from where they are further moved, either by rail, road or air, across the Siliguri Corridor to the rest of India.

Borphuken's BPN Logistics owned ten such reefer trucks. And, of these, a small convoy of four reefer trucks was moving slowly along the meandering Bondhuroh–Guwahati axis. All the vehicles were carrying fresh fruits and vegetables. The containers would take two days to reach the next intermodal container station. After an eight-hour halt for administrative necessities, they would continue their two-week onward journey to their ultimate destination—Delhi's upscale organic fruit and vegetable markets.

The night's stars were hidden by a thick cloud cover, the forest black and ominous on either side of the narrow, winding road. The night was cool, with the temperature dropping with each passing kilometre as the trucks gained altitude. But the driver of the lead vehicle was sweating profusely.

He had a nagging sense of dread ever since he had left Bondhuroh. It clawed away at his gut, sapping him of strength. He tried to concentrate on the task at hand. He had been on the road for the last twelve hours and was already becoming an emotional wreck. If caught by the authorities, there was little chance of escape. He would be on his own. The company he worked for would deny everything and hang him out to dry.

The driver was told that he would be required to do at least two runs each month. Each time, separate instructions would follow. The reward would be money, a sum beyond his wildest dreams.

The driver looked at the GPS tracker in his vehicle once again to confirm that the rendezvous point was still there, about 3 kilometres ahead, at a prominent bend in the road. He knew exactly where, having driven along this route for many years now. The bend had a small cul-de-sac that allowed drivers to take a break without blocking traffic on the main road. Any passing vehicle would assume that the driver had taken a small break. No one would suspect anything. His instructors had chosen the point carefully; they knew exactly what they were doing.

The driver slowed down the vehicle 500 metres short of the designated point. As if on cue, the three trucks behind him also came to a gentle halt. The driver carefully guided the vehicle to the cul-de-sac and parked it neatly along the left side of the road. Any movement from the side of the forest would now be hidden by the massive length of the truck. The release of the vacuum brakes made a dull hiss in the still of the night. He switched off the headlights and killed the engine. Except for the faint, eerie green glow of the driver's console, it was pitch dark. He waited nervously.

He felt the movement next to his cabin at the exact moment that he heard a gentle knock on the side of his door. Strictly instructed not to turn towards the source, he followed the directions to the letter. He pressed a pneumatic button just above his right knee, next to the steering column. A small door, barely 3 feet in height and 2.5 feet in width, unlocked with a gentle click.

This door was at the head of the reefer, just behind the driver's cabin. It fit snugly within the exterior wall of the container and was unnoticeable. The door opened into a cleverly designed compartment that was 8-feet wide—the width of the entire reefer—and 4-feet deep. Anybody carrying out a visual inspection of the reefer from the door situated at the rear wouldn't notice that the container length had, in effect, been reduced by 4 feet.

Taking care to keep his head still, the driver slowly shifted his eyes to the left and tried to discern the unfolding scene through the left rear-view mirror. It was a very awkward angle and he could barely see anything in the dark of the night. But he could hear the faint rustle of the wet grass—shuffling feet, perhaps because they were being pushed from behind. The kind of noise you would hear when someone's feet are tied together. The driver dared not turn his head but he knew from the instructions he had received that there would be roughly ten individuals per container.

Exactly ten minutes later, he felt a light tap again on his door. The signal to move. The driver quietly started the vehicle and climbed onto the road. The other vehicles slowly followed him.

The 'cargo' secure in the hidden compartment would be delivered to its interim destination on the outskirts of Guwahati in a few hours.

8

Lieutenant Colonel Sumer Singh sat in his cramped office, smoking a herbal cigarette and hating every moment of it. He had begun trying it only recently, hoping it would finally rid him of his habit, but he did miss the nicotine rush. Today, he felt its absence even more.

Midmorning sunlight spilled in from a window. Sumer had never met the two figures seated before him, though he had heard Chris speak of his wife, Gene's, wit and infectious energy. He'd had no clue that she was also very beautiful. Returning her intense gaze, the officer now understood why Chris was completely smitten by her.

Seated next to her, was a man introduced as Mihir—imposing height, close-cropped hairstyle typical of soldiers, who, after years in uniform, know no other way of grooming their hair. Even with his clothes on, Sumer could make out his chiselled, muscular frame.

Mihir's face stood out—sparse eyebrows covering deep-set black eyes, a sharp nose on a weather-beaten face with high cheekbones; clean-shaven, with a wide jawline. Sumer noticed a jagged scar that ran down from behind his left ear down to his collar bone, probably the result of a serrated knife. Proof of a violent past. Mihir returned the officer's gaze with a deadpan look. Sumer pitied anyone who would be unfortunate enough to cross paths with the man seated across him.

The unit's second-in-command had offered them coffee. It was a terrible brew in typical soldierly fashion: Well-intentioned, with a misplaced sense of hospitality. The result was a milky-white, sugary concoction that stayed in its cup after the first tentative sip.

'I am very sorry for your loss, ma'am,' Sumer said, tipping ash into the ashtray placed on his desk. 'You have travelled a long way from home; you needn't have taken the trouble. We would have sent whatever was required to your home. Nevertheless, how may I be of help?'

'I have come to collect his personal effects,' replied Gene.

'Yes, of course. We already have them packed and ready for dispatch.'

Mihir interrupted, impatiently.

'We can't seem to figure out what exactly happened. From the little we know, he seems to have left the unit premises alone. Quite unusual and, if I may add, a clear violation of standard operating procedure,' he stated.

'And how would you know it was a violation?' a visibly upset Sumer retorted.

'I have also served in the army. Clearly, he was alone. No one had a clue what he was on to. He was without protection. I think he did not trust anyone and, hence, did not share information with anybody. And your outfit had no idea of his whereabouts,' said Mihir, looking stonily at him.

Sumer stared at Mihir, trying to figure out how to tackle this stranger. After a long moment, he shifted his attention to the widow and softened visibly. 'We were also wondering why he was so impetuous. Sadly, it cost us the life of one of our finest officers,' said Sumer, restraining his emotions.

'He was not impetuous,' said Gene, stung by the word. 'He must have had a very good reason to do what he did. Unfortunately, he isn't here to speak for himself.'

'I apologize. I wasn't being disrespectful. It's just that this loss could have been avoided had he confided in us,' said Sumer, softening his tone further. 'An investigation is underway, headed by me, to find out the circumstances leading to this unfortunate incident … this murder. I will get to the bottom of this and find the culprits.'

'I'd like to take a look at his room and collect his personal effects,' said Gene, deflecting the conversation.

'And I'd like to visit the spot where he was shot, if that's okay,' said Mihir, looking at Gene for tacit approval.

'If it's not a problem?' she added.

'Well, there are some things that we have to retain since the investigation is still unfinished. But the rest of the stuff you can have. About the shootout site, since it's a crime scene, I will have the Military Police escort you there,' said Sumer, looking directly at Mihir. 'But I would rather not have the lady visit the site. It could prove deeply disturbing. And now, I will have you both escorted to the hut.'

Gene walked with heavy steps on the path to the hut, where she remembered having spent one of the happiest days of her life with Chris, barely a couple of months ago. It already seemed like a lifetime apart to her. Chris had always said no matter what happened to him, he would love her, forever and beyond. The words seemed strangely prophetic now.

Mihir followed closely behind as she entered the hut. It was a simple two-room set up with a small kitchenette. The outer room was slightly larger and contained a bamboo cane sofa set, as well as a dining table with seating for four.

The bedroom, smaller in size, contained a king-sized double bed with two side tables. Next to the bathroom door was a television mounted on the wall, a wooden wardrobe and a simple study table with a chair.

Gene took it all in in one go and the memories came flooding back. The realization that Chris would never be there for her hit hard. She collapsed on the floor crying. Mihir helped her to the sofa and offered her a glass of water.

'Whatever will I do without him?' she sobbed.

'You need to give yourself time, Gene,' said Mihir, trying to calm her down.

'Why did he have to go and die, Mihir? He just went away and left me to pick up the pieces. I can feel his presence. I can smell him everywhere, the bed, his wardrobe, his clothes and …'

She couldn't finish the sentence. Seeing her so helpless, Mihir felt cold anger like he hadn't felt in a long time. He vowed then that no matter what it took, he would make them pay in ways they hadn't even imagined.

He allowed Gene to grieve. All that had been bottled up inside of her needed to come out. That was the only way she could think of a future without the man she loved so dearly and who was never going to come back. When Gene was able to compose herself, she picked herself up and said she had to pack Chris's personal effects, and needed some time alone. Mihir nodded and quietly closed the door to the hut.

As he stepped outside, he saw Lt Col Sumer Singh standing with another officer—6-feet tall, ramrod straight and thin as a reed. A colonel with a red beret and a white web belt. Mihir knew what that meant—Military Police.

The colonel stepped forward. 'Hi, I am Colonel Shamsher Singh Randhawa. Care to join us in the office?'

They trooped back to Sumer's office and sat down in the same chairs they had vacated a while ago. 'Major Mihir Pratap Singh, decorated thrice, Shaurya Chakra and Bar, Sena Medal for gallantry, Para SF. Also court-martialled, unfortunately. A pleasure to meet you,' said the colonel.

'Likewise,' replied Mihir.

'Why are you here, Mihir?'

'The lady asked me to escort her here. Besides, Chris was from my old unit.'

'How long do you intend on staying here?'

'Hopefully, not long. But before we go, may I see the murder site?'

'I don't see why not,' replied the colonel.

It took them fifteen minutes to drive to the site of the murder. They rode in the colonel's Gypsy, with 'Military Police' emblazoned on the sides. They got down about 500 metres short and walked towards the spot that had tragically been the meeting point between Chris and his source. Mihir saw the dead tree, which was on an elevated piece of ground, and knew instantly why Chris may have chosen this site. Easy to recognize on a moonless night.

Mihir imagined the sequence of events as it would have possibly unfolded. Sumer had told him when they had met in the office that the man Chris was supposed to have met, and who was found dead alongside the officer, was from Bilbor—the town they had crossed en route. This meant the informant would have started early for the rendezvous spot on a predesignated signal, maybe a missed call from Chris.

Mihir was now at the exact spot where Chris lay after being shot. Unlike what is shown in the movies, where a person when shot is literally lifted off his feet and bowled over backwards before hitting the ground, the reality is different.

The bullet, depending upon the weapon, range and type, travels at nearly 1,000 feet per second. It exits the body before the target even realizes he has been hit. If it is a fatal wound, the victim just crumples to the ground, lifeless. One instant, there is life; the next, nothingness. And if the wounds don't kill you, the agony is unimaginable.

There was only one place from where the shot could have come and that was 15 feet west from where Mihir was standing. It was a matter of simple deduction—the shooter would have had to crawl through the thicket that covered the western slope, the only direction that provided that kind of cover.

The wound ballistics on Chris's body had indicated a 9-millimetre round. The empty shell casings of both the fired bullets had never been found. Maybe the shooter was careful and had picked them up later, or perhaps they may have had just sunk into the soggy, grassy ground. The shooter's weapon seemed to have been a handgun, of which there were plenty in this part of the country.

For Chris to have not detected the shooter who lay in the thicket merely 15 feet away meant only one thing—a level of training in field craft that could have been imparted only in the army, or in an insurgent unit. The shooter was no common criminal. He knew exactly where the meeting was to take place. This was a premeditated murder. It was more serious than Mihir had initially thought. No wonder Chris did not tell anyone. He must have suspected something. So how did they, whoever they were, know? Only one way. The source, who had eventually lost his life with Chris.

Mihir scanned the horizon behind the likely position of the shooter. Something at the base of the hills, about 6 kilometres away, caught his eye. He stored the observation in one corner of his mind, to be tackled later.

As they headed back to the Gypsy, the colonel asked Mihir what he had gathered. 'Nothing much, really. Just wanted to see the place where Chris was killed,' he replied, walking ahead.

Randhawa watched Mihir's receding figure for a moment before following him back to the vehicle.

9

The man with the white metal earring was called Mwhaay by his close friends (pronounced 'mhee' in Burmese). It meant snake.

Mwhaay was standing at the front door of a large Spanish-style hacienda. Due to its red roof, it was referred to by the locals as 'Lal Bangla' (Red Bungalow). Located on the outskirts of Guwahati, in an isolated hilly area that bordered a forest reserve, it was situated north of the main highway and could be approached by only one narrow road that meandered around the terrain for about 15 kilometres before reaching the house.

About 17 acres of thickly forested private land surrounded the structure. Since it was adjacent to the main forest reserve, both territories merged seamlessly. The bungalow was enclosed by a 10-foot-high security wall, with an electrified double-layered concertina coil fence for added protection. There was a web of CCTV cameras with thermal capability and searchlights that covered every inch of the estate. Then, there were miniature drones that constantly flew overhead, keeping a relentless watch on the premises. Security guards from an elite private security company, whose boss was the owner of the house, were deployed across the estate. Entry to the house was only possible through a massive, remotely operated iron main gate that was manned 24x7 by three guards. The entire security apparatus of the estate was centrally controlled from the guardhouse next to the gate.

The front door opened before Mwhaay could ring the bell. He was escorted by an armed guard to a veranda, which opened into a spacious courtyard, with a large swimming pool in the centre, and a jacuzzi and a pool bar in one corner. Splashes of water around the pool and glasses strewn about were ample evidence of a party that had continued into late morning or early afternoon.

Mwhaay knew what these were—secretive sexual orgies with drug abuse. Girls were brought in special SUVs and usually let off before first light; but not this time, it seemed. Many were young college students spoiled by the lure of easy money, drugs and an opulent lifestyle. A select clientele gathered and lived out their wildest fantasies in the safety of Lal Bangla. Here, favours were exchanged for mutual benefit.

The sun had almost dipped below the horizon. Warm pools of golden light emerged as the house lights were switched on. Mwhaay looked at his watch; it was 4.45 p.m. The master of the house did not like to be kept waiting. Mwhaay declined a drink offered to him and chose to wait by the pool.

He shifted his gaze from the pool to a door behind it that had just opened. Mwhaay looked at the small man who emerged from it—5 feet, 5 inches and about forty years old—and crossed the open space to enter the patio. He was known as 'Maalik', the Master. He was dressed in a pair of flashy swimming trunks and had a dressing gown thrown loosely over his shoulders, untied at the front, leaving his large, hairless beer belly exposed. The fat frame was supported by a pair of thin, spindly legs. The head was bald. His fat, alabaster face gave one the impression of a puffer fish having a bad day.

Intense beady eyes stared from underneath sparse eyebrows. A thin moustache completed the picture. Many had mocked the man's appearance openly and paid for it with their lives. Even Mwhaay feared him.

Maalik sat down in a cane chair, flanked by two bodyguards, one of whom covered him with a light woollen shawl. Without bothering to look at Mwhaay, he took a glass vial out and snorted its contents—a fine, white powder—from the glass table in front of him. Raising his head and laying it back on the headrest of the chair, he pinched his nose and allowed the opioid to take effect.

'I trust our little problem has been settled?' Maalik asked with his eyes closed, sarcasm dripping.

'Yes.'

'Hmmm. I don't think so! It was supposed to have looked like an accident. But now, it is being shown all over the media as the cold-blooded murder of an officer and a civilian.'

'It will die down, eventually.'

'Well, it's been more than a week and it hasn't. Is that why the woman is here with her friend?' Maalik asked, angrily.

'She's not a threat. Don't worry about it,' said Mwhaay, defensively. He could see the 'rush', or euphoria, common among heroin users, take effect on the man seated in the chair.

'I know she isn't. But who is the man with her?' Maalik asked.

'An old friend of the prick I killed; I assume he is just escorting her. They haven't caused any trouble so far. They are easy to follow. I have their every move covered.'

'The man looks dangerous. I can't take any chances. This is your job. Make it go away. I want no meddling in our business,' said Maalik, and dismissed Mwhaay with a careless flick of his hand.

Mwhaay broke out in a cold sweat; the last remark and the dismissive signal sent a shiver down his spine. The threat was more ominous because it was unsaid. He knew the price of failure. Maalik's brutality was legendary. Death was an easy choice compared to what might await him, should he fail. Mwhaay quickly left the patio from a side door that led to a staircase, which descended 6 feet underground and entered a stone corridor, dimly lit with low-wattage light bulbs. Lined on each side of the corridor were cells about 8-feet long and 6-feet wide. The entry to each cell was controlled by a small steel grille door, approximately 5-feet high and 2-feet wide. Most of the cells were dark, except for a few where dim overhead bulbs illuminated the space directly underneath, leaving the rest of the cell in the shadows.

The voices that emanated from these cells were barely audible—all of them female. Mwhaay knew why. Maalik was a connoisseur of pretty women. Some he liked were brought to Lal Bangla to entertain the master. After he had had his fill, Maalik dumped them in these cells, only to be discarded after he got bored. All of them were heavily drugged. Maalik wasn't too concerned about the manner of disposal; his close subordinates saw to it.

The naked fear Mwhaay felt a moment ago awakened in him a sudden sexual urge that begged release. There was one particular girl Mwhaay had taken a liking to. He now walked towards the cell where the girl was kept and nodded at his escort, who opened the steel door. The girl, knocked senseless by heroin, could barely comprehend what was happening.

Mwhaay lifted her from her sparse bed and, with one hand supporting her, he used the other one to strip her torn clothes. He unzipped his fly and entered her. The girl looked at him with vacant eyes and an empty smile. After he had finished, Mwhaay dropped her on the cot, zipped up his trousers and left the building quietly.

Meanwhile, back inside the house, Maalik was still seated in the same cane chair. Spread out in front of him were a number of glossy photographs of girls and boys, aged twelve to eighteen. He picked these up one by one and began to examine them closely. The angles made it clear that the subjects were blissfully unaware of the interest they had generated.

One photograph, in particular, drew Maalik's attention. The subject was a girl, barely seventeen. The photograph was taken from an oblique angle, while she was seated in a café. The natural light from a nearby window shone on her perfect skin and delicate features. Maalik had never seen a prettier face; he felt an all-too-familiar feeling stirring in him. He knew she was special. If a photograph could do this, he wondered, what would she be like in person. She was ideal for the start of a new venture. He would pass on suitable instructions for her not to be touched.

10

Meanwhile, not too far away, Sumer had invited Mihir and Gene for dinner at the small, makeshift officers' mess inside the compound. Gene had politely declined, preferring to spend the evening in Chris's hut one last time.

'So, who was the source who was killed along with Chris that night?' Mihir asked the lieutenant colonel, the only other person at the mess, while nursing a fresh lime soda, carefully staying away from alcohol.

'Ahmed Islam, a resident of Bilbor, aged thirty-two. Worked as a two-wheeler mechanic in the town. Married, wife, Khatun Bibi, one girl child, aged three. Mother, a widow, lived with them,' Sumer informed him.

'His credibility as a source?'

'Was on our roll for more than five years. He was A-one. Chris was his handler.'

'A-one' meant the source was completely reliable and trustworthy, and his information could not be doubted.

'What about their call records?'

'The civil police have the cell phones of both victims. We have the details of the call records from them. The initial printouts do not reveal anything. Chris did not contact his source through his cell phone at least—that much we know now. If there is anything else that the call records can reveal, we will know soon enough. In the meantime, we are analysing his WhatsApp messages. So far, we have drawn a blank there too. We will get a breakthrough soon,' replied Sumer.

Despite his confidence, Mihir was sceptical; he didn't expect much from mobile phone records. Professionals in this line of work rarely conducted their business on the phone. Instead, they relied more on age-old, time-tested methods, such as a face-to-face meeting. Something Chris was doing before it all went south.

'Any other leads in your investigation?' asked Mihir.

'Not yet. Whatever Chris was after, he did not share it with anyone. Played his cards close to his chest. We are pretty much in the dark here,' said Sumer.

'Did he have any professional disagreements with the commanding officer or any other officer in the unit?'

'Not to my understanding. Our cases are pretty much watertight and no one interferes in the other's work. The boss is kept in the loop. Counter-intelligence is a painstaking and tedious process,' Sumer said tentatively, not sure where the conversation was heading.

'Could it be possible that there was a civilian angle to the case he was working on that no one in the unit was aware of? Maybe the cops will be able to help,' Mihir suggested.

'Was he on his own trip? It is possible, but unlikely. Chris would not do that,' said Sumer with finality.

Mihir was about to ask one last question, but, for some reason, decided to keep it to himself. He would save it for later. Maybe.

His conversation with Sumer seemed like a dead end, but two possible conclusions could be drawn.

One, Chris was killed at random by militants in an area riddled with militancy. This was unlikely because the heyday of militancy was in the past, except in a few pockets.

Two, whatever Chris knew was so damning that someone was willing to kill for it. Killing is, for the most part, the last resort even among hardened criminals. Dead bodies always attract attention and leave a trail. So, the double murder was an act of sheer desperation. Whoever did it was willing to take the risk.

Mihir was still thinking about his conversation with Sumer as he walked back to the guest room, next to the mess. Short of the front door, he stopped and turned left, skirting around the hut and walking into the darkness behind.

Compared to other army camps in insurgency-infested areas, this one was small—spread over an area of approximately 200 metres in length and 100 metres in width—and it contained twelve op-shelters. The camp was organized in clusters. The first and largest cluster contained living barracks for approximately 100 soldiers, with toilets, a cookhouse and a dining hall. The second cluster comprised the office complex, an armoury (also called a kote for weapons) and other stores. The last and smallest cluster had the makeshift officers' mess, with a guest room and separate accommodation for two officers.

The complex was enclosed with a double concertina-coil fence with 10-foot-high angle iron pickets at regular intervals of 20 feet. Thirty-four-feet high perimeter towers made from steel girders—four of them—dominated the area around the camp. Entry and exit were possible only through one gate, manned round the clock by an armed guard of four soldiers with loaded weapons. Nobody could enter or leave the compound unseen. Yet, Chris had.

Standing in the shadow of his hut, Mihir could see that the towers were well-sited. Their height made it easy to observe all approaches into the camp. The bottom of the double concertina fence hugged the ground. The spread of the perimeter wire fence was about 6 feet across, so crawling underneath it would be very difficult without being seen from the towers.

Turning left and keeping to the shadows, Mihir started walking slowly, observing each section of the fence carefully. Low clouds flitting across the moon made his movements easier to conceal. After 50 metres, he came to another hut, located slightly away from the office complex. Probably a store of some sort. He stood in its shadows and looked at the fence carefully. He then turned in both directions to look at the towers, but could not see any.

Suddenly, it became clear as daylight—this was a dead zone; a 15-foot gap in the perimeter fence that could not be observed from any tower. A chink in the armour.

Mihir broke from the shadow of the hut and walked towards the fence. He knelt down and carefully began examining each inch of the ground in the dead zone. Two minutes later, he found what he was looking for. Hidden by grass approximately a foot tall, there was a gap between the ground and the bottom of the fence, enough for a trained soldier to crawl through. He now knew the exact spot from where Chris had left the camp unobserved. Cheeky bastard.

Mihir retraced his steps back to the store hut and continued his reconnaissance. From the rear of the office complex, he could quite easily observe the front gate. A rough track led from the gate on to the Karimpuhl–Bisota Road, about half a kilometre away. The road could be observed for almost 800 metres from the eastern tower nearest to the main gate. There was no traffic at this time of night; all was quiet.

As he was turning to head back to his hut, a brief flicker of light, like that of an illuminated cell-phone screen, caught the corner of his left eye. It was there for a split second and then it was gone. Its source was located somewhere on the main road. Countless hours of watching a target can be mind-numbing, and even the most experienced professionals get careless and make mistakes. The watcher had just made one, enough to show that Mihir and Gene's movements were being tracked meticulously. He smiled, turned around and headed back to his hut.

Back in his room, he sent a brief message from his cell phone to Rehaan. He then closed his eyes, took a deep breath and fell into a deep slumber. Tomorrow would be a long day.

In another part of the camp, Gene woke up with a start, as if from a nightmare. She got up sleepily, reached for the handbag kept on a side table and retrieved a small object. Without switching on a light, she found the study table. Five minutes later, she walked back groggily to her bed empty-handed, lay down and drifted off into a deep sleep.

11

They left the next morning at daybreak. The first rays of the sun were breaking through the low cloud cover. Inside the hired taxi, however, the mood was dark and sombre. Gene looked back at the camp one last time as they left the main gate. Mihir knew she was finally coming to terms with a life of loneliness ahead.

It was a long ride back to Guwahati and, by the time they checked into their hotel, it was dark outside. They ordered room service and ate in silence. Gene retired to her room to catch a few hours of sleep before her early morning flight to Kochi. Mihir's flight to Delhi was scheduled an hour later.

At precisely one in the morning, Mihir went to Gene's room to wake her up. She was already awake and dressed. Mihir realized she hadn't slept a wink.

'It's time,' he said.

Luggage in hand, they rang for the elevator and waited. Mihir was dressed in dark-grey slacks and a black jacket over a T-shirt the same colour. His only luggage was a fawn-coloured, medium-sized duffel bag. Gene was dressed in slacks and a light jacket to keep the cold at bay. She carried a handbag and a small cabin suitcase.

'I suppose this is where we part company,' she said. 'And thank you for being with me all this while. I won't forget it.'

Mihir nodded and opened his mouth to say something, but then decided to keep quiet. Gene looked at Mihir, hoping for some reassurance and words of farewell. When none came, she hugged him. After a moment of hesitation, she reached up and kissed him on the cheek. The hug and kiss lingered a moment longer than usual. Then, Mihir retraced his steps into his room.

Gene stepped out into the main lobby. No check out was needed as Mihir had already settled their dues an hour ago. She was the only one in the lobby, quite conspicuous and impossible to miss. Watching her every move from under the shadow of a tree in a dark corner of the hotel lawns was a man of medium height. He saw her waiting for her taxi. She was of no interest.

Exactly an hour after she had left, a man fitting the description of the target that the observer had been given walked down the stairs and onto the porch for his taxi. The man's features were hidden by a baseball cap. The observer would follow the target to the airport and wait till he had boarded his flight. He watched as the man got into the taxi. It drove past him and exited from the 'out' gate, heading to the airport. He quickly ran towards a waiting car to follow.

From a dark room on the second floor of the hotel, Mihir watched as the man tore himself from the shadows and ran towards a car that took off behind the taxi taking Rehaan to the airport.

Mihir had wanted to keep it quiet, preferring to leave Gene out of his little deception. After receiving his message the previous night, Rehaan had taken the first flight to Guwahati. He had then checked into the same hotel as Mihir and Gene before their departure for Delhi and Kochi, respectively. After Gene's departure, Rehaan had met with Mihir in his room. It was going to be tricky, but the gamble had paid off. Rehaan and Mihir were of a similar body type and height. The rest was taken care of by some astute dressing and the use of ambient hotel lights.

After an hour and a half, by which time he knew Rehaan was inside the airport and most probably about to board his flight, Mihir quietly picked up his small sling bag and left the room. He used the fire escape to leave the hotel and exited the complex from an unguarded gate at the rear. The road behind the hotel was dark and deserted; there were no street lights. Mihir began walking and, within a minute, was swallowed up by the pitch-black night.

Outside the airport, the tail, who had followed Rehaan unwittingly, punched in his report, giving an all-clear to his boss.

12

A flight from Delhi landed at Gopinath Bordoloi International Airport around the same time Rehaan was going through security check. It was always possible to get tickets at the last moment for flights at odd hours, and that was the case for the man and the woman from Delhi who waited at the baggage carousel.

Tuhin Khanna, in his late forties, was over 6-feet tall, thin and lanky, with a balding pate. He was clean-shaven, his complexion pasty pale—the result of spending hours in the comfort of an air-conditioned office. He was busy picking up his luggage as it crept up the belt. His female companion was dressed in black tights, knee-high boots and a matching jacket. Rubina was at least twenty years younger, barely 5-feet tall and voluptuous. She was standing a couple of feet behind Tuhin, helping him get the luggage on to the trolley. Still groggy from sleep, her actions were sluggish and uncoordinated.

Once outside, the couple walked to the car park, where a white SUV with a driver and an escort were waiting to take them to their destination. The presence of the reception party showed how important the venture was, or so Tuhin thought. If he had looked at the other vehicles in the car park, he would have noticed three more SUVs of similar make and colour, each with a driver and an escort waiting to pick up their passengers. They would be arriving in different flights from various cities across India. Once on the road, Tuhin relaxed, closed his eyes and rewound the last twenty-four hours of his life.

Tuhin Khanna was the CEO of a human resource firm headquartered in Gurugram. His company was a consultant to a number of multinationals located in the National Capital Region. Besides consultancy, the firm also made up for the shortfall of skilled manpower in various organizations, public and private. His association with government departments for a few years lent his firm credibility. His success had made him a well-known face in business circles.

Over a period of time, he began to get requests from select clients for a specific type of merchandise. Tuhin was considered reliable and discreet—his reputation travelled mostly by word of mouth and his new clients were headquartered overseas. Tuhin refused at first, knowing he would be unable to meet their demands. But the lure of large sums of unaccounted-for money, all in cash and tax-free, was irresistible. That was when he relented and began to look around. His attention was drawn to a part of the country about which he had only read. The Northeast, India's hidden gem.

From then on, business had never been better. Tuhin began thinking about making this the mainstay of his company. The law did not bother him; he had bought his protection with the local cops and was confident that he was safe.

Normally, in this line of work, Tuhin's firm would place a demand to the suppliers based on the client's requirement. And these were always specific. The suppliers would then send the merchandise to a preferred port, being careful while selecting routes, never repeating them, lest a pattern emerge. From there, the cargo would be dispatched to its destination on board luxury yachts chartered for that very purpose. The owners of these sleek machines never asked questions—the money easily ensured their silence. It was Tuhin's job as a third party to organize the exchange safely. The consideration for the whole deal was always more than adequate.

So, the call that came late the previous evening had been a surprise. They were being summoned immediately. It was urgent. The caller said new business opportunities were beckoning. Everything after that had been a rush, but they had just about made it by the first available flight.

Busy in his own thoughts, Tuhin failed to notice that the SUV had crossed the outskirts of Guwahati and was heading towards Barojat, at the junction of national highways 27 and 6. The former continued eastwards, while NH-6 turned south towards Shillong. The night sky was thick with heavy clouds and it had begun to drizzle. The driver slowed down in the reduced visibility.

They turned onto NH-6 and slowly began to gain altitude as the road wound its way up the hills. After fifteen minutes and maybe 3 kilometres, the vehicle slowed and turned right on to a dirt track, flanked by 6-foot-high barbed wire fences. This was private property. The canopy of trees that lined the path on either side provided a thick overhead cover.

Soon, they reached their destination and Tuhin woke up Rubina. As they stepped out and stretched their cramped legs, the two other SUVs from the airport also caught up with them. He observed the passengers as they tumbled out of their vehicles and recognized no one.

By the time they were escorted to their rooms after breakfast, it was already daylight. They were informed that their meeting was scheduled at 8 p.m., followed by dinner.

They would be picked up by 7.30 p.m. They were told to stay within the premises. The vehicles left shortly after.

Tuhin checked his and Rubina's cell phones. No signal. There was no landline on the premises either. They were completely isolated from the rest of the world and no one knew where they were. The seemingly endless waiting built up a sense of foreboding, not knowing what was to follow or expect. He had no idea what was in store for them. He understood now—it was all intentional, conveying a sense of hold and power over the invitees cooped up in this temporary habitation. For the first time since his foray into this business, Tuhin regretted getting involved. A nagging fear took hold of him. He was scared for his life.

13

Kankan was lying flat on his back in a hotel room, naked. The woman on top was in the throes of ecstasy as she rode him with wild abandon. Silki could barely contain her loud moans of pleasure as she lost control and climaxed multiple times—each orgasm more intense than the previous one. She collapsed on top of him, exhausted.

Later, sitting on a low diwan next to the bed and smoking a joint, Silki watched Kankan sleeping contentedly on the king-sized bed. She hadn't told him her name and knew he didn't even care. As long as the sex was great, who gave a fuck about a name?

Kankan stirred in the bed and looked at her sleepily, hoping for a final romp before they got down to work. One look at her and he knew it was not to be.

'Time to get to work. What time is she going to meet you?' Silki asked.

'Eleven,' said Kankan, looking at his watch. It was only 8.30 a.m., so they had two-and a-half hours. Plenty of time to get ready.

'What did you tell her?'

'Exactly what you told me to—that I had a chance meeting with a fashion photographer from Mumbai looking for some fresh faces from the Northeast, for the launch of a new designer collection. And that she was staying in a hotel in Guwahati and would like to meet,' he said, recalling his conversation with Maymunah.

'And her reaction?' Silki asked.

'Sceptical at first, but I managed to convince her. She trusts me. I even handed her the money you gave me for the trip,' Kankan said with a sly smile.

'Good boy. She has been noticed. Handle her with care. She must not be harmed in any way.'

'Yeah, sure! Haven't we gone over this a number of times already?' he replied, rolling his eyes. 'And if this silly conversation is over, come back to bed and fuck me. We have time. And then I need to have breakfast. I am famished.'

Silki smiled and rolled over on to the bed. Kankan took the joint from her and smoked it, savouring the high as it washed over him. She fondled his erection and took it in her as he moaned with pleasure.

∼

Maymunah alighted from the private taxi, hired thanks to the cash Kankan had handed her. He had said the money was from the mysterious and generous talent scout, whom she was quite excited to meet later in the day.

The taxi dropped her in front of a medium-sized three-storeyed hotel five minutes from the airport—one of the many on the borderline of seedy and downmarket that dotted the locality. But for the poor girl, who had never been to any hotel, even this one seemed fine. The ground floor contained a large reception area, with one corner occupied by a receptionist in her mid-twenties seated behind a large desk with an all-in-one desktop and a couple of telephones.

The rest of the space was taken up by two five-seater sofas sets with worn-out red velvet upholstery. The room was embellished with green granite tiles. An elevator in a corner and a staircase next to it led to the guest rooms above. Next to the staircase was a door with the top half in glass, with a sign stating 'Restaurant'.

Maymunah walked up to the reception and asked for the room number where she was told the meeting would take place. The receptionist rang ahead and gave her the details. She took the stairs.

Nervous and anxious, she knocked on the door. It was immediately opened by Kankan.

'Hi,' said Kankan, as he hugged and kissed Maymunah.

She hugged her boyfriend back, but broke away, embarrassed. A woman, whom she presumed to be the talent scout Kankan had told her about, walked into the room from the balcony.

'My goodness! She is pretty, very pretty! Just as you had described her,' exclaimed Silki, pretending to sound astonished at the sheer beauty of the young woman.

'Oh, it's nothing really!' replied a flustered Maymunah, blushing in response to the seemingly genuine praise.

'Tea? You must be tired from the trip,' said Silki.

'Not really,' replied Maymunah, sounding unsure.

'I think you need to relax. We will begin once we are set up. I need to take a few snaps of you in various postures and then a few close-ups. That will complete your portfolio, which I will present to my ad firm when I return to Mumbai.'

'Okay.'

'Have you got the change of clothes, as I told you?' asked Kankan.

'Yes,' replied Maymunah, holding out the best clothes from her meagre wardrobe.

'They will have to do,' said the woman condescendingly, rolling her eyes.

With that, she began to set up her equipment while Kankan watched.

'Why don't you use the restroom and freshen up? Wash your face with the face wash kept on the bathroom sink. I will need to apply minimal foundation and make-up, though you don't need it,' said Silki.

While Maymunah was in the washroom, Kankan quickly helped the woman set up the equipment.

'How long do you intend to continue this drama?' he asked, sounding impatient.

'Aww, let me have a little fun. We will wrap this up soon enough, I promise,' she assured him, noting his impatience.

Inside the washroom, Maymunah was trying to control her anxiety and excitement. Her dreams were finally coming true. She would do her best to make this work. Taking several deep breaths, she opened the door and walked out.

'Okay, let's get this done,' said the woman as she saw Maymunah walk out of the washroom.

14

After leaving the hotel, Mihir walked for nearly 10 kilometres at a brisk pace. For an ordinary person, this would have amounted to a slow-paced jog. The cold night helped. He took the main road out of Guwahati, which led him past the outskirts and on to the national highway. After an hour and forty minutes on the highway, he came to a quiet hamlet called Sepetia, east of the main junction of Barojat.

The road on either side of town was lined with small hotels, which provided decent lodging for tourists who came to visit the Nazirakhat Archaeological Park. He chose a small hotel 2 kilometres further away from town, which fit the bill nicely. The aim was to attract as little attention as possible. When he rang the bell to rouse the slumbering front desk manager, it was nearly 3.30 a.m.

The room gave a good view of the front of the hotel. Mihir left the lights off, parted his window curtains slightly and scanned the parking lot. Other than a car in one corner, it was empty. No tail. He was, for all practical purposes, heading to Delhi on a flight; and that flight he was supposed to have been travelling in would have taken off from Guwahati approximately half an hour ago.

Mihir reached into his duffel bag and extracted an envelope. Rehaan had handed it to him before returning to Delhi. The envelope was small and plain, made of a thicker-than-usual white paper to protect the contents, but still as common as the millions that travelled from thousands of post offices across the length and breadth of the country. Rehaan had also handed him a small, folded note; this one without an envelope.

Seated in a cane chair by the window, with only a corner lamp for illumination, Mihir examined both items and opened the folded note first. It gave the registration details of the vehicle that had tailed them from Guwahati to Karimpuhl—a car rental company based in Guwahati. A classic, foolproof smokescreen, designed to leave no trails. Though Mihir memorized the details of the rental company, he knew it wasn't of much use—they would be unable to help beyond a point. The documents that would have been deposited to hire the car would be fake and would lead to a dead end.

Mihir then examined the envelope in detail. Important clues were invariably lost when envelopes were torn open in a hurry. It was addressed to him, but to his office address. Strange. He rarely got letters on that address.

The faint postage stamp on the cover indicated that it had been posted from Ijgadora nearly two weeks ago. That was a small town roughly midway between Nagaon and Guwahati. The sender's details were mandatory, since it was sent by registered speed post. The name was Islam Khan; the address unknown to Mihir. He knew no one in that small town, leave alone an Islam Khan. How did this man get access to the firm's address? It was purely a word-of-mouth organization, not a company with details in Yellow Pages.

Mihir opened it. Inside was an A4-sized sheet of paper, torn in half by hand. Written across it were six digits. It looked like a telephone number. But whose?

Mihir rang the number using the hotel landline extension in his room. An automatic voice asked him to check the number that had been dialled. He tried adding the local code before the number. He got the same response. He stared at the number for a long time but could make no sense of it. Maybe he had the code wrong. He dialled the STD code of Ijgadora, the place from where the envelope came. No luck there, either.

The next step was to call the major towns and district headquarters in Assam. All the automated voices gave the same answer. So, it was not a telephone number. Could it be a pin code? He fed the number in the India Post website, but no such pin code existed. He let the problem lie in his head for now; the solution would come to him eventually. It always did.

Mihir then did some research on Ijgadora. It was a small town in Morigaon district, with a total population of just under 18,000. It was just like any other small town in the state, except for one thing: It had the largest dry fish market in the world. Another feather in its cap was the Ijgadora Paper Mill, the first in the world to produce paper made of 100 per cent bamboo. With an average literacy rate of over 87 per cent, it had three colleges and many good schools. And that was that; there was nothing more. He figured it wouldn't be too difficult for him to trace the sender in the small town.

Finally, with nothing left to do, Mihir lay down on the double bed. The cane creaked under his weight. He checked the time—4 a.m., an hour to daylight. He decided to catch up on sleep; he needed to be fresh and clear-headed.

15

Ranjan Basumatary did not go to work that morning. For a daily wage earner, that meant a day's income lost and less food on the table. The municipal office where he worked did not take too kindly to absentees. But his decision was an act of desperation.

'Is she answering?' asked his wife, Santati, in tears.

'No, it's the same response. It says that the mobile is switched off,' said Ranjan, on the verge of a nervous breakdown himself.

Their three other children were huddled together, scared. They could not fathom the reason for their mother's grief and father's worried expression. They missed their older sister's presence—she would have been able to handle everything.

The last message Ranjan had received from Maymunah was on WhatsApp. It said she had reached the hotel and would call once her interview was over. He had been so happy. Finally, some hope in their miserable lives. But the call never came. That was two days ago. Since then, nothing.

For the first few hours, the parents thought she had simply forgotten. Maybe the interview had gone on longer than expected. They tried to call her a couple of times, but could not get through. Maybe they were being paranoid. Everything would be all right by morning, or so they thought. They slept fitfully.

But the next morning, when there was no change in the situation, Ranjan decided to skip work. It was futile to call Maymunah. Obviously, she was in some kind of trouble. He decided to go to the police.

The Basumatarys lived in a two-room shanty in one of the countless by lanes on Dhabmandi Road, a narrow lane in Bondhuroh main market, in the heart of the town. It was also home to the largest brothel in the area, where most of the business was run out of small shanties and decrepit buildings that lined the road and small gullies. Each structure housed a number of prostitutes and was run by an owner, who was called 'madam' or 'maalkin'. The nearest police station was the Bondhuroh Sadar thana.

'Are you sure she is not in one of the whore houses?' asked the assistant sub-inspector as he looked at Maymunah's photograph. It was a well-known fact that the maalkins connived with human traffickers and the local police to supply girls to these brothels. But it was unlikely that a local girl would be picked up and placed in a nearby brothel.

'No, sir, she left for Guwahati two days ago and promised to call. Her phone is switched off and we don't know where she might be,' replied Ranjan, barely able to control his tears. He was not even sure the police would help him; poor people's pleas were rarely heard.

Somehow, the ASI was convinced about the genuineness of the wretched soul sitting in front of him. An unexplained sense of empathy overtook the man in khaki.

'Where in Guwahati?'

'Hotel Narzi,' Ranjan said.

The cop knew the place. It was a decent three-star hotel next to the airport, catering to local tourists from the neighbouring states.

'Why did she go there?' the ASI asked.

'She was called for an interview with a talent scout from Mumbai, looking for models from the Northeast,' Ranjan explained.

'Did somebody accompany her?' wondered the officer, acutely aware of the modus operandi of kidnappers in these parts.

'She went alone.'

'That's quite stupid, to send a young daughter alone all the way to Guwahati.'

'We had no choice. I would have lost two to three days of daily wages had I gone with her. My wife has three small children to look after. Besides, she was quite sure it was going to be okay,' said Ranjan, forlornly.

'How did this talent scout get in touch? Was it a he or a she?' asked the ASI.

'I don't know.'

'Any close friends in her school that you know of?'

'No one close, I think, but she was popular in her school.'

The ASI could see why. The girl was one of the prettiest he had ever seen. To the ASI, this looked all too familiar—young girls disappearing without a trace. Girls often ran away from their homes, enticed by fantasies of stardom and fame. Most were sold into prostitution in the countless cities and towns of India. Those too young were palmed off as maids. This girl could be anywhere. He felt sorry for the man. Chances were that he would never see his daughter again.

'I will see what I can do. This incident happened in an area next to the Guwahati airport. That falls under the jurisdiction of Razak police thana. I will send the details to them. Meanwhile, I will visit the school,' he said, trying to assure Ranjan, and hide his own lack of conviction.

He watched the poor father get up, bent and defeated, bowing with folded hands. He slowly walked away, pinning his hopes on the police to find his daughter.

The ASI picked up the phone and dialled the number of the Razak thana.

~

Meanwhile, Maymunah had no recollection of how she managed to get into the dark cell she was in now. She remembered the photo shoot, though. It had lasted for more than two hours. It was a revelation to her that modelling could be so exhausting. The photographer would not proceed until she had every shot exactly the way she wanted. It had to be perfect in every way. And that meant countless retakes.

Suddenly, in the middle of it all, the woman said they all needed a break. So, the trio trooped down to the restaurant where they had fizzy drinks and snacks. Kankan then invited Maymunah for a walk outside, while the talent scout excused herself and went up to the room to reset the equipment.

As they were walking side by side, Maymunah, who was practically glowing with happiness, noticed that Kankan was unusually quiet and constantly looking around. He seemed nervous. Even in the chill of the cloudy winter afternoon, he was sweating. Suddenly, her surroundings began to sway. Maymunah felt faint and wobbly. She remembered trying to steady herself by leaning on the side of a minivan that appeared out of nowhere. That was her last recollection.

Since then, Maymunah had lost all sense of time and direction. A weak bulb allowed her to make out that the room, more like a cell actually, was maybe 8 feet by 6 feet. There was a steel cot welded to the floor, on top of which was a mattress that stank of sweat. In one corner was a steel wash basin, next to it, a Western-style toilet, also of steel. Both were stained with overuse. There was no window, only a steel door, the top half of which was covered by an iron grille.

Maymunah felt as if the walls were closing in on her. Claustrophobic, alone and very scared, she began to cry, her sniffles barely audible outside the confines of her cell. She thought of her parents and the trauma that her unexplained absence would inflict on them. Then she remembered her cell phone and began looking for it. It was not there. Her purse was also missing. It had been her father's gift to her on her sixteenth birthday. She searched desperately in the dingy cell. Finally, giving up, she shrank back into the bed, sobbing. Where was Kankan?

~

Back at the hotel, Kankan was feeling sorry for Maymunah. There was some guilt about what he had just done, betraying her trust. After she had been bundled off in the van, he had gone for a long walk, trying to shake off the feeling. For the first time, he did not like himself. Finally, he walked back to the hotel room, where Silki was waiting for him, all packed up.

'Where the hell have you been? I was waiting for you. You have done well, my darling,' she said, kissing him.

'I don't feel nice about what I have done to her. What was so special about her anyway?' he complained, brushing her aside for the first time.

'You will see. My boss wants to meet you and thank you in person. The reward will make up for any bad feelings you have about your betrayal,' said Silki, smiling.

'I need to get back home,' he said, impatiently.

'It won't take long. It is on the way to Bondhuroh. Besides, this is one boss you do not want to piss off,' she replied with finality.

∼

Maymunah had no idea how long she lay on the bed. Her tears had dried up; she was hungry and thirsty. She tried calling out for help, but her voice was weak with fear and exhaustion.

After what seemed like an hour, the door to the cell opened and the light bulb was switched on, blinding her by its glare. Maymunah couldn't see the person in front clearly, but cringed as they advanced towards her. Seeing it was a woman, she relaxed a bit.

'Come with me,' the woman said.

'I want to go home … please,' she implored.

'All in good time,' said the woman as she helped her up by her elbow and led her out of the cell into the corridor.

∼

By the time Kankan and Silki left the hotel, it was already dark. Silki drove. They took the highway to the Barojat crossing and turned southwards towards Shillong. After half an hour, they came to a turning on the left side of the road that led to a narrow track. It was 5-kilometres long and led to a clearing at the base of a hill. As they reached the end, Kankan saw a large green shed. It seemed like a warehouse.

Silki parked the car. It began to rain just as they headed towards the main entrance. The sky above was heavy with black clouds. Kankan shivered as the first drops of cold rain fell on his bare neck. Quickly, he walked inside.

Kankan estimated that the structure must have been at least a 100-feet long and 50-feet wide. The ceiling was about 30-feet high. Except for a small bulb that illuminated one corner of the cavernous interior, the shed was dark and silent. Underneath the bulb was a single chair. Empty.

'Sit here. The boss will be here in a minute,' said Silki, pointing towards the empty chair.

Kankan sat. Silki stood behind him. A minute later, another side door opened and a man walked in. Kankan guessed he was the boss that Silki was referring to. As Kankan rose to greet him, the man gestured for him to remain seated.

As the boss approached the chair, Kankan realized that the face in front of him was covered by some kind of a pollution mask. The head was wrapped in a black 'patka'. Only his eyes were visible. As he walked up to Kankan and stood a foot away from him, Kankan saw him up close and realized that the face had no eyebrows. The skin looked pale and smooth.

'You have done well for us. Thank you,' said the boss, in a thin, raspy voice.

'You are welcome, sir,' replied Kankan, as he looked up at the man and then turned towards Silki, seeking more approval. He was standing so close to the chair that Kankan could reach out and touch him. Obviously, he dared not. But he had to look up at him, his neck straining at an awkward angle.

'Your reward,' said the masked man, holding up a medium-sized polythene bag. 'Take it. It's yours.'

Kankan took the bag.

'Take a look,' the boss prodded.

Kankan opened the bag. The rustle of the polythene sounded unusually loud in the otherwise empty shed. There were three wads of 200-rupee notes, each a hundred notes thick. Sixty thousand rupees in total. Kankan chuckled with delight; he had never seen so much money in his life.

'Thank you,' he said, his eyes bright with glee.

'Savour the moment, young man,' said the masked figure.

The man turned his back to Kankan, who got up to leave. Silki put a restraining hand on his shoulder, pushing him back down on to the chair.

'There is a slight problem, though,' said the masked stranger as an afterthought, raising his right hand and forefinger, while turning around slowly to face Kankan once again.

'What?' asked Kankan, sounding a little puzzled.

'In our line of business, discretion is very important. Identities are carefully concealed.'

'I understand. I won't say anything. You have my word.'

'The missing girl must have been reported by now,' the man continued, ignoring the boy's assurance. 'The police will be searching for her. And your absence over the last two days will also have been noticed. You were in the same school, isn't it?'

'Yes, but I won't tell the police anything, I swear,' said Kankan, suddenly feeling apprehensive.

'But when you go back, you will be questioned by the police. What will you say then?'

'I will tell them that I had gone to visit my relatives in Guwahati. Nobody knows I had asked Maymunah over to the hotel,' said Kankan, now clearly panicking. He realized with a sinking feeling that this man was dangerous.

'That I doubt. The young girl must have surely told her parents. It will not work, I am afraid. They will cross-check.

Besides, the police will not only question her parents, but check with yours too. What will they say, I wonder? Visiting relatives without informing them? The police are very thorough in their work when they want to be. You will have to disappear,' said the boss, shaking his head, unconvinced by the boy's desperate attempts to get out of the situation.

'Yes … Yes, with this kind of money I can do that,' said Kankan, scared.

'Good. We will help you do that,' said the man they called the Monster.

'Thank you, thank you so very much,' said Kankan, relieved.

The Monster smiled and looked at Silki standing behind the seated boy.

Kankan also turned around to look at his lover. In the same instant, a long scarf tied with a weight at one end materialized in the woman's hand, as if out of nowhere. Using her right hand, she flicked the weighted end around Kankan's neck with such speed that he did not even notice it till it was way past his throat and back in Silki's left hand.

Before Kankan realized the mortal danger he was in, the noose had tightened so much that his attempts to escape the death-grip were futile. He could not breathe. His lungs, desperate for air, felt as if they were on fire. His eyes bulged, pleading with the man in front of him for life. The Monster stared back with emotionless eyes. In that instant, Kankan knew death was near. He tried to scream, but no sound came out. His windpipe was being crushed against his cervical vertebrae. He started thrashing about, hands flailing, trying to loosen the grip of the cord around his throat. His legs started stiffening and kicking out under him. His body desperately tried to fight for survival. Silki snapped the cord tighter. Kankan's neck jerked back with a sickening crack. In his dying moments, as life was being sucked out of his body, he watched with disbelief as Silki looked down at him, wicked glee on her face. Kankan went limp, his shocked dead eyes staring at the woman he had made love to only a few hours ago.

The macabre dance of death kindled a familiar desire in the Monster; it arose from within his dark soul. The woman saw the look in his eyes as she loosened her grip on the scarf. She leered at her boss with cold delight as she reached for her trousers. Later, once everything was quiet, the Monster picked up the bag of money and walked out.

16

The young girl, no more than ten and dressed in a flimsy white frock, was playing outside, oblivious to the cold weather and the rain as it lashed her fragile frame. Her back was turned to her brother, who was running towards her, as if to protect her from danger. He called out, but she couldn't hear him. As he reached out to her, she turned to face him. She looked up at the grey sky and her face exploded into a fountain of blood, soaking her brother in crimson.

Mihir woke up with a start, his clothes drenched in sweat. He looked at his watch, it was ten on the same morning he had checked into the small hotel off the road. He had slept fitfully for six hours. He looked outside the window; after the previous night's heavy downpour, the sky was painted an azure blue.

He showered and shaved, shaking off the cobwebs of a bad night. Then he went through his morning physical regimen, a routine he performed no matter where he was. It took his physical and mental alertness to the next level. After an hour's intense workout, he showered again and got ready for lunch.

The hotel's restaurant was on the ground floor. As he entered the dining room, Mihir heard the sounds of utensils being arranged on the kitchen counters and gas stoves being lit. Mihir ordered tandoori naan and chicken, mixed veggies, daal and a glass of lassi to wash it all down.

As he began to eat, the nightmare faded from his consciousness. Though the dreams took a heavy toll on him emotionally, he actually welcomed them—they were a reminder of his shortcomings and also the only means to connect with Sneha, who was no longer a part of his world.

Snapping out of the downward spiral of thoughts, Mihir forced his mind to the task at hand, as he recalled the events of the last couple of days. He went over the information he had so far.

First, they were being followed continuously since the time they had landed in Guwahati. That meant somebody had information about their visit. But who? And why?

Second, why was Chris murdered? Mihir was no nearer to the answer than the first time he learnt of the murder from Gene that fateful night. The visit to the unit had only thrown up vague, uncorroborated suspicions.

Third, this letter he had received at his office address from a person he didn't know, from a place he had never been to—was there a connection?

Mihir finished his lunch and checked out of the hotel. He preferred to pay in cash as cards always left a trail that was easy to trace. It was also a convenient arrangement for night-time managers who could show the room as vacant and pocket the cash without informing the hotel owners. Not his problem, anyway. There would be no trace of him having ever stayed there.

Back on the road, he decided to follow the only lead he had at the moment. The distance between Sepetia and Ijgadora was about 45 kilometres. A forty to forty-five minute drive by car, longer by bus. Better to hitch a ride; one tends to get noticed when bus tickets are bought. No matter how much he tried, he couldn't blend in with the general public; so it was best to stick to the national highway as much as possible—they were way less crowded. He decided to hitch a ride in a truck, but it was nearly an hour before he got lucky.

By the time he was dropped off where the national highway intersected the arterial road that led to Ijgadora, the sun was already low on the horizon. By Mihir's estimate, it would be dark in about thirty minutes. He could see ominous grey clouds on the horizon. It would rain that night. A good time to search for the mysterious sender.

He looked at the address once again. There was no house number in which Islam Khan stayed, only a plot number—715—located on Hanusha Bahi Road. A public sector bank was opposite plot number 715. The map display on his mobile showed the bank, but nothing opposite. Islam Khan's address seemed a blank space. Mihir decided to check it out. The junction was about 5 kilometres from the destination. He began walking.

The walk itself was quite uneventful. Mihir realized that Google Maps was, in fact, updated. There was hardly any habitation on the road, except for a few houses scattered here and there at random. The road skirted Ijgadora from the north and was quite narrow, as it was constructed atop a bund—there were water bodies on both sides of the road. Two vehicles crossing each other would require some deft manoeuvring. Dark clouds hung low in the sky and with no lights to illuminate the road, visibility was down to zero; that suited Mihir just fine.

After walking for almost an hour, he could make out the faint silhouette of a large, two-storeyed building, its porch illuminated. It was the bank. The address on the envelope should be opposite the bank. About 100 metres short, Mihir began to have serious doubts about the authenticity of the address and they were confirmed once he was standing on the road with his back to the building. The porch light showed a vacant patch of land; there was no house within 500 metres of the bank on either side of the road.

So, no human habitation. Mihir looked carefully once again at the vacant piece of land. He saw something in the darkness and crossed the road to confirm. Yes, no human habitation—at least not the living variety. He was standing at the entrance to a graveyard.

~

Around the same, Colonel Randhawa, aka Randy, was seated in Sumer's office, in the unit headquarters 20 kilometres away from the Delta Company Operating Base, twirling a warm goblet of brandy. It was close to midnight. The mess staff serving them had retired for the night an hour ago. The office was completely dark, except for an overhead lamp pulled low over Sumer's desk. Under its yellow light, Randy was carefully reading a copy of the inquest report ordered by the executive magistrate of Karimpuhl into the cause of Major Christopher Zachariah's death.

The court of inquest was a mandatory requirement in the event of an unnatural death under suspicious circumstances. In Chris's case, the death was quite unnatural and highly suspicious. It was a no-brainer—death by multiple GSW (gunshot wounds). The military police officer had seen numerous unnatural deaths in his career spanning three decades; a general examination of the wounds on Chris's body, specifically the entry and exit points, clearly established that the rounds were fired from a lower level, from a range of about 15–20 feet. The weapon was most probably a handgun, calibre 9-millimetre. But the crucial information which the report was not mandated to cover, and could not, was the identity of the murderer.

Randy was frustrated, as his own investigation was leading nowhere. But now he had cause to celebrate. His cautious optimism came from an item Sumer and he were now examining. Beside the inquest report lay a small notepad, 3-inches wide and about 5-inches long, which flipped open at the top—the kind that army officers always carry in their combat-jacket pockets, handy to jot down points quickly. Hardly enough reason for their controlled excitement.

But they were excited for two reasons. First, it was found in a hidden compartment in the top drawer of a study table kept in Chris's hut. The officers had chanced upon it while carrying out a thorough search once again after Chris's personal effects had been handed over to his wife. Second, the first two pages of the fifty-page notepad were filled with a hurried scribble; the rest were empty. The scribbler was Chris; Sumer recognized his handwriting.

Beyond that, they couldn't figure out anything more. There was a series of numbers written without a break from the top of the first page to the bottom of the second. Ten rows, twelve digits to a row, with five rows to a page. The numbers were completely random, with no discernible pattern. Both officers had tried to make sense of the numbers for more than an hour, without success.

While Randy was ruffling through the pages, a small piece of paper fell on to the table, startling them—they hadn't come across it when they first studied the notepad. It was no more than 2-inches square, neatly folded in the centre. Randy opened it. He stared at the neatly written figures in pencil. Somebody's cell number.

∼

Nearly 400 kilometres away, Mihir was down on his haunches, a small LED torch in his left hand. Acting on a hunch, he was moving from one grave to another, trying to read the names of the fifty or so dead who lay peacefully, six feet under. Halfway through the eerie task, just as he was going to give it up as a silly endeavour, he was rewarded.

The twenty-third grave he examined was a small one—3 feet by 2 feet—maybe of a child, about three or four years old. It was located in a small depression in the ground, flanked by two larger graves. Had he not been on his fours, feeling his way through, he would have missed it. It was as if the child's grave had been jammed in the congested space between the larger two. May be the child's parents? As he removed the mud off the grave, Mihir read the name on the small stone slab. Islam Khan.

Mihir sat on the ground, his back resting against a large rock, trying to figure out if this was somebody's idea of a sick joke. Who would do such a thing? It had to be someone with intimate knowledge of the local area, especially this graveyard. Someone who had visited it and seen the name on the grave. But what if it was not a joke? Was somebody deliberately trying to draw his attention to this very spot?

While he was trying to figure out the answer, Mihir switched on the torch of his mobile phone and ran it along the small gravestone. There was a gap between the earth and the stone slab. He reached into his knapsack and took out a Swiss knife, and, prising open the largest blade, began to carefully widen the gap.

He then inserted his right hand into the gap tentatively and was surprised when he found he could insert his hand so far in that it was completely under the slab. He realized then that this was no grave; it was just a three-inch thick slab kept on the ground with a fictitious name inscribed on top. Mihir inserted his other hand in and lifted the slab, pivoting it to the far edge. The ground beneath had depressed grass, a host of insects and some scorpions. Mihir quickly brushed them aside, using one hand to hold the slab, while, with the other, he shone the torch on the ground he had freshly uncovered.

At the centre of the false grave lay a small rectangular dugout, about 6-inches long, 4-inches wide and 3-inches deep. Inside, lay a small diary, carefully enclosed in a transparent polythene bag. Mihir picked it up. Through the bag, he could see a small piece of loose paper. Written on it was one word: TIGER.

Mihir knew instantly who the mysterious sender was. In the army, juniors always refer to their seniors as 'sir'. More informally, they sometimes use a surname, followed by the word 'sir'. Only Chris, with affection and deep respect, addressed Mihir as 'Tiger', a nickname usually reserved for commanders of troops.

'Glad you found it,' said a voice from behind him.

Mihir whirled around to find a hooded figure standing at the entrance to the graveyard. His search had distracted him and the desolateness of the place had lulled him into a false sense of security.

'I thought you would never come,' said the hooded figure. 'I have been coming to this spot every night for the last fifteen days.'

'Did you hide it under the slab?' asked Mihir, still trying to gauge the figure in the shadows.

'Yes, I did.'

'Why hide it? Why not give it to me straight?'

'Chris sahab wanted it done that way, for safekeeping. He was sure only you, whom he called Tiger, would be able to find it. This way, even if I was caught, there would be nothing they would find on me.'

'Who are they?'

'I don't know. Chris sahab knew, but wouldn't tell me. He just said they were very powerful people. He feared for my life too, after this task he had entrusted to me.'

'Surely, they don't know about you; otherwise, you would not be here alive. And, what's in the diary?'

'I don't know and what you don't know can't kill you. But he did say that all that you needed to know was written there.'

As Mihir stood up to face him, the figure added, 'Chris sahab was a good man. I owed him a lot and I would do anything for him. But now that he is dead, killed by the people he suspected, I have no other task left to fulfil.'

'Where will you go now?'

'Bangladesh. The border is very porous. I will take my family with me. We hope to be safe with our relatives there,' said the man. Mihir then watched the silhouette dissolve into the pitch-black night.

Turning his attention back to the object in hand, Mihir carefully uncovered the diary and examined it under his torch. It was one of those typical, hardbound New Year's diaries provided by vendors supplying office stationery to army units. This was from 2018, with two calendar dates to a page, and standard information about holidays, zodiac signs, etc.

Only the first three pages were filled, with neat text written in blue ink in manuscript hand. There were fifteen names, numbered serially, five to a page. Mihir scanned through the names twice; they did not mean anything to him. Chris had clearly expected him to know the names. As he was glancing through them a third time, the last name in the list rang a bell. He had heard the name being mentioned, but by whom? He could not quite recollect. As always, he would eventually remember.

With nothing left to do, Mihir got up, collected his knapsack, replaced the slab in exactly the same spot and left the graveyard. The diary was safely zipped into his jacket pocket. As he was walking back, he once again mulled over the information he had gathered so far.

A set of numbers written on a piece of paper contained in an envelope, which Chris clearly expected Mihir to know. The numbers weren't making any sense at the moment.

Then, a diary found under a false grave, again kept there by his dead friend for him to find, containing unknown names, except for one vaguely familiar name. He wished Chris hadn't been mysterious. He could have just written all this down and sent him a secure message.

Retracing his steps, Mihir headed back towards the junction he had left a few hours ago. By the time he reached the intersection, it had begun to rain, the dark clouds so low one could almost reach out and touch them. The wind was cold. Shivering slightly, Mihir was about to decide on his next course of action, when his cell phone rang. Unknown number.

'Mihir. This is Colonel Randhawa. Where are you?'
'Why?'
'I'll explain once we meet. We have something you might like to see. You need to come over immediately,' said Randy.
'It may take time. I am in Gurugram.'
'You never took the flight out of Guwahati.'

17

Tuhin Khanna slept fitfully, his mind tense with the events of the previous evening, which kept playing on loop.

The group had been picked up at 7.30 p.m. in a twelve-seater minibus. They could see nothing outside; the curtains were drawn across the windows, with strict instructions not to open them. They dared not disobey the orders, as a man stood just behind the driver and observed them carefully. Tuhin had seen a bulge in the small of his back. No one disobeyed a man with a gun.

They had travelled for nearly thirty minutes before the vehicle stopped. After two minutes, a gate opened to let them through. Five minutes later, they stopped again. This time, the engine was switched off. They had finally arrived at their destination.

The guests were received in style. It was a party like no other. But before they could indulge in its many pleasures, they were whisked away to a nearby room for a meeting with the owner, or Maalik, as the staff preferred to call him. Tuhin went in alone. Just before he entered the conference room, he saw his girlfriend, Rubina, pleasantly surprised, being led to a poolside chair by a semi-nude gigolo.

The room for the meeting had a large oval conference table, with seating for twenty, and a large LED screen on one wall. The lighting was muted; visibility was limited to a few feet. Tuhin noticed that besides the four guests who had accompanied him in the bus, there were eight others. All men. They must have stayed somewhere else. The chair at the head of the table was vacant, presumably awaiting the arrival of Maalik.

Ten minutes later, he appeared. In the partial darkness, all that could be made out of the host was the silhouette of a man in a suit and tie. Tuhin assumed it was a deliberate move to keep him in the shadows—the fewer people who recognized him, the better. He was accompanied by two men, most probably his security detail. They quietly stood behind him as he sat down in in the vacant chair.

'I thank you all for having taken the time out to come all the way here for our meeting. I assure you it will be worth your while,' said Maalik, in a thin, gravelly voice, as if each word he uttered was an effort.

'Business has never been better. The credit for this achievement goes to all of you,' he added. 'I want to take our mutual interests to the next level. We are gathered here to ensure success.'

The attendees nodded in unison, not sure where this was heading.

'As you are aware, cash flows from our business have been substantial. Our business is thriving. But that is the root of our present problem. We haven't found ways to make the complete lot legitimate. In bits and pieces, yes, but not the whole lot. Our efforts haven't been enough.'

'How can we help?' asked one eager guest, realizing too late that he had spoken out of turn.

'I am sure you will find a way. All of you, besides being our partners in this line of business, have legal companies. Naturally, you will use them,' Maalik said.

'What if we can't?' asked a doubtful eager beaver. Tuhin hoped that these idiots would learn to keep quiet, lest they all suffer for this indiscretion.

Maalik said nothing in response. For a full minute, the conference hall was quiet. You could cut the tension in the air with a knife.

To everyone's relief, the host spoke again. 'The money will be routed to your firms in cash by my associates. They will contact you from time to time for details of the transactions. I am sure you will look after my assets as if they were your own.'

He began to get up to leave, but then said, 'Oh, I almost forgot! There is a short video. Sit back, relax and watch. After it, you are all invited to the party outside. Do enjoy yourselves.'

The dim hall became completely dark as he left and the LED screen lit up with grainy footage. The guests saw the exterior of a large warehouse. The next shot showed the warehouse from the inside, virtually empty, except for a lone chair directly underneath a dim light.

A young man was seated on the chair, speaking to someone who was standing and had his back to the camera. He seemed to be wearing a mask. There was no audio, so the guests could not make out what was being said. After a minute, the man with the mask turned to go. And, as if on cue, the young man got up to leave. That was when a hand emerged out of the darkness and pushed him down—a woman who was partially in the shadows, unseen until now. The masked man turned again and the young man on the chair gaped at him.

That was when the whole scene became surreal. In the blink of an eye, a cord of some kind had wound its way around the young man's neck. It tightened; he was being choked. There was a collective gasp from the seated audience. They watched in disbelief as the boy desperately struggled for life ... and failed. The screen went blank.

After an eternally long minute, the ashen-faced guests were escorted out of the conference room to the party at the poolside. The warmth and gaiety outside were in sharp contrast to the cold death they had witnessed inside the room. The nonchalant manner in which the young boy had been killed was too much for Tuhin to handle. He ran to the restroom and retched his guts out until he nearly fainted. What had he got himself into?

Earlier that morning, Susuma Majumdar had been looking at the assistant sub-inspector nervously—he had been in her office for more than thirty minutes, and she was doing her best to answer all his questions truthfully. As the school's principal, she was also worried about its reputation: One missing student and a police enquiry was enough to damage its name. The school was only a decade old and she had been its principal from the start. It was her life.

'I will need a list of all her friends. Who she was close to, or with whom did she spend most of her time? Any other relevant details you can think of that can assist us in finding this girl?' the investigating officer said.

'This is Mr Samanta, Maymunah's class teacher,' said the principal, pointing to a man who had just entered the office.

Samanta placed his right hand across his chest and bowed respectfully. The ASI nodded a greeting in return and gestured towards a chair next to him. The teacher sat down.

'How is she as a student?' asked the ASI.

'Not the brightest, but she more than makes up for it with her popularity among her fellow students.'

'Anyone she is close to?'

'There are a couple of girls in the class who are her close friends. I can get them here if you want.'

'It would be better if we met them outside; that way, we will attract less attention,' the officer said.

They walked around the school premises; it was the midday recess, and a gaggle of students had collected under the shade of a tree. The teacher walked up to the group and called two girls towards him.

'This is ASI Gogoi from the police station nearby. He wants to ask you a few questions about Maymunah,' said Samanta.

The girls looked at the policeman unsurely.

'I believe you two are close to Maymunah. When was the last time you met her?' ASI Gogoi asked.

'About four days ago in class,' said one of the girls.

'Did she say anything about going somewhere?'

Both girls shook their heads.

'Anyone she was going to meet?'

'No,' said the girls in unison, looking at each other.

This was getting frustrating. 'Anyway, if you think of anything that can help, please let me know. Your principal has my contact number,' said Gogoi, turning to go.

'She has a boyfriend. They are quite close,' one of the girls blurted out.

The inspector turned around slowly. 'What did you say?'

He noticed one girl was trying to stop the other from saying anything more. But she brushed aside her hand and spoke.

'He is a boy from the twelfth class. They would often leave together after school.'

'Name?'

'Kankan.'

'Okay, thanks. Next time, don't keep anything from me. You don't know what small information might help,' said the ASI.

Once the girls had been excused, the investigator and the class teacher began talking again.

'Know this boy?' Gogoi asked.

'Yes, I used to teach him when he was in the tenth.'

'Let us go and meet him.'

The recess was not yet over and some of the students were still in the classroom. The teacher called out to one of the boys, who sauntered up in a way so typical of teenagers—loose ties and shirts untucked.

'Where is Kankan?' asked Samanta.

'Don't know, sir. He hasn't been to school in four days now,' replied the boy.

The policeman glanced at the teacher. This was too much of a coincidence.

'Any idea why he has been absent for so long?'

'He said he was going to Guwahati for some work.'

Gogoi looked at the teacher and nodded. He had what he wanted.

~

Inspector Sarma, in charge of the Razak police thana in Guwahati, was impatiently drumming his fingers on the table, watching CCTV footage from the front of a hotel, recorded over the last four days. Earlier, he had shown the photograph of the girl sent over to him by the Sadar police station in Bondhuroh to the receptionist. She remembered directing the girl to the hotel room where a woman and a young man had checked in the previous evening. She had thought they made an odd couple—the man barely out of his teens, much younger than the woman. No one had seen the girl after that brief encounter. She hadn't been seen leaving the hotel by the staff either.

'I would like to see the CCTV footage from the time the odd couple checked in,' said Inspector Sarma.

'Sure, sir,' the hotel manager replied.

When the footage was up, Inspector Sarma asked the staff and the manager to leave the room.

He forwarded the video to the date of the alleged disappearance. After a few minutes, the footage showed the girl walking into the hotel and speaking to the receptionist. There was no audio, but the policeman could make out that the girl was being directed to the room where the odd couple was staying. As Inspector Sarma forwarded the video, he caught footage of the boy and the girl leaving the hotel through the central lobby. After fifteen minutes, the boy returned. This time, he was alone. He looked in the direction of the reception, but the receptionist was not at her station. He quickly moved out of the frame, probably heading to the room to meet his partner.

The whole operation was sloppily done. There were too many crumbs left on the trail, too easy to follow. Inspector Sarma took out a USB drive and connected it to the security DVR. It took a few seconds to get the entire footage on to the drive. He then disconnected the drive and inserted a compact disc, typing out a few commands. The virus soon corrupted the entire hard drive.

The inspector smiled. Now, there was no evidence of the girl having ever been to the hotel. He quietly left the room, thanked the manager waiting outside, advised him not to utter a word of this to anyone, and walked out of the hotel.

Once outside, he dialled a number on his cell. It was picked up after three rings.

'I have taken care of the problem here, but the parents of the girl have lodged a complaint with the local thana and the police there are now involved.'

'I will take care of the parents. They wouldn't be a problem. Handle the cop from Bondhuroh,' said the voice on the other end, before disconnecting the line.

18

Outside her cell, Maymunah could barely see in the dark corridor. She noticed similar cells on either side. It took her and the unknown woman a couple of minutes to cross the dingy passage, after which they began to climb a flight of stairs—the woman leading, her left hand clasped firmly around the frightened girl's right. At the top of the landing was a pantry and a spacious kitchen, where a couple of cooks were preparing a meal. They barely glanced at the woman and the girl, who continued past them to another corridor on the same level. Unlike the one in the basement, this one was well-lit, and had the kind of opulence that Maymunah had only seen in Bollywood movies. The floor was granite; the lower halves of the walls were panelled with teak, while the upper halves had floral wallpaper. Ornate paintings adorned the walls. The corridor had doors on both sides.

But the rich surroundings did little to assuage Maymunah's fears.

At the end of the corridor, the woman stopped in front of the last door on the right side. It opened into a suite. Maymunah was instructed to sit down on the sofa in the living room and wait. The woman left, shutting the door behind her.

The room that Maymunah was now in was so different to the grimy cell that she had trouble believing that they were in the same building. Just then, the wall clock gently chimed three. Seated at the edge of the sofa, she wrung her hands nervously. Gathering some courage, she got up and walked tentatively around the suite, exploring it. The living room led to a small dining room, with a table at the centre set for four. A door at the other end led to a bedroom with a king-sized bed. A medium-sized walk-in closet and a dresser were situated at one end of the bedroom. The closet opened into a bathroom with a bathtub and a shower cubicle.

The living, dining rooms and the bedrooms were adorned with French windows that overlooked a covered patio with a swimming pool in the centre. The rays of the late afternoon sun reflected off the water, and bathed the courtyard in light and warmth. Maymunah wondered what kind of people could afford such opulence. As she was walking back to the living room, she heard the front door open and saw a woman she had not seen before enter the living room. She was carrying a medium-sized duffel bag and a purse, which Maymunah recognized as her own.

'Can I have my bag please? I want to call my parents,' she stammered.

'In fact, that is exactly what I think you should do after we have had a little chat. But first, you must eat. I am sure you must be starving,' said the woman, with a disarming smile.

~

In another part of Lal Bangla, Maalik leaned back and smiled with satisfaction as he watched the girl speak with her parents back in Bondhuroh. They seemed to have been reassured. It was not too difficult to doctor the narrative; first, the girl needed to be convinced, and once that was achieved, everything fell into place. A lie told convincingly was almost like the truth.

Maalik was now confident that the parents would withdraw their FIR from the local police station. It was important to throw the cops off the scent. He did not want his venture to flop. The girl was the first in a new line of business he had just decided to explore. And it was important that nothing came between him and his success, least of all an eager, honest cop.

Once Maymunah disconnected the call, she was glowing with happiness. She put down the past few hours to some horrible misunderstanding. Now, things were finally back to normal. Her dreams were coming true, her family would no longer be poor.

'You did well. I will make sure the money reaches your parents by tomorrow,' said the woman.

'How long will I be in Mumbai?' asked Maymunah.

'Shouldn't take more than a week. Once the shoot is over, you can take the flight back to Guwahati and be with your parents before they begin to miss you,' said the woman with a smile.

'Will I be travelling alone?'

'Of course not. We have organized an escort who will be your guide for the duration of your stay. In fact, they are a nice couple. I am sure you will be safe.'

'Where is Kankan?' asked Maymunah, suddenly, as an afterthought.

For a moment, the woman's eyes went cold, then she regained her composure. 'He had to get back home. Don't worry, he will be there in Bondhuroh once you get back from Mumbai,' said the woman, the smile back on her face. 'By the way, have you ever travelled by air?'

Meanwhile, Tuhin and Rubina were still at Guwahati airport. Their flight had left more than three hours ago, but they were not on it. Tuhin's hosts had cancelled their tickets at the last minute, citing a change of plans. They were now booked on a flight leaving Guwahati at about midnight and would be accompanying a young girl of sixteen. They were to be her guardians till she was picked up outside the arrival terminal in Delhi. They were to await further instructions once they landed. Though irritated and angry at the change of plans, Tuhin was wise enough to not argue with his hosts. He knew the orders came from the very top.

Maymunah arrived at the airport exactly two hours before the flight was due for take-off. Tuhin had received her photo on his cell phone and recognized her as she walked towards them. She seemed happy. Tuhin didn't know why and, frankly, he didn't care. He just wanted to board his flight and head to the national capital. On home turf, he would be in a position to take a call on his future association with this sordid business.

∼

While Maymunah was being innocently led to Delhi, and to whatever fate had in store for her, her parents and siblings were cramped together on a dilapidated diwan—the only piece of decent furniture in the house. A naked, low-wattage bulb hanging from the ceiling on a wire illuminated the small confines of the room that doubled up as a bedroom and a living room. A small kitchen and a toilet completed the picture.

The children stared goggle-eyed at the sophisticated woman seated on a plastic chair. Their father, Ranjan, was barely able to control his excitement. Meanwhile, their mother, Santati, had rushed off to the kitchen to rustle up a cup of tea for their surprise visitor.

'This is such good news. I really don't know how to thank you and your company,' said Ranjan, who was now clutching a brown envelope.

'The envelope contains 20,000 rupees. Please count them. It is Maymunah's first commission as a model,' said the woman.

'I am sure it is all here. Frankly, I have never seen so much money in my life.'

'This is just the beginning. Much more will follow. Your daughter is quite extraordinary. She is destined for success.'

'We worry for her safety. After all, she is just a child.'

'We will look after her. Our company is very particular about its models. I assure you she will be safe. Besides, you can keep speaking to her. I think you already have her number. Isn't it?' questioned the woman, smiling.

'Oh, yes, and she was so excited about her new assignment. She said she would be going to Mumbai for a while.'

The visitor had no intention of correcting him.

Santati returned with a cup of tea. The woman reached for the brew hesitantly, thanking her.

'Will she return in time for her studies? Her next academic session begins in a month,' said Santati.

'I don't see that as a problem. She should be back in two to three weeks. You should be happy for her and not worry so much. Your daughter is going to change your family's fortunes,' said the woman.

'Can we have your number also, just in case?' asked Ranjan.

The woman stared at the parents for a loaded minute.

'Sure. Why not?' she said finally, and handed over a card with her name and number embossed on it in gold.

'And there is one other thing,' continued the woman. Ranjan looked quizzical.

'I believe you have lodged an FIR in the police station about your missing daughter.'

'Yes, I am sorry. We did not know what else to do. She hadn't spoken to us for two days and we—' began Maymunah's father.

'Yes, yes I understand,' said the woman, cutting him off. 'But now, you know there is no need to worry.'

'Yes, we are very happy. I will withdraw the complaint first thing tomorrow,' said Ranjan.

'That's settled then.'

With that, the woman left the shack. The tea was left untouched. Once outside, she took out her cell phone and speed dialled a number. She spoke briefly, hailed a cab and left as quickly as she had come.

The next day, Ranjan arrived at the police station as promised. He walked up to ASI Gogoi's desk and wished him.

'You look quite happy today,' remarked the inspector, taking a few seconds to recognize the man.

'I am sorry to bother you, sir. I have come to withdraw my complaint,' said Ranjan.

'Why? Has your daughter returned?'

'No, but I spoke to her and she is absolutely fine. In fact, she has been signed up by a modelling agency based in Mumbai.'

'You are sure of this?' asked the policeman, sceptical.

'Yes, a representative of the agency met us yesterday. She even handed us 20,000 rupees as the first commission for my daughter's modelling assignment.'

'What is the name of the agency?'

'She left her card,' said Ranjan, handing over the embossed card to the ASI.

Gogoi examined it. The background was French grey. In the centre, in bold italics, were the words 'Belle Modelling'. Underneath, a name, Aimee, a mobile number and a web address. This was all embossed in gold.

'Okay,' said the inspector. He noted down the details before returning the card to Ranjan. 'Do you have your daughter's mobile number?'

'I have her usual number. But I was told that they would give her a new number once she reached Mumbai and that she could retain it since she would be travelling often for her modelling assignments.'

'Alright. Once she contacts you from Mumbai, give me the new number,' said Gogoi.

'Yes, sir,' said Ranjan. As he got to the doorway, the ASI called out to him.

'By the way, do you know someone by the name of Kankan?'

'No, who is he?' asked Ranjan.

'A student, also from your daughter's school. Never mind.'

Gogoi sat staring at the empty doorway, deep in thought, long after the girl's father had left. If all was well, where was Kankan? And more importantly, why had nobody reported him missing? Time to visit his parents.

He went to Vinayak Apartments, a housing society west of Meherpur Road. Three towers, each eight-storeys high; four apartments to a floor, ninety-six apartments in all. He walked over to the gate and identified himself. Kankan's parents lived in Apartment C303. As he entered the society premises, he noticed individual parking spaces. The space allotted to C303 was empty. As he was going up in the elevator, he realized that he had forgotten to ask the guards at the gate whether Mr and Mrs Sharma, Kankan's parents, were at home.

Gogoi stepped out of the elevator on to a long corridor. The false ceiling had subdued lighting. The society was ultra-luxury; each apartment had a small alcove before the main door.

Gogoi rang the doorbell and waited patiently. After a minute, when there was no response, he rang the doorbell again. He turned the doorknob and the door creaked open. Instincts tingling, he stepped inside.

'Hello, anyone home?'

No response. The door opened directly into a small passage that led to the living room. Gogoi noticed a strange odour, like food that had gone rancid. The flat was dark, but the light from the setting sun streaming through the French windows was enough to illuminate covered dishes on the dining table. A table was laid out for two—both plates were half-full. He opened one of the bowls tentatively. The stench hit him. A fish curry covered with fungus.

Gogoi looked around further. On the centre table in the living room, he saw three glasses, each half-full of cola. He walked around the rest of the apartment—three bedrooms and three bathrooms. All empty.

He returned to the dining hall, which, he knew from the evidence, was where the action had unfolded. Most probably, they were interrupted by unexpected visitors. Gogoi took out his cell phone and called the police station. While he waited for the forensics team to arrive, he decided to question the security guards at the gate. He was now sure they were hiding something. His instincts shouted that all was not well with Kankan's parents. Where in hell were they?

19

Mihir was back in the camp near Karimpuhl that he had left barely seventy-two hours earlier. He had travelled the whole night, having hitched a ride in a cargo carrier, arriving early in the morning. He was now seated in the same chair as he had when he met Lt Col Sumer Singh for the first time—a meeting that had nearly turned acrimonious. But not this time. The mood in the office suggested an unstated understanding between Sumer, Mihir and Randy that they could all benefit from each other's help and expertise. Sumer was not only in charge of the court of inquiry to unearth the facts of the murder, but also was, temporarily, the commanding officer of the company whose commander had been so mysteriously killed.

Randy placed the small notepad in front of Mihir, who carefully began to examine the contents. A total of 120 digits combined on both pages. Twelve to a row. The sequence reminded him of the six-digit number that he had received in his mysterious envelope. He took it out and placed it on the table alongside the notepad.

'What's this?' asked Randy, the Military Police colonel.

'The source of my predicament over the last forty-eight hours,' replied the former special forces officer. 'But why did you want to show me this notepad?'

'Because it had your number on it,' replied Sumer, who had been quiet so far.

'How did you know the number was mine?'

'On a hunch. I remembered reading the personal details that you had filled up at the entry gate when you had visited us last. The number struck me as unique because of the combination of zeros and nines in it. I looked up the visitors' book and, sure enough, it matched your number,' explained Sumer.

'How did you know I was still around?' Mihir asked Randy.

'My sources at the airport. There was no Mihir on the flight to Delhi,' replied the officer. If the Military Police could find out, Mihir's adversaries would be on to his moves soon enough. They hadn't so far, otherwise, he would have been followed.

Randy examined the figures on the slip, shrugged, and passed it to Sumer, who stared at it equally puzzled. Mihir looked at the digits in the notepad again and compared it to the digits on the slip of paper. In that moment, it became crystal clear, popping up from one of the hidden recesses of his mind.

Mihir took a pencil from a holder on the desk and proceeded to draw a line after every sixth digit. After he had finished drawing the last line, he was looking at ten lines on two pages in the notepad, segregated into two six-digit combinations on each row. A total of twenty combinations. Each was a unique six-digit number. He turned the notepad around for the two curious officers to see.

'Is it what I think it is?' quizzed Randy.

'Yes, I think so too. It was begging to be decoded. It would have been obvious to any soldier had it been accompanied by the other two pieces of missing information, which are not here,' said Mihir.

Essentially, the numbers referred to the Military Grid Reference System—a method of reading maps common to all militaries of the world.

This is actually a combination of two systems—the Universal Transverse Mercator (UTM) grid for all regions between 84 degrees north and 80 degrees south, and the Universal Polar Stereographic System (UPS), which is designed for the polar regions, specifically further than 84 degrees north and 80 degrees south.

Together, they form a grid that covers the entire globe. The precision varies from 100 kilometres to 1 metre. A six-figure grid reference essentially means an accuracy of 100 metres, common to all military maps. The notepad left by Chris had six-figure grid references, indicating locations whose accuracy could be pinpointed to within 100 metres. All that was needed now was a military map that would show these locations. But a unit held scores of such maps. The question was, which one?

'Suppose you had the grid reference of the place which you could identify on the ground, or which you had been to. It would be easy to find out the map sheet reference,' stated Mihir.

'That would be easy,' confirmed Sumer.

Mihir took the six digits he had received in the envelope and asked for the specific map sheet for Ijgadora. Military maps held by units are of two types—metre maps and quarter-metre maps. A metre map is divided into square grids, with each side of the grid measuring 2 centimetres. The 2 centimetres represent 1 kilometre on the ground; thus, each 4-centimetre square covers an area of 1 square kilometre. The first three digits show the 'eastings', the last three show the 'northings'. Using the map, Mihir located the graveyard he had visited the previous night and wrote down its grid reference. A six-digit number. He then compared it to the six digits he had received in the envelope. They were exactly the same.

'A clue in the reverse order,' said Mihir.

'Meaning?' asked Randy.

'Meaning Chris wanted to indicate the map sheet to me in reverse order. Rather than indicate the map sheet directly, he did it in a roundabout way by making me go to the actual location, which was already indicated by the address on the back of the envelope and the six digits contained within it. He gambled on the hunch that I would be able to decode the six digits once I met with you.'

'But the notepad?' asked Sumer.

'It was meant to be discovered by me, someone he could trust completely, but which you clearly did,' replied Mihir, looking at both the officers.

'Why the secrecy?' questioned Randy.

'Looks like he was apprehensive about the information falling into the wrong hands. Which also seems to indicate why he went out alone without telling anybody,' said Mihir, watching both officers very carefully.

'That means someone local is involved. Not telling anyone meant that he did not know who that really was and did not want to risk the information falling into the wrong hands,' said Randhawa.

'But how did he know we were not involved in whatever he thought it was?' asked Sumer.

'He did not. This notepad was meant to be discovered by me in case of his death. I did not. You did. The very fact that you called me shows that you have no clue what is going on. Anybody involved would have known what these grid references were pointing to and what was there, and would have destroyed it quietly. Stroke of pure luck,' explained Mihir.

'So now, we are looking at twenty locations on this map sheet and possibly the adjacent ones. What are in these locations?' questioned Randhawa.

'Beats me. The information is still not complete,' said Mihir.

'How so?' asked Sumer.

'This is what I found in the graveyard. It was marked for me,' said Mihir, as he dropped the diary he had found in the false grave on to the desk.

Randy picked up the diary and read through the names written on the first two pages. His eyes briefly stopped at a couple of places in the list.

'Recognize any?' asked Mihir.

'Some of them. Nicknames from a distant past,' said the military policeman, as he stared back at Mihir and Sumer.

'One name belongs to an outfit which had surrendered en masse to the security forces more than six years ago—the result of a peace accord signed with the central government. They were all pardoned. He was one of their most deadly assets: Kidnappings for ransom, assassinations, etc. The other one was confirmed killed in an anti-terror operation four years ago. He was quite infamous, especially for his brutality towards women. He is not alive. Must be some kind of a mistake,' explained Randy.

'Are these nicknames?' asked Sumer.

'Yes, normally, outfits use nicknames when they refer to each other. That way they can hide the guy's true identity. Helps protect his family. The first one was called Mwhaay, pronounced mhee, meaning snake in Burmese. The second one was called the Monster, because of the burns he had suffered on his face in one of the counter-terror operations launched by the security forces to eliminate him. They believed that he had been killed in the action. However, no body was produced as evidence, so it was only conjecture. As it always happens, military intelligence picked up stories about a militant who had managed to survive the carnage, who had been scorched beyond recognition. But nothing was corroborated,' explained Randy.

Mihir didn't say anything, but he noticed that the last name, which rang a bell in his mind, had escaped the notice of both army officers.

All three of them fell silent, each mulling over the information that now lay in front of them. It seemed that Chris was reaching out from beyond his grave and pointing them in a definite direction.

'That's it, then. Time to hit the sack,' said Mihir, getting up to leave.

'Not really, there is something else,' remarked Sumer. 'When we began to process Chris's final claim settlements and emoluments, we found a major error.'

'Go on,' said Mihir.

'Well, it seems his next of kin is his mother and not his wife, Gene. His marriage occurrence was never published by his previous unit.'

'An inadvertent error?' questioned Mihir.

'Maybe, maybe not. But it means he was never married to Gene. Officially, at least,' said Sumer.

20

As the forensics team swept the apartment, ASI Gogoi conferred with them briefly. Then he took the flight of stairs down to the lobby of the tower. Being a new housing society, the occupancy was just 50 per cent. He walked up to the main gate and asked to see the security head. One of the guards led him to an adjacent tower, where one of the spaces under a parking stilt had been enclosed and converted into an office.

Seated behind a desk was a man in his early thirties. He introduced himself as the society manager as well as the security in charge. Gogoi introduced himself.

'I would like to see the footage of the main gate over the last forty-eight hours.'

The manager led him to a computer connected to the security DVR, which took its feed from various cameras installed in the society premises. The screen displayed ten cameras, including the main gate. He ran footage from the main gate. The manager and one of the guards from the main gate assisted Gogoi in identifying vehicles belonging to occupants. There wasn't much movement through the day and it thinned out completely by eight in the evening. Nothing happened for an hour. Then, at around nine, a small hatchback stopped at the gate. The footage showed the guard walking over to the vehicle on the driver's side, with a register in his hand, to note down its details and the apartment number the people were visiting. The footage then showed the guard pointing out, perhaps, where the guest parking was located. The car then moved out of the camera's frame. It was picked up by a different camera, moving into the stilt parking of tower 'C'. And that was the limit of the CCTV coverage.

Gogoi fast-forwarded the footage till about forty-five minutes later, when the same vehicle was picked up by the main gate camera, moving out of the society. It had two occupants when it entered the society, but left with four. Kankan's parents, the ASI thought. The security guards were inside their hut and did not inspect the vehicle as it was leaving.

Gogoi saw anger in the manager's eyes—those responsible for the carelessness would get pulled up. He did not pursue the matter further. He had what he wanted.

The policeman thanked the manager and asked for the CCTV footage to be handed over to the forensics team. He walked over to the main gate to examine the visitors' register. Among the details were a name, a mobile number and the registration number of the vehicle, which he knew from experience would all be fake. He noted down the number, nevertheless. He rang up the police control room, gave them the make and model of the car, and asked them to send an alert to all mobile patrols and traffic cops to be on the lookout for the hatchback.

~

Maalik was sitting beside his pool, relaxing after a leisurely swim, eyes closed. A Havana cigar hung loosely from his mouth and, in one hand, he held a glass of expensive chardonnay. His other hand absentmindedly drummed the chair, in rhythm to Beethoven's Symphony No. 5 wafting in from somewhere within Lal Bangla. Maalik's cell phone buzzed. It was Inspector Sarma from Guwahati.

'There is a problem,' the policeman said, his voice conveying fear.

'What?' asked Maalik.

'The ASI refuses to give up.'

'Why? Wasn't the FIR withdrawn?'

'Yes, it was. The father had personally gone and withdrew it,' confirmed Sarma.

'So, what's the problem?'

'Well, it was all okay from the girl's side, but the boy has also been missing for the last three days and his absence has been noticed by the cop.'

'Has he connected the two?' asked Maalik, his voice apprehensive for the first time.

'Can't say, but he went to visit the boy's parents at their house and found out that they were missing.'

'And?'

'A forensics team is dusting the place down and he has issued a lookout notice for a hatchback which he thinks was used for the kidnapping. It can't be kept quiet now.'

'Send me the details of the cop and let me handle it,' said Maalik and disconnected the call.

He sat in his chair, deep in thought, his fingers silent. After a few minutes, he picked up his mobile and rang a number. It was picked up after three rings.

'I am sending you a face. You know what to do. Keep it quiet.'

'Yes,' said a woman, before the call was disconnected.

～

The man was small in stature and bent with age. He was cursing the unpredictability that had befallen the seasonal cycles in recent years, threatening the livelihood of traditional communities like his. It had rained heavily even in winters and in the traditional dry months from October to March, in which he would normally have been busy farming. This time, the Hatchla wetlands, about 15 kilometres south of Bondhuroh, had not dried up. So, instead of farming in the dried wetlands, he was fishing—an activity he would normally have undertaken from April to September. Still cursing under his breath, he slowly stepped into the shallow water.

It was an hour before dawn. The old man was about to use fishing gear called the 'jong'—a long, pointed iron rod fitted with a wooden handle, ideal for hunting the Kuchia fish that normally lived in the digs under the soil on the banks of wetlands. Suddenly, he noticed something jutting out of the water barely 20 feet from where he was standing. He would have easily missed it in the darkness if his movement in the water had not caused minor ripples. He walked tentatively over to the object, but before he could reach close enough to touch the surface, his feet hit something hard beneath the water—something heavy that would not budge. He bent down and felt it with his hands. It was the rear end of a car and the object he had noticed was the vehicle's roof. He did not know the exact make of the car, but it looked like one of the smaller ones. Alarmed, he got out of the water quickly and hurried to inform the police.

Gogoi was at his desk when he received the call at about ten in the morning. A car matching his description had been found dumped in a wetland 15 kilometres south of Bondhuroh. There were two occupants, both middle-aged: A male in the driver's seat and a female in the other at the front.

~

Mihir couldn't remember the last time he had slept so soundly. Maybe the exhaustion of the past few days had finally caught up with him, maybe it was relief that there was some progress in his quest to find Chris's killers. He ordered a hearty breakfast from the cookhouse. Relishing the parathas and eggs with a glass of full-cream milk, Mihir recalled his days in the army. Some things never change, like a good breakfast from the unit langar.

He left his room at about ten, but here in the northeast corner of India, it felt more like noon. He went to the company commander's office, knocked gently and walked in. Sumer and Randy were gathered around the office desk, poring over military maps. Sumer looked up and beckoned him over. As Mihir looked over their shoulders at the maps, he noticed about twenty red circles drawn at random locations.

'What lies within the circles?' asked Mihir.

'No idea, but each one of these circles is some distance away from any major habitation or residential complex. At the same time, they are also right next to a main road or highway,' replied Sumer.

'What are these?' asked Randy, indicating small square blocks in red within each circle.

'I can only assume they are buildings of some sort, to be used for work. They definitely do not look residential,' said the lieutenant colonel.

'The circles are clustered around in a major concentration, with a bias towards the east and the south along the national highway to Shillong,' said Mihir, examining the map and the circles in detail.

'Whatever it is that is happening within these circles is sufficiently away from population centres. The relative isolation is planned to attract the least attention. Also, the highway provides an easy entry and exit,' said Randy. 'But what could possibly be in common between these circles and the list of nicknames in the diary?'

'No idea, but they are connected in some way. Only one way to find out,' replied Mihir.

'Locate and search the premises on the ground,' said Sumer.

'These locations might shed some light as to why Chris may have been murdered. Unfortunately, we have no jurisdiction in civil areas, unless we involve the local cops. And we can't do that without taking our chain of command into confidence,' said Randy.

'Yes, and assuming that even if we were able to convince our bosses, the civil police would need more than just a diary with grid references and a hunch to enter what could be somebody's private premises,' added Sumer.

'It would create enough publicity to alert interested parties,' said Mihir, knowing where this conversation was leading. The 'grey' zone is not exactly within the ambit of the law, but things move faster and are more effective that way.

Later, in his room, Mihir spent an hour poring over the maps once again and memorized the encircled locations. He never forgot things, because he had a near-eidetic memory, which precluded the need to write down or carry any notes. Any information that he needed was tucked away safely in his mind. He then traced his pencil along the national highway connecting Shillong to Guwahati. There was one location there that was relatively isolated from the rest of the cluster, on the south-eastern outskirts of Guwahati. Isolation meant that it was likely to be of lower importance and, therefore, the least well-guarded. He decided to pay a visit to this spot first, hoping to uncover something.

He left the next morning at dawn, having given a rough plan of action to Sumer and Randy the previous night. They organized a ride for him in an army convoy, which would drop him off at Guwahati. He would be one of the scores of soldiers going on leave or a posting, which would be easy and less likely to attract any unwanted attention. Mihir estimated he would arrive at Guwahati around four in the evening and it would be almost dark. He would stay in the Military Police unit at Guwahati, courtesy of Randy. No questions would be asked. He would be the guest of a fellow army officer.

~

In another corner of the state, ASI Gogoi was seated in his office, reading the forensic reports. He was unsurprised that the team had come up with very few clues. The house was clean, except for the fingerprints of the old couple who lived there. But that information was not important now. The bodies recovered in the wetlands were those of Kankan's parents.

They told an unfortunate story. The vehicle had been nose-down in the water—it seemed as if the driver had lost control and driven off a sharp bend in the road. On the face of it, it seemed to be death due to drowning. Fortunately for the pathologist, the bodies had been in the water for only a few hours and decomposition had not yet set in. So, the autopsy gave some vital clues.

First, both victims had injuries caused by a blunt object to the back of the head. Considerable force had been used, as the skull had fractured and caved in at the point of impact.

Second, there was no water in the lungs, which meant that the couple had been killed before they hit the water. They seemed to have been murdered and the murderers were at large.

These conclusions were all preliminary. Gogoi would wait for the final autopsy report. The viscera had already been dispatched to Guwahati. He had spoken to his contacts there to hasten the process. Even then, he knew it would take at least two weeks for the report to reach his table. In the meantime, he decided to intensify the search for the missing boy. The death of his parents had made it imperative that he be found at the earliest.

While his mind was grappling with the unexpected turn of events, his gaze fell on a cell phone on his desk. It belonged to Kankan's father and had been found in his bedside table drawer. The murderers must have missed it in their hurry to leave the flat. The cyber team had already cracked the password—a four-digit combination of his wife's date and month of birth. A common habit.

On a hunch, Gogoi opened the WhatsApp chats and scrolled down to Kankan's picture. There were no messages from his son in the last four days, but there was one from a day prior. The inspector could not believe what he was seeing. It was a geo-tagged screenshot, with the typical upside-down tear drop that indicated a location pin. Gogoi was now quite sure that this was Kankan's last known location, which he must have sent to his father. Unfortunately, his father had not seen it. It had probably got lost in the clutter of 300 or so unread messages. The pin was pointing to a place a few kilometres south of Barojat, next to the national highway from Guwahati to Shillong. At last, Gogoi knew where to begin his search for Kankan.

21

Barojat is about 300 kilometres from Bondhuroh, if one takes the route that skirts Shillong from the south. The journey was doable in about eight hours, but Barojat wasn't where ASI Gogoi was headed. His exact point of interest was about 5 kilometres east of the highway, near a small lake tucked away in the hills, called Aramgar.

Gogoi had left Bondhuroh early in the morning and it would take about six hours to drive up to his destination, with about two hours of daylight to spare. He considered that adequate time to find Kankan. There was a slim chance that the boy would be static—close to seventy-two hours had passed since his last message to his father. But it was worth a try.

In his career spanning a decade, there had been few occasions when Gogoi had conveyed the bad news to relatives of murder victims. He had no idea how the boy would react. Going by his phone records, Kankan rarely spoke to his father. Maybe the boy was closer to his mother. There was no way of knowing—at least not yet. They were unable to locate the mother's mobile, but they had her phone number and would have the call records in a couple of days.

On a hunch, Gogoi had decided not to divulge too much about his investigation to his boss. He had left it vague and promised to bring him up to speed once he returned from his trip. It was quite likely that his trip could turn out to be a wild goose chase. But, at the moment, this was his best chance to solve the riddle of the missing boy, his dead parents and the rather unusual happenings with the girl Maymunah. Somehow, he knew it was all connected.

Preoccupied with his thoughts, the ASI forgot to scan his rear-view mirror, else he would have noticed a somewhat unremarkable vehicle following him at a safe distance. The driver of the tailing car took care not to get too close, ensuring there were at least a couple of vehicles between them. The small hands that were carelessly drumming the steering wheel in time with the beats from the stereo signalled confident ease. They belonged to a woman whose delicate stature disguised the tremendous force and violence she could generate when needed, a fact discovered too late by many unsuspecting victims who were unfortunate enough to cross her path. Cunning as she was pretty, Naomi was an assassin par excellence.

For the man in the car ahead, who would soon be her next victim, she had wanted the hit to look like an accident. But the ASI's sudden trip had thrown a spanner in her well-crafted plan. Though frustrated at first, Naomi was now coming to the view that this unexpected trip could be a godsend. It had actually made her task simpler, away from the congested town where he was stationed. She was a minimalist and wanted her work to reflect that philosophy. This one was a simple assignment.

Naomi chose her instrument carefully—it was a prosaic object, easily available in any kitchenware store, but could become deadly in the hands of an expert, and would also pass police scrutiny at various checkpoints en route. Her hand unconsciously caressed the blade of the carving knife tucked away safely under the driver's seat. An ideal device to cut and dress meat. The smooth handle and the razor-sharp edge felt reassuring to her light touch.

Gogoi, oblivious to the danger he was in, decided to halt for lunch at a roadside restaurant. He turned into an open space between the restaurant and road, which, typically across India, is treated as an impromptu parking lot. There were seven cars already present there, which meant the eating joint would be moderately crowded. He could not afford to wait too long. He was on a tight schedule and had to get back to Bondhuroh early next morning.

Not far behind, Naomi watched his car turning towards the restaurant. She slowed down and let her car glide along the left side of the road until it came to a stop, engine idling, and bided her time. Following the target inside immediately after he had entered would alert him. From what she had gathered, the cop was observant, methodical and tenacious—all qualities of a good investigator.

Exactly five minutes later, she drove the last 500 metres to the restaurant. Parking at a safe distance, she got out of the car and walked at an unhurried pace to the entrance. Once inside, she stalled her stride for a moment, allowing her eyes to adjust to the restaurant's dark interiors, which she proceeded to scan quickly. Identifying her target in one brief glance, she sat three tables away from him, ordered a coffee and studied him closely from the corner of her eye. Gogoi had chosen his position well. It was a corner table and he was seated with his back to the wall, allowing him to observe anyone arriving or leaving.

Gogoi almost smiled. He was an avid reader and loved to absorb as much as he could in the limited time his job allowed him. A bachelor, he kept a few hours aside every night for reading. One of his favourite subjects was kinesics, the study of body language, or non-verbal communication—a major component of communication. Being of the firm opinion that it was essential reading in his line of work, Gogoi loved to hone his skills by observing people. That was exactly what he was doing in the limited confines of the restaurant's dining space.

The subject of his attention was a woman in blue stretch jeans, fawn ankle-length trekking shoes and a black round neck T-shirt worn loosely over her jeans. Looking not a day above twenty-five, she wore her hair short and straight. Gogoi noticed she was taller than him, maybe 5 feet and 9 inches, and quite pretty. She was not a local; maybe from further east. There was a brief halt in her stride, then she picked up her pace ever so slightly, and sat down three tables from his own. She ordered a coffee and was nursing it for the last fifteen minutes. Each time she raised her cup to sip it, she threw the briefest of glances at him. She seemed interested. Gogoi had no idea why—pushing forty, with a slight frame and the slenderest evidence of a belly, he was too practical to consider himself a catch, especially for someone as pretty as her. He could not fathom the reason, so he put down his analysis to faulty reasoning.

For the briefest moment, Naomi became acutely suspicious that she had been spotted by Gogoi. Deciding not to take a chance, she quickly finished her coffee, paid her bill and left the restaurant. She got into her car and hunkered down low in the driver's seat. She adjusted the rear-view mirror, so as to keep the front of the restaurant under observation. After ten minutes, the policeman emerged from the hut, walked over to his car and got inside, but not before briefly scanning the car park. Easing his vehicle slowly on to the main highway, he picked up speed and joined the traffic heading towards Guwahati via Barojat. A minute later, she did the same.

Gogoi drove the last few kilometres using Google Maps on his phone. The turning, hidden by thick undergrowth on both sides, suddenly arrived. Had it not been for the automated voice from the app, he would have missed it completely. He slowed down, turned to the right and drove cautiously onto the empty track. Over the last fifteen minutes that he was on the road, the sky had begun to darken, with unexpected clouds from the west. Cursing under his breath, Gogoi knew that this would reduce the daylight available by at least an hour. He would have to hurry up. Busy navigating the narrow track ahead, he did not notice that another car had followed him discreetly a few minutes later.

After about 3 kilometres, the track began to curve around a lake. Next to it was a park that had been developed into a picnic spot. It had a walkway and benches for people to enjoy nature's beauty, which Gogoi knew could be quite breathtaking under happier circumstances. After another three-quarters of a kilometre, the road left the alignment of the lake and curved away to the south, and then further on to the east. The thick foliage and the low clouds had reduced visibility on the narrow track considerably, forcing the ASI to switch on his headlights. Keeping them on low beam, he carefully negotiated the waterlogged curves. One could never guess the depth of water and the condition of these curves. It was easy to slip off the road and break a spring or an axle. The woman following behind could not risk driving with her headlights on; the best she could do was to align her car to the taillights of the policeman's vehicle, which was about 100 metres ahead on the dirt track, and hope for the best.

Glancing at the map display on his smartphone, Gogoi saw that his destination was another 500 metres ahead. It had to be, because he could see the dark, ominous outline of a hill range up ahead. Unless the track was meant to negotiate that too, he was nearly at the end of his trip. After a short distance, he came to a bend on the track, as it curved again to the south. He could not see beyond the curve, but noticed that the track had begun to widen. He turned and immediately came to an open space. On it, was a large green shed, about 100-feet long and 50-feet wide. There was only one door and no windows. The door was closed. There was no one around. A completely secluded spot.

As Gogoi switched off the engine and the headlights, a black opaqueness settled into the area, the eerie silence of early evening. He wondered who the owner was. Apprehension writ large on his face, the ASI got out of his car and began to walk towards the shed, just when it started to drizzle.

~

Mihir left his guest room at around noon, and decided to hitch a ride in an army vehicle which took him via GS Road and dropped him at the junction with NH-27 at Anakhpara. According to the GPS on his phone, the distance to his destination was about 40 kilometres. It would take about an hour on the road, depending upon his ride. A car would take about forty-five minutes, a load carrier much longer. His chances of getting a ride in a car were remote, but, after a few failed attempts, he got lucky, getting into one of the many shared taxis that plied on the Guwahati–Shillong axis.

It was a Tata Sumo, the workhorse of long-distance taxi drivers. It was always a wonder how drivers could manage to cram so many passengers in the limited confines of an MUV. It looked impossible for a big fellow like Mihir to fit, but the driver miraculously made it happen. In silent understanding, the other passengers adjusted and made space for him. It was barely enough, but once on the road, the swaying of the vehicle on the hilly road created room where none existed earlier. Mihir would have to suffer the cramped confines only for an hour.

As the driver took to the road, Mihir realized that his estimate was far too conservative. Thanks to the driver's mastery over the hilly terrain, the vehicle reached in forty minutes, dropping Mihir off at the confluence of the main highway and the track which would lead him to the lake. His watch told him it was nearly 3.30 p.m. He looked up; the sky had filled with thick grey clouds. It would begin to rain in a few minutes. The distance from the junction to his destination beyond the lake was approximately 5 kilometres. At a fast jog, it would take him twenty minutes, giving him about an hour of daylight for a quick search. Good enough. Mihir turned left on the track and began to jog. Feeling the first drops of rain on his face, he increased his pace.

Naomi slowed her car just before the curve. She saw the large green shed at the right corner of her rain-swept windshield. She parked off the track, confident that the thick foliage would shield her vehicle from the observant eyes of the ASI. She was quite sure that Gogoi had not seen the tail; he would be surprised to see her.

Would he remember where he had seen her last? Maybe, maybe not. She was not planning on giving him any time to recollect their last meeting. It would be over quickly. Naomi got out of the car, the carving knife in her right hand, shielded by her palm facing outwards. The blade was upright, its sharp edge towards her thumb. She began to walk slowly, edging towards the turn in the track, allowing the shadows of the trees and foliage to cover her silhouette.

Gogoi reached the door of the shed just as the drizzle intensified. He felt the first drops of the cold rain trickle down his neck as he stood flat against the door in a vain attempt to find shelter under its small awning. But the rain continued to pour down his exposed back. Cursing under his breath, the ASI quickly turned the door handle above the latch. The handle turned and the door creaked open. Quickly stepping inside, Gogoi noticed that the interior was cavernous and dark. He kept the door partially open, permitting the dying daylight to illuminate the interior as much as possible, while reaching inside his jacket pocket for a torch.

Under its white beam, Gogoi began walking slowly towards the other end. As far as he could tell, the inside of the shed was empty. Moving the torch slowly from left to right, the beam caught a familiar shape at the right rear corner of the shed. A wooden chair. Slowly running the beam in all directions, Gogoi saw a single naked bulb above the chair, hanging directly from the ceiling with the help of a long non-metallic sheathed wire, the kind used in almost all homes. The wire from the light bulb disappeared into the darkness of the roof. There was a switch on the wall next to the chair. He flipped it. Nothing happened; the interior remained dark. A couple of tries later, he gave up and continued searching the interiors, walking along the wall, trying to look for another door or window. There was none. The door he had come through was the only entry and exit point. The location pin he had extracted from Kankan's dead father's phone indicated that he was at the correct place. But the boy was nowhere to be found. It was entirely possible that he had been at the spot for a short while. In any case, who would want to remain in an isolated spot like this?

Outside, Naomi kept herself in the shadows, toying with the idea of entering the shed and finishing the job inside. She gave it up a minute later and decided to wait. She had no idea what was inside. The territory was unfamiliar and her prey had a head start, putting her at a distinct disadvantage. She saw the ASI's car a few feet from the shed and quickly shuffled towards it in a crouch, taking up a kneeling position next to a rear tyre. Using her knife, she carefully slit the outer sheath till the inner tube was exposed. Once the sharp blade had pierced the tube, the sound of the escaping air created a loud whoosh, but it was camouflaged by the din of the downpour. Extracting the knife, she moved in a crouch towards a tree directly in front of the shed, keeping the car between her and the door. No point in giving herself away at this juncture. Naomi looked at the car; the result of her handiwork was quite visible, despite the heavy downpour. The weight of the vehicle had shifted distinctly on to the left rear wheel. Unfortunately for her, the door to the shed was hidden from view, but that was okay, since her prey would have to step out into the rain before he reached the car. That was when she would take him down. She waited.

The ASI was already standing at the door, having missed Naomi by a few seconds, and was wondering what to do next. The deluge did not make his task any easier. This was the last known location of Kankan's phone and that was more than four days ago. Gogoi had tried ringing the kid's number, but it was switched off. He was beginning to get an uneasy feeling. If Kankan was okay, he would have got in touch with his parents. The father's phone was in Gogoi's pocket and it had been silent all this while.

~

Not too far away from the scene that was about to unfold, Mihir was grateful for the rain that washed the sweat away and cooled his body down. He was now well past the lake. It had become dark. He could hear the thunder of the clouds; the lightning had become more frequent. An occasional flash lit up the path in front for just a brief second, throwing up eerie shadows. Mihir was soaked to the bone, his wet shoes squelching in the mud. He was confident that his sturdy boots would survive.

Just as he was rounding a curve, a flash of lightning hit the ground somewhere behind him. It was really close. In that brief moment of illumination, Mihir saw a car parked on the wrong side. It was leaning awkwardly to the right as the ground dipped considerably off the track. He slowed down and left the track, instinctively hugging the treeline. Keeping the car between him and the track, he kept moving. Not leaving the cover of the trees, Mihir moved ahead and saw the clearing and the shed ahead of him. From his location, he was about 50 metres to the shed. He saw the police vehicle in front of the structure. Why were the cops here?

Deciding to wait for them to clear out before stepping out, Mihir moved further into the trees and turned to face the clearing the moment he was level with the shed. From his new position, the shed was now to his right, and the police vehicle in front and slightly to his left. He estimated his distance to the front door of the shed to be about 200 feet.

Just as he was about to settle down in his hiding position, Mihir saw a figure detach itself from the cover of the shed, where it had been shielding itself from the rain. It was Gogoi, who had decided to reconnoitre the area around the shed before heading back home. But before doing that, he dashed over to retrieve his raincoat, which he normally kept in the boot of his car for such emergencies. As Gogoi opened it, he recognized that the vehicle had developed a distinct slant to the left, accentuated by the slushy ground. Quickly wearing his coat, he took a step back and saw the flat tyre. Unfortunately, he did not examine it more closely. Closing his eyes in frustration at the stroke of bad luck, Gogoi decided to replace the tyre after he had finished taking a round of the premises.

The din of the downpour practically blocked out any noise that Naomi may have made as she swiftly covered the ground from her hidden position. Gogoi never got a whiff of the movement behind him. He felt a tremendous blow to the back of his neck, just below the base of the skull. Stunned, he fell to the ground, face down, barely conscious. Somebody grabbed him by his shoulders and turned him on his back. Trying to concentrate on the person towering above his prone body, despite the searing pain he felt at the back of his head, he recognized that it was a woman. She was now seated on his stomach, looking down at him. In her right hand was a rather long knife, the kind normally used for cutting meat and flesh. The blade was at least 9-inches long. At that moment, Gogoi knew he was going to die. He vaguely recognized the woman as the one from the roadside eatery. His life was about to be snuffed out. Why would she want to kill him?

Naomi had decided to kill her prey by attacking him from behind as he stepped out of the shed. A simple slicing action across the carotid artery passing through his throat, supplying oxygen-rich blood to the brain, would do the trick. He would be dead within a minute from blood loss. Unfortunately, Gogoi had decided to run to his car. But instead of opening the door to get inside, he had gone around and opened the boot. As he buttoned up his raincoat, she saw a strap, made of thick material, wind itself around his neck. With that, the attack from behind became a no-go. She would have to turn him around and open the strap to reach the arteries. For that, Naomi would have to immobilize him. So, she was now looking down at her prey—his neck exposed, his eyes fearful, his mouth moving as if to say something.

Mihir witnessed the sequence from his hidden position. The policeman dashed for the car, but, instead of opening the front door to get inside, he went to the rear, opened the boot and took out what looked like a raincoat. While he was putting it on, Gogoi took a step back as if to examine the car. In the same instant, Mihir saw another movement from the corner of his eye. Fast and lithe. A woman had broken out from the shadows of the shed and, in a few seconds, had moved behind the cop. Mihir knew then what was going to happen. The cop would be dead in a few more seconds. He left her with no choice.

Naomi never saw or felt the movement behind her. She was good, damn good, at her craft, but no match for the man who appeared as if out of nowhere and now towered behind her. Gogoi saw the giant black shadow the same instant that Naomi, who now had the knife out in her hand and was raising it to strike, suddenly realized that someone was behind her. She hesitated for an instant, sensing danger.

Too late. Mihir cupped his right hand under the woman's chin, while his left hand gripped the back of her head. Her face seemed puny in his large hands. Creating a powerful torque, he snapped her head and broke her neck like a dried twig. She died with the knife still raised in her hand; her eyes staring at Gogoi. She collapsed on top of him and lay still. The entire sequence had taken less than ten seconds. Mihir threw the dead woman to the side like a rag doll and offered his hand to the cop. Still in pain, Gogoi reached out, while staring incredulously at the man towering above him.

22

Gogoi's mind was still blank as he reached out to take Mihir's hand. Though in shock, he thanked Mihir profusely for saving his life. He had no idea why somebody would want him dead. Gogoi looked at Mihir, searching for answers; he had none to offer.

'Who is she?' Mihir asked.

'I haven't the faintest idea,' replied the policeman, before adding, 'Who are you?'

'Mihir. You?'

'Gogoi, assistant sub-inspector of the police station at Bondhuroh. And why are you here?'

'Thank goodness I am; otherwise, it would have been you dead in the mud instead of her,' replied Mihir, evading a direct answer.

'Yeah! Thanks once again.'

'There is a car parked on the dirt track about 200 metres from here. I reckon it is her car. She must have been following you from Bondhuroh. You didn't know that?'

'I saw her for the first time at a restaurant a few miles from here, where I grabbed a bite. Didn't think it was out of the ordinary, though,' said Gogoi, hiding the fact that he had caught her observing him a number of times. 'I've never seen her before that.'

The policeman wrapped the knife in his handkerchief, taking care not to smudge the handle, trying to preserve the fingerprints as far as possible. In this weather, the possibility of her fingerprints remaining intact was quite remote; nevertheless, he did the drill. He searched the woman thoroughly and came up with nothing except her car keys. She was carrying no wallet or identification of any kind.

'She has nothing on her,' confirmed Mihir.

'Why is that?' asked Gogoi, without turning around, continuing to search the woman from his kneeling position.

'A couple of reasons. First, she was a professional contract killer. They are paid to keep everything under wraps. Her employers would not want any hit to be traced back to them. Second, her car is parked a few hundred metres away on the same track you took to come here. Why would she carry non-essentials with her, especially in this weather, when she would go back to it anyway after her job was done?'

The cop got up, looked at Mihir, and together, the two quickly made their way along the track towards her car. Gogoi unlocked the car on the driver's side. The insides were clean to a fault—no personal knick-knacks, no documents. Gogoi knew that even the registration number would be false. The boot was clean too. No cell phone either. That was difficult to believe; she would need to communicate with her handlers. It had to be somewhere. Finding nothing of importance, they circled back to the spot where she had attacked Gogoi. Using a torchlight, they swept the area in a widening circle. The sweeping light caught a reflection. Mihir walked over to the spot and dug out the cell phone, half-buried in the wet earth.

'It must have been flung out of her pocket when you threw her to one side as she lay dead on me,' said Gogoi. 'Damn! It is password protected.'

'I doubt we would find anything of value there. I'll bet her contact list would also be completely blank. Most probably she would key in her success to a memorized number,' said Mihir.

'It is on and functional. No point switching it off. You never know; somebody may try to contact her,' remarked Gogoi.

'Worth a try. Why were you here?' asked Mihir.

'Looking for a boy who's been missing for eight days now. He is somehow connected to a schoolgirl, who I suspect has been kidnapped. Only, her father does not think so,' said Gogoi and proceeded to give the details of his case to Mihir.

'Why here?' asked Mihir.

'Last known location of the boy, based on his cell-phone data. But there is nothing here. The place is empty,' said Gogoi, looking around. They were standing under the small awning of the front door. Even though the rain had slowed down to a drizzle, both of them were soaked and muddy. The clouds still hovered low and ominous in the night sky.

'And the boy's cell phone?'

'Switched off. Has been like that for the last eight days now. He could be anywhere. This was the only solid lead we had.'

'Or he could be dead,' added Mihir.

'But who are you and what the heck are you doing here, in the middle of nowhere? And don't tell me you lost your way,' asked Gogoi.

Mihir gave the ASI an abridged version of the events so far.

'Para SF! I have seen you guys operate. No wonder the woman stood no chance,' said Gogoi, looking carefully at the ex-soldier.

'Didn't like killing the woman. She left me with no choice, though. It was either you or her. Also, I think the boy is dead,' said Mihir.

'Why so?'

'He is a teenager. School kid. Even if he had a fight with his parents—no matter how rebellious—how long do you think he would have stayed away from home? Two, three, four days tops? Ultimately, they all head home, especially after they run out of money. And he hasn't checked in for eight days now? That is unusual. Unless he had planned to run away from home in the first place. And what about his parents? Haven't they reported him missing?'

'They are dead. Found in a car in a shallow lake. Murdered, most probably.'

'How is he connected to the girl?'

'He is her boyfriend. Took her to Guwahati to meet a talent hunter. The girl hasn't been seen since.'

'I think the boy is still somewhere around here. And very dead,' said Mihir, with finality.

'No harm in looking around,' said Gogoi. He began to move in an ever-widening arc around the shed. His flashlight focused on the ground, trying to pick up anything out of the ordinary. Mihir moved alongside.

'Something is out of place,' mused Mihir.

'What do you mean?'

'Look at it this way. Your investigation is on to something. You are close enough to make someone very uncomfortable. So, you are obviously a target. Someone wants you dead. So much so that they sent an assassin to eliminate you. It's a big decision to eliminate a cop. Most of the time, they just buy your lot—no offence intended, it's easier that way. With you, they did not do that. They knew you were incorruptible. That speaks very highly of you. Also, nobody sends a lone wolf for a kill. There is always a backup and I have been trying to locate one since the time I picked you up from the mud. There is no one here. That is very odd.'

'Maybe they were very confident they could handle me with just one. Why are you here?' asked Gogoi again.

'I lost a friend. Murdered. He was at Karimpuhl. Used to be in the army. Found this location mentioned in his diary along with a few others. This was the first one in his list. So, I decided to investigate,' explained Mihir.

'That's a remarkable coincidence! You selected this location at the same time I did. And thank God for that. Have you found anything here?'

'I was hoping to find possible answers to my friend's murder,' replied Mihir, solemnly.

They continued to sweep the area. Untouched ground is tough, especially with thick vegetation around—the heaviest downpours cannot break the mud crusting. The water simply seeps through, finding a path through cracks and pores, and around the roots of trees and plants in the soil. It continues to flow down, helped by gravity, till it reaches the rock layer, filling the empty spaces around it as ground water. Mihir was looking for any break in the continuous layer of thick grass that saturated the ground around the shed, which would be a sure sign of recent digging. He could find none, even as they finished the circuit around the shed.

'Well, he isn't here. If he is dead, maybe they took the body away from here,' said Gogoi, slightly dejected.

'And risk being caught lugging a dead body? I don't think so. Maybe we are looking at the wrong place. Give me another few minutes,' said Mihir, and left for the back of the shed once again.

Ten minutes later, he called for Gogoi, who found him standing over a patch of earth just inside the treeline. An area they had not covered before. The earth that Mihir was pointing his flashlight at seemed freshly dug. Without a word, both men got down to work on the small patch. It did not take much effort. One, the recently dug-up earth had become soft because of the rain, and second, the topsoil was still loose. Twenty minutes later, 2 feet below the surface, they came upon a human hand. Half an hour later, they had uncovered a shallow grave with the body of a young male inside.

Just as Mihir had thought, the killers had presumed too much. After all, who would come looking for a dead boy missing from one state in an isolated spot at the end of a dirt track on a private property in another state? They had become careless. The body had been dumped with the victim's wallet and mobile phone still in his back pocket. He was definitely the boy Gogoi was looking for. Now, Gogoi was lumped with two bodies, both unexpected. He had a difficult choice to make.

'The ligature marks tend towards the top of the neck on the laryngeal prominence, or the Adam's apple, and under the jawbone, indicating the position of the killer as being behind and standing. Which means the boy was sitting down on the lone chair in the shed. The murderer was standing behind and took the victim by surprise. He could have been interrogated before being killed,' observed Gogoi.

'Did you approach any other police station to be on the lookout for the girl?'

'Shit! I remember calling the SHO at Razak in Guwahati. I knew the hotel she had been called to for her audition. I haven't followed it up.'

'Have they got back to you?'

'Not yet, but I will once I get back. I will also have to call in the Bhiroi police. I hadn't expected any of this to happen,' said Gogoi, explaining that the Aramgar area fell under the jurisdiction of the Bhiroi district. He was also aware of the kind of explaining he would have to do to the local police.

'I understand. It now seems as if your missing girl is a part of a much larger plot.'

'Seems so. What will you do?'

'Leave. Can't wait for the local cops to turn up.'

'I agree. How can I contact you, just in case?'

Mihir handed over his cell number to Gogoi, and added, 'Let me know if you receive a call on the dead woman's number.'

He left the scene quickly. There was only one way in and out, and he did not want to cross paths with the local police when they arrived in response to Gogoi's call. Back on the road, he continued to walk towards Barojat. It would be daylight by the time he reached the town. It was already past midnight. Without a second thought, he rang Randy, the Military Police colonel, who picked up on the second ring. Mihir brought him up to date on the events of the past few hours.

'What's your future course of action?' asked Randy, sleepily.

'That place threw up nothing. It does not seem to have any connection to Chris. I'll keep looking,' said Mihir.

'Keep me posted,' said the officer before signing off.

Mihir had been right; there was a back-up. Only, it wasn't anywhere nearby. In fact, the back-up saw Mihir exiting the dirt track at exactly the same time Mihir laid eyes on him. The man was huddled low in the driver's seat of another small hatchback parked by the side of the road, about 200 feet from the turn. He was getting restless for he should have heard from her quite some time ago. Just as he was about to start his car, heading out to assist his companion, he heard distant police sirens. Staying low in his seat, he looked at the dirt track heading into the woods once again when his eyes fell on Mihir. He knew something had gone wrong. He rubbed the windscreen and tried to focus his eyes on the road ahead. The visibility was poor, but he could discern the silhouette of a tall figure walking quickly away from the junction of the road and the track. He looked at his watch—it was 12.30 a.m. What was someone doing in an isolated spot so late in the night? And Naomi's car had not left the site yet. The sirens were coming closer and would reach the turn in under a minute. The back-up decided to exit quietly. Whatever had happened to Naomi, she was beyond help.

Without switching on his headlights, he drove past the junction, just as his rear-view mirror caught the headlights of the police vehicles. The cops would miss him as well as the man on the road, who, by now, had disappeared into the shadows of numerous trees along the road.

Mihir saw the car without the headlights move past him. He knew that the back-up was leaving the site and was also aware that he would have been spotted. His description would be with the man's bosses within an hour.

23

No lights were on in Tuhin's flat, which stood on the twelfth floor of a tower in an ultra-luxury apartment complex on Gurugram's Golf Course Road. However, the heavy drapes on the French windows in the expansive living room were drawn back and the city lights filtered in.

Tuhin was seated in his favourite armchair in a dark corner of the room, looking out at the nightscape. His left leg was constantly bouncing—annoying to a casual observer, had there been one, but it was a sign of anxiety. Tuhin was petrified; the last few days had turned him into a nervous wreck. He thought he was going to die back there, which had left him numb. Back in his house, he felt safer and could think clearly.

This trip was the first time he had seen his business associates up close; his earlier interactions had been through faceless third-party suppliers. Most of the work was done via phone calls and encrypted messages through the internet. This time, their summons were polite and inviting at first; intimidating and very threatening later. This was also the first time he had seen a sample of the merchandise he was trading in—the girl he had so reluctantly escorted had been picked up at the parking lot the moment they stepped outside Terminal 3.

In one of the bedrooms, Rubina stirred sleepily and glanced at her watch. It was five. She walked naked to the living room to find her lover sitting in an armchair, wide awake. She gave him a sleepy kiss, which Tuhin reciprocated half-heartedly.

'I'd better get dressed and leave,' she said.

'So soon?'

'Your wife is due in an hour, silly. She's coming from Mumbai, in case you had forgotten. You don't want her to see me here, and in this state,' she said, teasing.

'Shit!'

'Exactly. I need to leave.'

'When will I see you again?'

'Soon.'

Rubina got dressed and took the elevator. The ground floor lobby was empty, except for the security guard, who was asleep in his chair. He stood up reluctantly, wished her good morning and returned to his slumber. Pushing open the glass doors, she walked out into the open. It was still dark, daylight an hour away. Rubina walked the 100 metres or so to the society's main entry gate, manned by two personnel. The security cameras made a note of all who entered and left. She paused on the pavement for a second, spotted the car standing a few feet to the right, walked around it, opened the passenger side front door and sat down.

'So?' the driver asked.

'Worried. No, shit-scared, actually,' she replied, lighting up a cigarette and taking a deep drag.

'Can he handle it?'

'Maybe, maybe not. He is quite close to losing it,' she said, looking at the driver.

'Then you must ensure that he doesn't. The girl is a first; many will follow. We have to make it work. So, don't fuck it up,' he said, delicately brushing her hair to one side and gently caressing her neck. His gentle touch accentuated the underlying threat in his deadpan voice.

~

At that moment, the girl being discussed was fast asleep in another corner of the city, in a spacious farmhouse, surrounded by high walls. Except for her and a woman who guarded her, there was no one else on the vast premises.

On arrival, Maymunah's phone had been taken away and she was assured that one with a local SIM would be provided soon. Her plea to speak to her parents was politely declined. However, Maymunah had snuck in a WhatsApp message to her father, between the aircraft landing and deboarding. At least her parents would know she was safe and well.

~

It was already daylight in the northeast corner of the country, around the time that Maymunah was being taken to her room in the capital. It had rained heavily the previous night, but the morning had ushered in blue skies.

Maalik was taking a walk in his garden in Lal Bangla when he received confirmation of the girl's arrival at the safe house. She was the first of a few who would gather there. Accordingly, clients had been informed to be ready to arrive at short notice. Many would come from across the Arabian Sea. Things were moving as per plan. But, closer to home, Maalik was yet to receive any message about the outcome of his instructions regarding the assistant sub-inspector from Bondhuroh. He was beginning to get a little impatient. It was unlike Naomi to take so long. Maalik decided to wait for a few more hours.

~

In his small home in Bondhuroh, Maymunah's father was feeling elated and relieved at the same time. He had received a short message about her safe arrival in Delhi and was a bit surprised—she had specifically mentioned in their last conversation that she was heading to Mumbai. Must have been a last-minute change of plans. He would have been much happier if she had called, but she must have been really busy. He would try later.

~

Gogoi was back in his office in Bondhuroh. It had been a mess up at the Aramgar site—two dead bodies and a lot of explaining. He wasn't too convinced by his own version and doubted whether the Bhiroi police were either. The boy was easily explained, but the woman was a different proposition. It took a phone call from his boss in Bondhuroh to the cops in Bhiroi to sort out the matter. It was not over by a long shot, but it would do for the time being. Now, two state police forces were involved; he was no longer in control.

'Any progress on the missing girl? I spoke to you about her, remember?' Gogoi asked Sarma, the Razak sub-inspector, whom he had called earlier too.

'It was a false trail. Checked out the hotel and spoke to the staff. No record of a girl of that description or the boy for that matter.'

'What about the CCTV footage?'

'Nothing there either. Are you sure you have the correct name of the hotel?'

'Pretty much. Will get back to you once I have more details,' replied Gogoi, hanging up on Sarma. He was not convinced. On a hunch, he looked up the hotel on the internet and rang the number on the website. It was picked up on the third ring.

'Narzi Hotel.'

'I need to speak to the manager please,' said Gogoi, introducing himself.

Once the manager came on the line, Gogoi explained his requirement.

'Yes, I do remember an inspector from Razak police station had visited us. He did go through the CCTV footage,' said the manager.

'Did he find anything useful?'

'He didn't mention it to us.'

'Can I speak with the receptionist who was on duty that day?' asked the policeman, on a hunch.

'Sure, I will get her for you.'

The phone's receiver was put down on the table and, after a minute or two, it was picked up again, and a young woman's voice came on the line.

'Hello.'

'Do you recollect a girl coming to the hotel that day?' asked Gogoi as he gave her the date of Maymunah's meeting with the modelling agent.

'Yes, I do. She asked to meet a couple in room 103.'

'Notice anything about the couple?'

'Nothing much, except that they had registered themselves under the same surname. But, as a couple, it was quite strange. I mean, the woman was way older than the boy.'

'Age difference?'

'The woman was in her mid-thirties and the boy was barely out of his teens.'

'Could they be siblings?'

'They did not look like siblings.'

'When did they check out?'

'Though they had a reservation till mid-morning the next day, they left that very evening around six, I guess,' said the receptionist.

'Thanks. Ring me up on the number I have given the manager in case you think of something,' said the ASI before hanging up.

Gogoi's suspicions were confirmed; he knew Sarma would have taken care of the CCTV footage. The inspector from Razak was lying. He was in the game too.

There was one more loose end to tie up before his next line of investigation began. Gogoi dialled the number of the modelling agency. The automated voice on the other side asked him to check the number he had dialled. A bogus number. The girl had been kidnapped.

He rang the girl's father, Ranjan.

'Any news of your daughter?'

'Yes sir, I received a WhatsApp message from her yesterday. She is okay.'

'Any idea where she is?' asked Gogoi, surprised by the lucky turn of events.

'Maymunah is in Delhi,' replied the father.

'I thought she was going to Mumbai. Can you give me her number?'

'I thought so too. Could be a change of plans. But I'll send you the number.'

After a moment, Ranjan added, 'But there is a problem. I have been trying to call her since yesterday. Her phone is switched off. I have no way of contacting her.'

'Let me know if you hear from her,' said Gogoi. More suspicions confirmed—the girl had been kidnapped and taken to Delhi. Gogoi knew where he would get his next lead.

~

The few hours that Maalik had promised himself had come and gone. There was no news of the ASI, who should have been dead by now. Maalik prided himself in not giving in to panic, and his team took confidence from his stoic demeanour. They thought it was his nature, but very few outside his inner circle knew that the calmness was a result of detailed planning and meticulous execution. The wargaming and contingencies worked out were almost endless. And even though things were progressing according to plan, he was becoming slightly nervous and agitated. Maalik had thought that the irritant had been dealt with. But now, there was no room for doubt. The call he had just received had made sure of that.

The dead officer's friend was still here and poking around. How the hell had he missed this? The assassin also seemed to have failed in dealing with the policeman. Maalik was quite sure the friend had a hand in this. The bright and sunny morning did little to alleviate his dark mood.

His cell phone rang. Trepidation was writ on his face as he recognized the caller. It was a long-distance call. Maalik answered.

'It seems you have problems and you are incapable of eliminating them,' said the voice on the other end, soft and smooth. No evidence of panic, only some concern and irritation.

'I have done what was needed,' Maalik said, a mild protest in his voice at the accusation.

'Clearly not enough. You are making people unhappy and nervous.'

'I'll take care of it,' said Maalik timidly.

'We led him to you so that you could take care of the problem.'

'We need to go slow. Can't afford a fuck up. Maybe put things on hold till the current problem is solved.'

'No, we can't afford to do that. Too much at stake. On the other hand, I would advise you to speed up your deliveries. Deal with the problem on your own. It's on you. No comebacks this time,' said the voice before hanging up.

~

A few hours prior, the object of Maalik's frustration had managed to hitch a ride in the most unlikely of transports—a light truck delivering milk to the neighbourhood. But before that, Mihir had had to foot it at a brisk pace for nearly two hours along the deserted main highway connecting Shillong to Guwahati, before he reached the outskirts of Barojat. It was early dawn before he could tempt the driver of the delivery vehicle with some extra cash. By the time he hit the sack, it was daylight. Mihir was fast asleep in less than a minute, blissfully unaware of the trap being set for him.

24

The ex-soldier would have to be tracked down first; elimination would follow. He was good. Very, very good. Maalik knew that without a doubt—a grudging acknowledgement from one professional to another. And that was precisely why killing him would give him deep satisfaction, almost like a trophy. Compensation for the loss of one of his valuable assets and, more importantly, for the humiliation he had suffered in front of his faceless partner. He was riled by the chiding he had received on the phone. He had looked like a complete fool in his own backyard, his territory. It would never happen again. He promised himself that.

Maalik would have to play it carefully. There could be no room for mistakes, otherwise his well-cultivated public persona would be over. As a politician, he had the power to influence the course of the local government. His dark side was cleverly concealed from his public avatar. Any slip up and the influence he wielded would diminish. Despite the considerable resources he could muster, deep down, he was worried.

The Monster received the summons late at night. He was a few hours away from his mentor. He dressed, packed and got into his car. He would be at his destination before first light.

A similar call was received by Silki. It was unusual for her boss to call so late at night. She dressed, packed and took off on her bike.

The Monster and Silki reached Lal Bangla at about the same time. Morning had just broken. They were ushered inside by security and were made to wait for their master by the porch next to the swimming pool. The Monster noticed an increase in the level of security. Silki had also observed the change. Clearly, the boss was expecting some threat.

Maalik walked in a few minutes later. He was up early and dressed for the day, which was quite unusual. He was known for his late-night binges. So, the threat was real.

'The officer's friend is still here. Sniffing around,' he said, without preamble.

'Thought he had left along with the wife,' remarked the Monster.

'Well, he hasn't.'

'How do we know he is still here?' questioned Silki.

'Because he killed one of ours. At least, that is what I think. It was beyond the Bondhuroh cop to take her down. Your friend Naomi is dead. The man who was the backup saw him emerge from the site. He is the only one who could have done it,' said Maalik, looking at her.

Silki stared at Maalik in disbelief. It wasn't easy to kill Naomi.

'I'll kill him,' she hissed.

'Easier said than done. The ex-soldier is very good. I have asked for more information about him. More importantly, he is in the area, but we do not know where exactly. Since the time he was to have boarded the flight one week ago, he has evaded detection by our informants. He knows how to move. He is like a ghost.'

Maalik walked over to the breakfast counter. 'Anyway, I need you both to take care of the threat. Hunt him down and kill him. It has to be done immediately. We can't allow our new business to be threatened by this unwanted complication.' He piled his plate with eggs, ham and bacon. He picked up a glass of orange juice with his free hand before walking over to a chair and table by the poolside. He invited his lieutenants to join him for breakfast.

'How much does he know?' asked the Monster, taking only a meagre helping.

'Next to nothing.'

'Then why bother with him?'

'For the simple reason that he will keep looking for his friend's killers. If he succeeds, he will come within sniffing distance of our work. And we do not want that,' said Maalik, speaking between mouthfuls.

'One last question. How did she die?' asked Silki.

'He broke Naomi's neck with his bare hands. Our police friends think the cop from Bondhuroh did it, which even they are finding difficult to believe. It won't be long before her profile and past are made public. Such things do not remain hidden for long,' replied Maalik. A few minutes later, he finished his breakfast and walked inside the house.

The Monster and Silki were left alone to work out their plan. By the time they stepped out of Lal Bangla, the sun was well up. Time for action. Silki parked her bike in one of the spare garages in the estate, collected her gear and joined her colleague in the car.

~

Around 2,600 kilometres away, Maymunah's emotions had plunged to the depths of despair. Her mind was a mess of incoherent thoughts. A dreadful realization had finally taken hold—she knew in her heart that she was trapped. After her repeated requests for her mobile phone, she was told firmly that she would not get it; she was also physically threatened. The farmhouse was constantly guarded by a bunch of armed men. She could not speak with anyone. Her meals were frugal, but regular. She was told to stick to a schedule and stay within the confines of her room. Escape seemed impossible.

Unknown to Maymunah, similar episodes were unfolding elsewhere in the farmhouse premises. The number of girls had now increased to ten, all kept in separate rooms. They had been brought from different parts of the country.

Messages had been sent to prospective buyers, some from within the country and some abroad. Everything was progressing as per schedule, till a message was received late at night to put all plans on hold for the time being. The prospectors were told to postpone their travel itinerary until further notice. The handlers had no choice but to do as told. Though the inmates were unlikely to cause trouble, preparations were made to deal with any problems arising out of the delay.

~

Elsewhere, events were unfolding at a rapid pace. The modus operandi had changed, which made Samanta Borphuken of BPN Logistics very nervous. The risk had gone up. After all, the merchandise was being transported in his fleet of trucks. According to the earlier agreement, his responsibility ended at the delivery point in Guwahati. But the other party now wanted him to take the load all the way to Delhi in his fleet of reefers. Apparently, they did not want to risk discovery at any of the transshipment points, where the probability was quite high.

Borphuken didn't know that the party was Maalik, but he did know that the party was also planning to speed up the present consignment to its destination. Maalik was thinking of ceasing all operations temporarily, till the irritating problem of Mihir (he had learnt the man's name) was sorted out. He did not want anything out on the road till then. Too risky.

This time, the reefer convoy was ten vehicles strong. It left Bondhuroh early, before first light, the same morning that Maalik received the news of Naomi's death at the hands of the ex-major. The fleet of trucks was transporting organic vegetables specially grown in the Northeast to Delhi, the demand for which was almost insatiable. Hidden in the secret compartment of each vehicle was the usual load of unfortunate human beings also being transported, but to a different market in Delhi. The demand for them was equally unquenchable. It would take a week for the vehicles to reach their destination. The tricky part was to get them past the various checkpoints manned by private contractors and government agencies, whose prying eyes were always looking for violations by truckers.

If caught, it was Borphuken's unfortunate neck on the chopping block. He would be hung out to dry. He tried not to think about it.

~

In another part of the state, ASI Gogoi was looking carefully at the CCTV footage he had recently received from the police in Delhi. The request had been conveyed by the police district headquarters at Bondhuroh via POLNET, or police net, a thousand-terminal strong, satellite-based wide-areas communication network. It connected all state capitals, district headquarters and other selected locations where central paramilitary forces and police organizations were located. The request was accessed and immediately acted upon by South-West District, New Delhi Range of Delhi Police, who, in turn, placed another request to the Central Industrial Security Force (CISF), whose units controlled the security of all domestic and international airports in India.

For the time being, Gogoi wanted to term his investigation as a case of kidnapping. There was little evidence to the contrary. His instincts, though, said otherwise. He may have stumbled onto something more sinister.

Close to 20,000 girls were transported within India at any given time. Their purpose was commercial sexual exploitation (CSE, as law enforcement agencies call it); 60 per cent of those trafficked were below the age of eighteen. Though Maymunah's disappearance did seem like a case of human trafficking, he would need more evidence to back his claim.

For now, he was more focussed on the footage on the screen in front of him. It showed domestic arrivals at Terminal 3 in Delhi. He had obtained the initial departure details from authorities at Guwahati airport. Gogoi spotted Maymunahon on the escalator, a small handbag slung on her right shoulder. Behind her were her escorts, a man and a woman. He continued to trace their movements till they exited from arrival gate number one. Outside, the trio was met by another man—well-built, clean-shaven and young—who took the girl to one side. No words were exchanged between any of them. The couple walked towards a chauffeured car; Maymunah was escorted by the man to a pre-paid taxi and ushered to the rear seat. The man then sat down next to the driver before the car drove off. Gogoi was satisfied with the footage, not because it reinforced what he had suspected all along, but that the cameras had caught the couple's car registration number as well as the taxi's. The trail was still warm.

25

Nobody would have given the balding, pot-bellied, middle-aged fellow a second glance. He was dressed in a pair of shabby pyjamas and a mud-stained, half-sleeved kurta, with a gamucha cloth tied loosely around his head. A week's stubble completed the facade. He was tending carefully to his vegetable cart, soliciting customers.

Like all the other fruit and vegetable vendors, he was allotted a designated spot for his cart by the local goon. The whole stretch occupied by the vendors was actually a pavement for public use, but had been encroached upon with the tacit approval of local authorities.

This particular vendor, though, was different—he was actually part of an elaborate, three-part web laid out by the Monster and Silki.

First, there were observers at vantage points, keeping a discreet watch on all hotels and entry and exit gates to the cantonment. Second, there were mobile patrols on cars and two-wheelers, prowling around, on the lookout for their prey. And third, there were the cops on Maalik's payroll, who had spread word to their informants for any details on the man. A massive manhunt was underway in Guwahati—information was being gleaned from every possible place where the soldier could be holed up. It would be nearly impossible for Mihir to step out without being noticed.

Mihir, meanwhile, was observing that same vegetable vendor very carefully, seated by a window in his room, a cup of Assam tea in his hand. He was impressed by how swiftly his adversaries had reacted—it had been barely twelve hours since his encounter with the assassin and they were already out looking for him. They must have replicated the same surveillance model all over the city. He had really upset them. But now that he had their attention, the question was, what should he do about it?

The rundown hotel was quiet and he was confident the management would not give him away, because it was owned by a close relative of one of his Assamese ex-colleagues in the army. He had been assured of secrecy.

As he continued to observe the vegetable vendor, Mihir noticed that every hour or so, a small hatchback would drive slowly past, and the man would look up at the car as it went by. Mihir knew the car would be touching base with a number of other observers and that there would be more such cars or two-wheelers quietly doing the rounds. Even though he was safe for the time being, Mihir did not want to endanger his hosts anymore. He would have to make his move. Soon, but not yet.

While still seated by the window, Mihir took out the diary he had uncovered from under the grave. He went over the names once again. Besides Mwhaay and the Monster, the other names were still a mystery. Then his eyes fell once again on the last name, which he had felt was vaguely familiar. Then he remembered where he had heard it. He was stunned. It seemed impossible. Must be a mistake. How could it even figure in this list? If true, then his search for Chris's killers had taken an ugly turn. Some pieces of the puzzle were beginning to fall in place.

It was close to midnight when Mihir got up from his position by the window. He hadn't moved the whole day. He ate and drank there, using the time to observe the routine of his adversaries. This particular vegetable vendor, like the others in the trade, had packed up and left at eight. His place had been taken by another guy sitting next to a tea shop, consuming endless cups. The vehicle was still moving, but not quite as frequently. It was obvious they were frustrated by their lack of success. When that happens, it makes people impatient and careless. He had learnt that over the countless ambushes he had laid in his decade-long career in the army—there were times when one had to wait for three to four days before success. The key was to be patient and stay absolutely still. But then, those searching for him were not soldiers. And they made mistakes. This mobile patrol had. The car took exactly an hour and twenty minutes to make one round. It did so twice; then there was a gap of about forty-five minutes, after which the same routine would repeat. The gap between rounds was probably when they reported back. Mobile conversations get overheard, so, this physical process was to keep the content of their reports under wraps. If he divided the time in half, leaving aside five-odd minutes for reporting, Mihir assumed the reporting base was twenty minutes out. That was where the command elements were located and that was where Mihir would be heading.

But he had a problem: Transportation. To solve that, Mihir had called his office earlier in the day and it had taken them just a couple of hours to follow through on his instructions.

He switched off the low table lamp in his room and stepped out into the parking lot, dressed in a pair of dark-grey jeans and a black T-shirt, his carry bag slung loosely around on his left shoulder. Mihir could not help but admire the efficiency of Rehaan. Standing silently in a corner and matching Mihir's dark attire was a black Royal Enfield 500cc motorcycle, commonly called 'Bullet'. It was a superb beast, powerful and strikingly silent at low rpm. Just the thing he was hoping for.

'You do not have to go out of the front gate. There is a small gap in the rear wall, enough for a two-wheeler to pass through. It opens out into a lane. No one is watching that gap,' Mihir's host told him when he had brought dinner to his room.

'I suppose not. I'll be gone soon. Thanks for your help,' said Mihir.

'In fact, it is I who should be thanking you for saving my nephew's life. Thanks to you, he is with us today,' said the host, gratefully.

'He would have done the same for me. We are a band of brothers and we look after our own,' remarked Mihir, remembering his army days with a deep sense of pride.

He had checked out in advance, tipping the host handsomely. This was off the books, of course. There must be no record of his ever having been there.

Mihir, wearing a black helmet, with a visor hiding his face, squeezed out of the gap into the narrow street behind the hotel. The alleyway and the houses lining it were totally dark and silent. It was a cloudy night. He pressed the self-start button. The four-cylinder air-cooled engine gently purred to life. Without switching on the headlights, Mihir slowly manoeuvred the motorcycle towards the end of the alley and stopped just short of the main street. Traffic was sparse; except for the odd car or two-wheeler, the main road was deserted. The tea shop was closing and the man watching the front gate of the hotel was preparing to reposition himself for the night watch. It would be a long night.

Mihir waited for the car. By his calculations, it would arrive in another ten minutes. Soon, he saw the dipped headlights. The car was moving slowly from his right; it would take thirty seconds to reach his location and another fifteen seconds to reach the man watching the front gate, to Mihir's left and on the other side of the road. That was enough time for him to make his move—for a brief moment, the car would block the man's view as it crossed him. It was a momentary blind spot that Mihir would take advantage of.

The car had two occupants, who had been on the road for nearly sixteen hours. Mihir knew that they would be tired and low on patience. That would also work in his favour. As the vehicle crossed him, Mihir allowed it to move for another 50 yards before he eased his bike, still with its headlights off, on to the main road at the exact instant the car was between him and the observer across the road. The car continued its slow movement—it slowed for a brief moment in front of the observer—then picked up speed and moved on. Mihir followed at a safe distance. The man across the street watching the hotel did not bother to look at the motorcycle as it crossed him.

By Mihir's reckoning, it would take about fifteen minutes to reach the command centre. For the occupants of the car, it would be another disappointing report. Mihir kept his bike at a safe distance. He could see flashes of lightning; the clouds were waiting to vent their watery fury on the city below. Ahead of Mihir, the car took one of the side roads to reach NH-27, running south of Guwahati. Short of Ahorgaon, and a little ahead of a hamlet called Kutchalbet, the car slowed and turned on to an isolated road, just wide enough for one truck. Mihir followed them in the dark, using his instincts to align his bike with the road.

∼

At the end of the narrow road, inside a small warehouse in a secure compound, Silki and the Monster waited impatiently for some good news. It had been a frustrating day. Despite their considerable resources, the man now being called the 'Major' had remained elusive. The Monster had begun to develop a grudging respect for him—it was quite an achievement to remain undetected for so long, especially in a city where the underground was practically owned by his boss. Catching and killing the Major would be deeply satisfying. He despised anyone in uniform; not that the ex-soldier was wearing one now, but he had, once upon a time, and that was reason enough for the Monster. Just then, his phone rang. He picked it up.

'I have some background information about the Major,' said Maalik's voice at the other end.

'And?'

'Do not take him lightly. He was Para SF. Decorated thrice for gallantry. Left under a cloud. They court-martialled him. His impeccable record saved him. He is as lethal and as dangerous as they come.'

'I have dealt with his type,' scoffed the Monster.

'I wouldn't be so sure. I spoke to some of our friends who were unfortunate enough to cross paths with him. His tenacity is matched by his brutality towards his enemies. Our friends were saved from a painful death only because of the intervention of saner heads in the army. He feels the judicial system is wasted on the likes of us.'

Maalik paused, then asked, 'Any luck?'

'Not yet, but soon.'

'Don't take too long,' Maalik said, before the line went dead.

~

Just as he had been about to step out of his room in the hotel, Mihir had received a short, edited video clip and details of a car registration number from ASI Gogoi. The girl had been kidnapped to Delhi.

Mihir was furious at the people who perpetrated these odious acts. An innocent girl, probably underaged, had been kidnapped to be exploited by those who viewed her as a commodity. The poor invariably bore the brunt. As a former soldier, Mihir felt cheated about the rot in society. But deep down, he felt that there was still some hope. There were still good, conscientious people around. That was worth fighting for.

Still deep in thought, Mihir passed on the details to his agency, where they were received by Rehaan. The instructions were crisp. Rehaan liked that about his friend and boss—his clarity and single-minded focus had been well-known within their unit. These qualities were the sole reason for his team's successful track record during anti-terror operations. Rehaan had accompanied Mihir on at least twenty-six missions, each a 100 per cent success, with no casualties to the team. The men had complete faith in his ability to deliver success every time they hit the field.

'We have a task from the Tiger,' said Rehaan to their colleague Yudhvir, another brother from their old days in the army.

'You will have the details by the end of the day,' said Yudhvir.

∼

This time, winter in Delhi had been surprisingly mild. The customary cold wave had never occurred and, by end of January, the ambient temperature was already in the late twenties. Warmer-than-usual gusts were accompanied by dust from neighbouring regions that hung like an opaque pall over the city. Visibility was reduced. The powdery dirt was so pervasive that it spared none and entered virtually every possible fissure. The farmhouse on the outskirts of Delhi was no exception. Despite the best efforts of its occupants, who had shuttered every door and window, it managed to seep inside, creating a claustrophobic airlessness even in spacious confines.

Inside the dining hall, the girls, together for the first time, were seated on straight, high-backed, ornately carved chairs around an equally ornate wooden table. The air-conditioning had been deliberately kept off and this added to the stuffiness. The room was illuminated by a low-wattage bulb hung from a wire.

Life had taken a hellish turn for the girls. They would see each other only at mealtimes. No conversation was allowed. A gruel was served to the poor wretches. Given half a chance, the guards would have had a go at the girls, but they had been warned to stay away—no customer would pay top dollar for 'second-hand goods'.

Maymunah who had now been missing for close to two weeks was painfully aware of her kidnapping and confinement, but did not know why. Her parents were not rich; they could not possibly pay any ransom to rescue her. Tears welled up the moment she thought about them. She quickly lowered her head, hiding them from her captors, whom she was terrified of. Poor Baba and Maa. They would be so helpless and desperate. She regretted the day she had struck up a friendship with Kankan. She understood now how she had been lured away by the boy. She wondered where he was now. She hated him for what he had done to her. She cried in silence, trying her best to finish her awful meal.

~

Not far from where the girls were trying to finish their meal, a figure stood concealed behind a tall bush. He was 200 metres from the front gate and the farmhouse's high compound wall. Dust and wind obscured his position. If he was spotted, he could easily pass off as a casual labourer or gardener. He was a patient man, with the ability to observe for endless hours with barely any movement—a skill he had picked up as a young soldier hunting down terrorists. His keen eyes missed nothing. This wasn't a normal house. It was deathly silent. Nothing out of the ordinary for a vacant house, but it wasn't empty. The guy who had driven the taxi that had ferried the girl to the house had confirmed it. He would not divulge the information initially, but was very cooperative after some polite coaxing.

The man flicked on his smartphone and spoke to the boss, confirming his findings. He nodded at the instructions and settled down to wait. He had nothing else to do.

~

At around the same time, an ultra-luxury apartment complex in Gurugram was also being watched, particularly Tower A's twelfth-floor flat, which belonged to the CEO of a human resources firm. The number plate caught in the footage outside Terminal 3 was clear. After that, it was really quite easy.

Fortunately for Yudhvir, the apartment faced the main road. Two spacious balconies, a part of the living room and a bedroom were clearly visible to him from his position on the opposite side of the road. He was standing on the roof of a partially constructed, three-storeyed elevated parking lot. The construction site had been abandoned over some legal dispute; it was deserted.

Tuhin was cooped up in his flat. He hadn't left for office and refused to meet anyone, including his wife, whom he had ignored when she had kissed and hugged him after her arrival. She left him alone, disgusted by her husband's rude behaviour. She had long suspected that he was having an affair.

Tuhin, on the other hand, was feeling sick. He hadn't eaten all day. A bottle of single malt stood nearly empty on the side table beside him. He kept thinking about the poor girl and felt very guilty. He was a businessman, always looking for a quick profit. But this was very wrong—he was not an abductor of anyone, leave alone innocent children. But now, he had become a party to human trafficking. He could have gone to the authorities and confessed everything, but he was mortally scared. He had seen the footage when he was in Guwahati.

The buzzing of his phone snapped him out of his stupor. He saw the number and began sweating profusely.

'Expect another package by evening. Go to the office and await its arrival. Be there at seven sharp. Dismiss your staff for the day. Be alone. After everyone has left, you will be met in the office by one of ours to assist you,' said the male voice at the other end.

'Yes,' Tuhin replied, weakly.

'By the way, you look like shit. Freshen up before going to the office. We can't have you looking sick,' mocked the voice, before hanging up.

26

Mihir decided to dump the bike for the time being and follow on foot. He realized that the narrow road taken by the car ahead of him would most likely lead to a warehouse, like the one where he had rescued Gogoi. It was pitch dark. He dismounted and parked his bike behind a tree surrounded by thick undergrowth; it could not be seen from the road. He waited for five minutes, allowing his eyes to adjust to the darkness. Then he began to walk in the direction taken by the car.

It was fifteen minutes before he saw the compound. The walls were high and obscured any view of the warehouse. At the centre was a large gate, which seemed to be the only point of entry and exit. He moved silently, using the cover of darkness. Another 100 metres and he got a clear view of the gate—it was made of a thick metallic grille, through which he saw what lay beyond. The car Mihir was following was parked outside, next to the gate. He noticed a number of reefer trucks parked in a neat line inside. Mihir had thought that the route taken by the car was the only one available, but it was too narrow for the trucks parked inside, so there had to be another, wider road from another direction.

Mihir saw the two men from the car walk towards a man and a woman standing in front of the warehouse, next to one of the trucks. It was too dark to clearly discern their faces but there was enough ambient illumination from the security lights on the main gate for Mihir to make out that the man's face was hidden under a mask. The woman was much shorter, looked to be in her thirties, and had straight, shoulder-length hair. Both were dressed in dark jeans and black T-shirts. The pair from the car exchanged a few words with the man and the woman, then took a few steps back and waited. Mihir knew why. A minute later, he saw headlights from another car moving down the same narrow road he had taken earlier. It was followed by two more. The short convoy parked itself inside.

The passengers of the six cars alighted and stood in front of the duo, and it became clear who the boss was—they stood with heads lowered and listened quietly to the masked figure. The man seemed clearly disappointed with the outcome of the day's proceedings. While the one-sided exchange was on, one of the guys in the group broke his silence and spoke, gesticulating with his hands, pointing towards the masked figure, body language bordering on impertinence. The masked figure listened quietly. It was clear that he did not like being interrupted. After the man had spoken, the boss looked at the woman by his side and seemed to nod.

The woman took two steps towards the guy who had spoken and, in one swift move, impaled him with a knife just below the sternum, aimed at the heart. The man collapsed in a heap. There was a stunned gasp from the others, who took a step back in alarm. The masked man then walked slowly towards the rest and spoke quietly. They listened, then scurried out of the gate with desperate energy.

Things at the warehouse quietened down after a while. The masked man and the woman beckoned to someone who had been standing in the shadows. They spoke a few words before getting into a car and driving off, taking the other route that Mihir had been wondering about. As he returned his gaze to the front of the warehouse, he noticed that a few more individuals had gathered, and were being addressed by the man who had seen off the masked man and the woman. He seemed to be pointing towards the trucks. Mihir gathered that these were most probably the drivers and cleaners of the reefers standing in front of the warehouse. He noticed that the man addressing the gathering wore a ponytail, and was tall and well-built. After he had finished, they trooped back inside the warehouse behind him. A few minutes later, two armed guards emerged from the warehouse and dragged the dead guy towards a dark corner of the compound. A minute later, Mihir saw flames leaping up from the same spot where the body had been dragged to. A quick funeral. Later, all the lights were switched off. It was suddenly as quiet as a tomb. The body continued to burn in one corner of the compound.

Mihir waited for ten minutes and then made his move. He jogged towards the front gate, keeping to the shadows. He crouched down next to one of the pillars and scanned the area inside, looking for the security guards. He found a pair standing in front of the main door of the warehouse, ex-military written all over them, both armed with pistols tucked inside their trouser belts. The positions of the weapons showed that both were right-handed. Their weapons were of a foreign make and fired 9-mm Parabellum rounds, and carried a 15-round magazine. A good weapon to have. It looked similar to the Indian Army's 9-mm automatic pistol.

The distance from the front gate to the guards was about 100 yards. To reach them, he would have to negotiate the gate, then run at a good lick for about thirteen seconds before he reached either of them. Mihir knew he would never make it beyond the first few yards. Even if by some stroke of luck he managed to take out the first guard, the second would shoot him dead before long. He would have to outflank them.

Mihir retreated from the gate and walked slowly along the wall. He was within its shadow zone. The walled fence ran for about 150 metres before taking a 90-degree turn towards the south. This corner was laced with thick undergrowth, with a few short trees next to the wall. To his advantage, this area was also completely dark.

Mihir stepped on to one of the thicker trunks and stretched his arms till his hands caught the top of the compound wall. Heaving himself up easily, he quickly lay prone on top of the 1-foot-thick wall and scanned the ground directly underneath. No panjis—sharpened sticks made of either bamboo or wood—were dug in the ground.

Panjis were normally planted immediately below the wall; dug deep enough that only the sharpened ends stuck out, which were easily hidden by the grass around them. Anybody jumping over the wall would quickly find his feet painfully impaled. It was a cheap and effective way of discouraging unwanted visitors. The absence of panjis could only mean that the property was rarely used for storing anything worthwhile. There was nothing to steal.

Mihir used the vantage point to reconnoitre the inner complex. The front side, facing the gate, was illuminated and he could see the two guards, along with the ten trucks. Their drivers and caretakers were not around. The other side of the complex was in darkness; he could discern a closed door in the shadows. There was no activity here. The ground on this side was covered with overgrown grass.

Mihir silently slid down the wall and went on to his knees, staying low for a minute, allowing his eyes to adjust to the new surroundings and the darkness. Then, moving quickly towards the warehouse, flattening his back against the wall, he slid slowly towards the end where the front and side walls met. He tried to locate the guards; he could see one, 7 feet away. The other was not visible. Mihir figured that if they were as stationary as before, when he had seen them from the gate, then the second guard would be about 10 feet away—a gap of two or three seconds. Long enough for him. He would be able to take both of them down.

There was another way—old school, but it invariably worked. He created a diversion by simply picking up a stone and throwing it away from his location, towards a patch of undergrowth. He then lay and waited for the reaction that would inevitably follow. The guard closer to the noise looked in the direction of the disturbance and then at his companion, who nodded. The first sentry started moving cautiously in the direction of the sound, his hand loosely touching his weapon. He stopped for a second before rounding the corner.

Mihir lay in wait. In total darkness and in a low crouch, he saw the sentry advancing in his direction, the weapon still in its holster. The man moved slowly along the wall, avoiding stepping on to the grass. He missed Mihir, who was about 4 feet away, lying behind some of the taller undergrowth. The moment the sentry crossed him, Mihir rose noiselessly. In one swift movement, he had him in a chokehold, his right elbow firmly around the man's throat, left elbow pressed behind his neck. Firm pressure for a minute and the man collapsed, unconscious. He would be out for at least a couple of hours. Mihir gagged and bound him with the man's own shirt. Except for the grass rustling, there was no other sound. Now Mihir waited for the other guard. He guessed it would be another couple of minutes before the other guy came over looking for his buddy.

It took a little longer. First, the other guard called out softly. No answer. Then, a little louder. No response again. Slightly alarmed, he began moving in the direction the first man had taken; his weapon was already pointed in front of him. He moved in a classic crouch which soldiers adopt when contact with the enemy is imminent. As he rounded the corner, it took only a second for Mihir to notice that the man's finger was on the trigger guard, not on the trigger itself. This would make it easy.

The man's eyes hadn't yet adjusted to the darkness and that was enough for Mihir, who was crouched low to his opponent's left. He rose and, in one swift movement, used his right hand to grab his opponent's right wrist and the left to remove the trigger finger from the guard, twist and break it. Mihir rendered the man helpless and, before he could cry out in pain, he pivoted on his right heel, bent his left arm, and, using the bone of his elbow, hit the man on the right side of his forehead. The man went down like a sack. It took less than five seconds.

The field was now clear. Mihir moved quickly towards the front door of the shed. It had a wide, steel-roller shutter. Bending down, he pushed the slide lock on both sides of the shutter into their end slats, firmly locking the only entry and exit. Anybody inside would stay there.

Mihir turned towards the trucks. They were ten in all, lined up neatly along the perimeter wall. A line-up designed for a quick move. The drivers were possibly scheduled to drive out before dawn; it would be a long journey to wherever they were headed. Mihir had a fair idea where.

He moved to the first vehicle. The reefers were large, each capable of carrying about 12 tonnes of refrigerated goods. They came with their own refrigeration units, which, besides the engine, consisted of a compressor, evaporator and condenser. Auxiliary power was provided by a diesel generator, which was used whenever the vehicle's driving engine was switched off, and the stuff inside needed to be preserved at the desired temperature. All ten generators were on; they hummed in unison, creating an ambient low-frequency din. The refrigerated units mounted on the rear chassis were mild-steel corrugated containers. The insides were made of food-grade stainless steel, with a polyurethane foam inner lining for efficient insulation.

Mihir moved to the rear of the first truck, where the entry to the refrigerated unit was through a double door. At the centre was the locking mechanism, which was a typical locking rod that ran the height of the container. There were two, close to each other in a pair, on either side of the junction where the two halves met and slammed shut. The locking rods in turn were secured with crossbar locks, which were resistant to bolt cutters and lockpicks. The outside surface of the container had standardized serrations for structural strength. The complete surface looked even, with no breaks.

But Mihir was not convinced. He ran his hand along the surface at shoulder height, looking for structural faults. Then, exactly 3 feet from the front end of the container, there was a small break in the metal—so minute that it was easily missed by the naked eye, but could be felt by the tip of a finger.

Mihir ran his index finger along the gap—it rose in height to about 3 feet from the bottom of the container. Then, it stopped abruptly and went left for about 2.5 feet, before running down again to the bottom of the container. He understood. It was a small door, beautifully crafted into the side. It was easy to miss, because, unlike other doors, this one had no latch to open it, no keyhole, no press-fit mechanism. This meant that the door could only be opened from inside the driver's cabin. Mihir walked over to the other side, got into the driver's cabin, and began looking around for a small lever. It took him over five minutes, but he managed to locate it slightly behind the vacuum brake air release lever.

As Mihir held the knob and pressed it down, he heard a soft popping sound. He walked around to the side of the small door and found it slightly ajar. Forcing his hand inside the gap, he opened it wide and peered inside. He was shocked by what he saw—children and teenage girls lay helplessly, packed like sardines, half-drugged, covered in human faeces and urine. The stench was unbearable. Stepping back, Mihir took a couple of snaps, tagged his pin location and sent it to ASI Gogoi.

Next, he opened the doors to each of the hidden compartments on the remaining containers. He did not stop to see the young women, girls and boys tumbling out of the packed space, dazed. He silently urged them to keep quiet and assured that help was on the way.

A while later, just as he was about to reach his hidden bike, he heard the wail of distant sirens approaching. Gogoi had been prompt; the police would reach in about three minutes by the narrow road. There was nothing more to be done here.

Mihir started his bike and rode out quietly by the alternate route. The proverbial ball was now firmly in the other side's court. He would be ready for them.

Back on the main road, and an hour out of Guwahati, Mihir headed out towards Barojat. A little distance short of the town, he stopped at a roadside restaurant, and ordered a cup of tea and some sandwiches. Savouring the Assam tea, he took out his mobile and rang Lt Col Sumer.

'Could you cross-check a location for me from the map-sheets we had identified?' he asked.

'Just a sec. Let me get the maps.'

Mihir heard some paper ruffling.

'Shoot,' said Sumer.

Mihir gave the location of the warehouse he had been to.

'Okay, stay on the line,' said Sumer, as he traced his pencil along the route taken by Mihir.

'Yes, it checks out with one of the locations on the map. It is the third grid reference from the top in the diary. So, what's going on?' asked Sumer, after a short pause.

'Bigger shit than we initially assumed. Human trafficking. Will fill you in later,' said Mihir, and hung up.

He drank his tea and waited for the call he knew would come soon enough.

27

The flames from the three wooden pyres leapt almost 10 feet high. Together they created such intense heat that the wood not only burned, it sublimed—changing state directly from solid to vapour. The temperature from such combustion normally reached 1,100 degrees Celsius.

The young woman standing a few feet away was oblivious to the heat that was nearly singeing her skin. Tears streamed down her delicate face, as she leaned on her aunt for support, and watched her parents and brother turn to ashes, snatched away by fate's cruel and remorseless hands.

Watching this tragic scene from a distance, leaning against his Gypsy, was ASI Gogoi. He had managed to trace Kankan's sister from the contact list in his mobile phone. She had flown in the previous day from Pune, where she worked in an IT firm. He glanced up at the overcast afternoon sky, before walking tentatively towards her. All Gogoi could offer were empty words of sympathy, as he watched the last embers of the pyres die down. The ashes would be ready for collection the next day.

'Where will you go now?' asked Gogoi.

'With my aunt, my mother's sister,' she replied, pointing weakly in the direction of a woman who was waiting with her husband and two teenage boys next to a car.

'Why would somebody want to kill my family?' she asked after a moment of silence, tears streaming down her face once again.

'We don't know, yet. We are investigating,' said Gogoi, looking at the girl sadly. He didn't disclose that her brother may have got mixed up with some bad people.

'How long do you plan to stay?' he added as an afterthought.

'I don't know. I have taken a long leave. Two weeks.'

'I will let you know the moment I get to know something. I have your number,' said Gogoi, and hurried back to his vehicle. Once inside, he reached into his pocket and dialled the number of the man who had saved his life less than seventy-two hours earlier.

'Quite a lot has happened since we last met, major,' said Gogoi, looking up at the sky just as it began to rain, 'and all because of you.'

'Thank you. I counted ninety-six people, all women and children,' said Mihir.

'They were lucky; we got to them just in time,' said Gogoi, watching Kankan's sister leave with her relatives. 'Some of them were critical and would have died had they not been rescued on time. They are undergoing the necessary medical check-ups before being discharged and taken back to their homes.'

'I left some others there too. I am sure they were a far more interesting catch.'

'Yes. There were ten drivers and ten handlers, and two groggy security guards. One of them had his finger and wrist broken pretty badly. He won't be able to hold a gun ever again. Even though the other fellow got away lightly, he will be in hospital for at least a couple of weeks. And a partially burnt body behind the warehouse. All yours?' asked Gogoi.

'The first two, yes; the partially burnt body is their handiwork, not mine. But only two security guards?' asked

Mihir. 'I thought there would be more, especially inside the shed.'

'We only found the drivers and handlers. Was there anybody else?'

'Maybe,' said Mihir, thinking of the ponytailed guy who should have been among those apprehended. 'And who do those trucks belong to?'

'An influential guy, deep pockets. He began his foray into politics a year or so back. We have sent a team to pick him up. Find out what he knows, since they were his reefers transporting the women and kids,' explained Gogoi. 'Any news of the girl?'

'She has been located in a farmhouse on the outskirts of Delhi.'

'That's good news,' said Gogoi, cautiously.

'We have eyes there. I will be in touch.'

A day of mixed news, thought Gogoi, as he drove out of the crematorium. Despair for one family, hope for another.

~

Gogoi was seated in a small space that served as the family's living room, dining room or bedroom, depending on the time of the day or night. Seated across him on the floor was Maymunah's family—the father tired and defeated; the mother dishevelled, barely holding on to her sanity; the other kids still staring goggle-eyed at the visitor, confused and scared.

Gogoi told Ranjan, 'I have good news and not-so-good news.'

'Have you found her?' the father asked, looking from the policeman to his tearful wife.

'We have,' Gogoi said, patting one of the children on the head. 'She is in a farmhouse in Delhi. We believe she is safe.'

'Then why has she not spoken with us?' asked the father, relieved, but also angry at Maymunah.

'Because she is not free to do so. She is a prisoner along with some other girls.'

'I don't understand; she went willingly from here.'

'It may have seemed like that, but appearances can be misleading. She was lured into it,' said Gogoi. 'Her kidnapping was aided by her boyfriend from school, whom she trusted completely.'

'Where is this friend? Have you arrested him?' asked the father, redirecting his anger towards the boy. The mother listened to the conversation, her hands on her face.

'Unfortunately, he is dead; most probably killed by the people who kidnapped your daughter,' the policeman said.

'But who are these people who murder and kidnap? Why haven't they been arrested yet?' the father asked naively.

'Very powerful people. We don't know who they are yet, but we will. In the meantime, keep this information to yourself. Your daughter has been located. Hopefully, she will be back here with you soon.'

A few minutes later, Gogoi left the house. It was a long time since he had felt hopeful. The sordid drama had finally revealed a silver lining.

∼

The events unfolding in Samanta Borphuken's life were exactly what he had always feared. It was a nightmare. He looked out of the window; it was raining heavily. His bedside clock showed 3 a.m. He had been rudely woken up by a panic call from a senior driver—all ten of his reefer trucks had been apprehended by the Guwahati Police. The rescued underage girls and children were being treated at a government hospital. It was only a matter of hours before the cops paid him a visit. He got dressed and walked around the quiet house, his mind blank.

They came for him just before dawn—handcuffed him and took him in a Gypsy, barely giving him time to talk to his family. Seated in the rear of the vehicle, he watched his expansive home and political dreams recede, just as the orange glow of a new dawn lit up the front porch.

Maalik was livid. His lavish breakfast lay half-eaten. His glass of fresh orange juice had become the target of his frustration and was splattered on the wall in front of him. He wished Silki and the Monster dead for their utter failure in dealing with the Major. The stupid fools had led him to their lair. Punishment for such failure would have been swift; Maalik would have gladly shot them. But that would have to wait till the immediate threat had been dealt with.

This was not the first time the cops had raided one of his properties. But each time, they returned empty-handed. Maalik was always a step ahead, thanks to a well-entrenched network of informants within the law enforcement agencies and the government. But this time, it was different. The most important step now was to limit the damage. Thankfully, nothing had been found at the site that would lead to him, directly or indirectly. After that, he would deal with the menace of Mihir, personally. Staring coldly into the eyes of the Monster and Silki, he dialled a number.

'I pay you not to get surprised,' he said to the voice at the other end.

'This completely passed me by. I had no clue, I am sorry. Won't happen again,' replied Inspector Sarma, from Razak police station.

'It had better not. Make it go away or the consequences won't be pleasant. I wonder how it feels to see your whole family cremated?'

'Please, I will do whatever is needed to be done. Please don't harm them,' Sarma begged.

'That, my friend, is entirely on you,' said Maalik, hanging up.

'One more chance is all I need,' hissed the Monster. 'I will personally make him suffer.'

'Your chance is over. I warned you he was no amateur. Leave him to me,' Maalik said, as he dialled another number. 'In the meantime, I want you to keep all operations on hold for the time being.'

Then, he said into the phone, 'I want to talk to the Major directly. It is time we spoke.' He hung up, without waiting for a response.

~

Back at his office by ten, Gogoi learnt about the successful raid and arrest of the owner of BPN Logistics. The scale of the operation in Guwahati and the arrest of Borphuken, a rising political star, in connection with what was clearly a human trafficking racket, meant that Bondhuroh was becoming the focus of media attention. Borphuken's political party had immediately distanced itself from the scandal, while the state government, belonging to the rival party, sniffed a political opportunity. The law minister came on television to announce the formation of a special task force under an additional director-general of police, which would submit its report to the chief minister's office in a month.

Suddenly, Gogoi had become small fry—nobody cared that it was his tip-off that had led to the massive human trafficking racket being caught. Ignoring the hubbub, Gogoi was determined to continue his investigation. He would only rest when the girl was reunited with her parents. Picking up his phone, he rang up his counterpart at the police station in Guwahati that was responsible for the raid.

'Thanks for the tip-off, Gogoi sahab. Our operation was a 100 per cent success,' said the sub-inspector, cheerfully.

'Who is the owner of the warehouse?' asked Gogoi.

'A private party. That person happens to own the land on which he decided to build a private warehouse. He leases it out for about two lakh rupees a month. This one was leased out to BPN Logistics four months ago. It seems Borphuken was the kingpin of the racket. Looks like a watertight case against him,' replied the sub-inspector.

'Thanks for the input,' replied Gogoi, quite sure that Borphuken was only the fall guy. Someone else was moving in the shadows, covering his tracks—the real mastermind who controlled the strings. Gogoi wished he knew who it was. Maybe Borphuken had the answers.

∼

Gogoi looked at the man seated across the steel table. A naked bulb, hanging low from the ceiling, partially illuminated the top of his head. Samanta Borphuken looked unkempt and tired. The state police had charged him under the Immoral Traffic (Prevention) Act, and the Protection of Children from Sexual Offences (POCSO) Act. The first was a bailable offence but the second one was not, so he was destined to spend his days in judicial custody until trial. If found guilty, he would spend the rest of his life in a cell far worse than the one he was seated in right now.

'Have some,' said Gogoi, handing the man a cup of tea. 'It may be some time before you get a chance to taste one as good as this.'

Borphuken reached out for the cup, eyes down, head hanging low. Gogoi sensed his shame. He leaned forward and spoke in a low voice.

'I know what you are going through.'

The other man did not respond.

'I can help you,' continued Gogoi, offering him some hope. 'You have to tell me who was forcing you to do this. I know it wasn't you.'

'It wasn't.'

'Then who? Tell me.'

'I have already told the others. I was paid a visit by a man the first time, four months ago. After that, I always got instructions on the phone via SMS.'

'Can you describe him?'

'Small, maybe 5 foot 5, very agile and strong. Expressionless eyes. Black hair cropped close. East-Asian features, definitely not from here. That's all I know,' said Borphuken.

'His phone number?'

'Always an unknown number. I tried to trace it, but could never find out.'

'Your phone record will show the conversation?'

'No. Somehow, it always got erased within a few minutes of receiving. I had to memorize the number so as not to make a mistake.'

'Why did you do it?'

'They threatened to kill my family,' Borphuken sobbed.

Gogoi got up to leave. He felt pity for the pathetic figure seated in front of him. If only he had come to the authorities in time.

Borphuken called out from behind him.

'Wait, I just remembered something else. The man who came to meet me wore a strange-looking earring in his left ear. It was a fat skull, made out of some shiny, white metal.'

28

Rehaan had had the farmhouse under surveillance for close to seventy-two hours. It was clear as daylight that the place was being used for human trafficking. About eight to ten girls were being held captive in the house.

The scourge had become a national menace, and with enforcement agencies like the Anti-Human-Trafficking Unit (AHTU) and the local police hot on their heels, the perpetrators were forced to change their modus operandi constantly. Based on newspaper reports, these days, they were using small railway and bus stations which weren't monitored that well. Boys and girls, some as young as eleven, were being picked up and bundled off to work in inhuman conditions in congested industrial units that dotted the country's landscape.

But there was a difference. These girls were in their late teens, old enough to be used somewhere else, for something even more vicious. Rehaan's earlier conjecture was sexual exploitation, but had it been so, they would have been picked up by pimps immediately on arrival and sold to a brothel. Nothing of the sort had happened and that meant only one thing: These girls were special and had been selected with great care. They were being reserved for a more discreet and wealthier clientele. They would be sold to the highest bidder, maybe from overseas as well. Humans for sale, bought by other humans.

This farmhouse belonged to one of the most wealthy and powerful families in Delhi. Old money; the owner was a rich carpet merchant. Rumour had it that he was also a power broker, patronized by the high and mighty. The operation seemed to have police cooperation. Involving the media would turn the affair into a circus and those responsible would be able to manipulate the justice system to their advantage.

No. That could not be allowed to happen. The criminals would pay dearly for their actions. This had to be dealt with outside the ambit of the law. Rehaan was dead sure that this operation ran across the length and breadth of India. If it was destroyed, along with the evil people who ran it, he would consider it as an oath fulfilled towards his motherland.

Rehaan rang his boss and brought him up to date on the matter at hand.

~

Elsewhere, Maalik was also keen to get in touch with Rehaan's boss. He dialled the number he had acquired. At the other end, Mihir saw the word 'SPAM' flashing on his screen. Normally, he would have declined the call, but this caller had managed to get past his expensive spam-blocker software. There was only one explanation: This someone had managed to get his number—an achievement in itself—and wanted to speak with him while concealing their identity under the guise of a spam call. Finally, the dominoes were beginning to fall.

'Quicker than I thought,' Mihir said as soon as the call connected.

'You have made my life inconvenient, Major sahab,' said the raspy voice on the other end.

'Not a major anymore.'

'Yes, court-martialled. I am aware. But don't they say, once a soldier, always a soldier?' mocked the voice.

Mihir did not respond.

'Why do you meddle in my business?'

'How so?' asked Mihir, leading him on.

'You killed one of mine at the shed.'

'No choice. She was not exactly out for an evening walk. Cop's good fortune, chick's bad fortune,' quipped Mihir.

'I am willing to forget all this happened if you walk away, now,' replied the man, keeping his temper under control.

What did the piece of shit think he was?

'How can I? You killed my friend,' Mihir said, taking a shot in the dark.

'An unfortunate incident. I consider killing an unpleasant business. How should I put it … It sours the sweetness of the prize and attracts unnecessary attention. Something I try to avoid as much as possible.'

'Then why kill him?'

'He was obstinate. Kept meddling. Wouldn't listen to reason, and continued on a path which crossed mine and threatened my business. That, I could not tolerate,' said the man, seething with suppressed anger.

'I do not want that same fate to befall you, my friend,' he continued after a short pause, the ominous tone accentuated by the breathy, raspy voice.

'I am not your friend. And on one condition,' responded Mihir, laying the trap.

'Yes?'

'I want to know who killed Chris,' said Mihir coldly.

'That would be a terrible mistake. No one gets to know him and lives. You want to stay alive? Leave quietly. Consider the woman you killed as having squared the account. You won't be touched on your way out of this place if you leave quietly.'

'And what about the boy you had killed in that shed. And his innocent parents, who died without knowing why? And the hapless victims of your sleazy work, which you dare to call a business?'

'Sad. Inevitable consequences in our line of work. I am sure you do not want to meet the same fate.'

'You made a terrible mistake when you touched my friend. It's too late now. It's on you,' warned Mihir.

Maalik stared at the blank screen in his hand as the call was disconnected. The piece of shit; he would die for his insolence. The problem, however, was to locate him. He was like a ghost, moving unseen. He had even escaped one of his most elaborate traps. Not this time. He picked up the phone and called in his assets.

~

Still seated at the roadside restaurant with his second cup of tea, Mihir knew now that Chris was killed because he had stumbled upon a human trafficking network. He had refused to back down. Chris could have reported the matter to the local police and allowed them to deal with the criminals. Mihir was almost certain why he didn't do it. But Chris had paid for it with his life.

His phone rang again. This time, it was the ASI, Gogoi.

'Just spoke to the owner of the reefer trucks. The man does not know who the boss of the whole set-up is, but he was always contacted by a go-between. Before it all began, he was paid a visit by a man.'

Gogoi then went on to describe the visitor exactly as Borphuken had.

'I think you are still not out of danger, my friend. They will come back for you hard. This time they will leave nothing to chance. They know where to find you. Be careful,' cautioned Mihir. 'By the way, I was contacted by their boss not a moment ago.'

'Did you get his number? What did he say?' asked Gogoi.

'The number was disguised as spam. He asked me to leave quietly. He promised to spare my life if I did.'

'So, the murder of your friend and the human trafficking ring are connected. How? It does not fall within the ambit of army duties. He could have reported the matter to us through his channels.'

'Maybe he did not want that to happen. Why? I do not know yet,' replied Mihir, keeping his suspicions to himself.

'What will you do now?' asked Gogoi.

'Wait for them to come for me,' said Mihir, quietly.

'You sure of that?'

'Oh, yes. They won't stop till I am dead,' replied Mihir, with finality.

~

The call was being monitored.

'I know where he is. The fool even has his location on. He is lit up like a beacon,' said a man, turning around to face Maalik.

'Good. But he is not a fool. It was deliberate. He wants us to come for him. We will, but not where he expects us,' said Maalik, feeling grudging respect for the ex-major. He was as cunning as a fox.

Quite certain by now that he was being tagged electronically, Mihir knew that it would only be a matter of time before they came for him. It was late afternoon when Mihir turned west and took the road back to Guwahati. Time to wreak havoc on the bastards. He would begin at the warehouse that was nearest to his memorized list.

'Let me finish him. He has caused us enough trouble,' said Mwhaay, the snake.

'Others are baying for his blood and I am inclined to give them a chance. For you, my friend, I have another task. I want you to take out the cop. Make no mistakes. Besides, the soldier is nowhere nearby. The policeman is vulnerable, alone. He can't be protected this time,' said Maalik.

Mwhaay gave a slight bow and left. Maalik watched him leave, and, after a moment's pause, summoned the Monster and Silki.

'You have your chance now. You will be given the details. Silki can stay; I need her here. Do not fail me this time,' said Maalik, dismissing the Monster with a flick of his right hand.

Yudhvir had noticed another man watching the flat within a few minutes of taking up station opposite Tuhin Khanna's apartment block. He was able to see both comfortably from his vantage point, which was higher than the one taken by the other man. The traffickers must have felt that Tuhin could not be trusted, otherwise, why would they keep one of their own under surveillance? The man in the apartment was at the end of his tether—that much was obvious from the endless glasses of whiskey he was consuming.

Yudhvir did not empathize with Tuhin. Based on Rehaan's briefing, he deserved no pity. For Yudhvir, morality and integrity were either white or black; there were no shades of grey.

By late noon, the man showed some signs of life, after a phone call he received with a degree of trepidation. Yudhvir noticed that the caller was the other man who had been watching the apartment—both had their mobiles next to their ears at the same time. Some instructions were being passed to Tuhin, who was reluctantly nodding his head.

'The target is preparing to move,' Yudhvir reported back.

'Tail him. Keep me posted,' ordered Rehaan.

Exhausted, drunk and feeling defeated, Tuhin got up to get ready. Despite his miserable state, he was sure of his decision. Half an hour later, he got into his chauffeur-driven car and headed for his office, a fifteen-minute drive from his apartment complex. The road was jammed with the first lot of office-goers returning home. Tuhin turned south, keeping Sun City to his left till he reached the intersection of Golf Course Road and Golf Course Extension Road. Turning right, he headed to Vikas Marg. There, he slowed down in front of a large, sliding iron gate that guarded the entry to a thirty storey–tall commercial complex. His office was on the tenth floor.

Following on a bike, Yudhvir quietly established his observation post in a ground-floor coffeehouse opposite the office complex. The café specialized in serving coffee brewed in a French press. Yudhvir noticed that the other man tailing Tuhin had also followed him and was stationed comfortably on the pavement outside the building, as if waiting for someone. It was twilight; the lights inside residential apartments and office complexes that dotted the neighbourhood had begun to come on.

After an hour, an armoured van pulled up outside the main gate of the office building. The man on the pavement nodded imperceptibly at the vehicle and quickly got into the driver's cab as it slowed down in front of the main gate. The armoured car then entered the premises and went down to the parking lot in the basement.

Yudhvir knew it was a cash-in-transit vehicle—an armoured van used extensively for cash logistics. This was an industry that employed close to 40,000 people, replenishing cash across 80,000 ATMs that dotted India, carrying about 15,000 crore rupees' worth of cash daily. It did all this with the help of 6,000 armoured cars, such as the one that had just disappeared inside the basement.

This type of vehicle would usually have at least three occupants: A driver and two armed guards at the back in the armoured compartment. The watcher was the fourth.

To Rehaan, who was receiving constant updates from Yudhvir, the purpose of the armoured vehicle was becoming clear. It was most probably being used to move large amounts of illegal cash from the business of human trafficking. Rehaan was quite sure that the cash logistics company, whose name was emblazoned on the vehicle, was being used as a front for the sordid affair.

Most illegal businesses deal with large amounts of cash, naturally, because cash is always untraceable. But after a point, too much physical cash becomes a liability. So, it needs to be laundered before being fed back into the system as legitimate money. So, criminals create elaborate systems handled by financial experts. One smart way is to piggyback on the proceeds of an existing legitimate business and infuse just enough cash into its transactions regularly so as not to be singled out. The trick is to keep the cash flow under control. This illegal cash is now mixed with legit cash, then physically deposited into banks that handle the company's businesses. Meanwhile, the rest of the cash waiting to be fed into the business needs a place where it can be physically stored, like a hidden vault.

It was evident that Tuhin's company was being used to store and launder cash. Rehaan was convinced that there would be other companies across the country assisting the traffickers. Rehaan did not envy Tuhin; the chokeholds these people came up with could be suffocating. Any attempt to break the stranglehold could invariably prove fatal.

Time to relieve the man of his suffering. Rehaan picked up his phone and spoke to an old friend, someone high up in the Gurugram police department. The cops loved anonymous tip-offs from old and trusted sources that netted big fish.

~

In another part of the country, Mihir continued on the national highway, past the warehouse he had visited the previous night. Short of the airport, he stopped at a small mobile store and purchased a cheap smartphone. Using a spare SIM, he activated the phone and rang up Rehaan. Mihir then took to the road once again, heading out to the warehouse that was next on his target list.

On the other side of Guwahati, in the control room of Lal Bangla, Silki and the Monster were monitoring the movements of the ex-major on the screen in front of them. It was clear where he was headed. It did not worry the Monster. The site was virtually empty. The Major would meet nothing there except his own death. He knew the man was cunning and it would be difficult to tackle him alone. Therefore, the Monster set about laying an elaborate trap to corner the ex-major. Though Maalik had asked him to kill the man on sight, the Monster had other plans. He wanted the ex-major taken alive. He would then have some fun with the soldier before relieving him of his miserable life.

~

Back in Gurugram, Rehaan, who had been briefed by Mihir, rang up the number he had been given. The call was picked up by Colonel Randhawa.

'You are sure this is what he said?' asked Randy, after Rehaan had passed on the instructions given to him by Mihir.

'His instructions were crystal clear. That is exactly what he asked me to convey to you,' replied Rehaan.

'Then it is time to meet an old friend,' replied Randy.

The Military Police colonel then rang up his counterpart in Guwahati on the Army Static Switched Communication Network (ASCON)—the secure, end-to-end encrypted voice and data telecom backbone of the Indian Army.

Time was short, but he was confident of success.

29

The man observing the farmhouse had now spent forty-eight hours at his post, beyond a high boundary wall. He hadn't been static all this while. Krish, as he was affectionately called by his army buddies, had used the cover of the night to sneak closer. Using the elevation of a tree next to the boundary wall, he had scouted the layout of the farmhouse and its security apparatus. The house had three storeys including the ground floor; Krish reckoned it had twenty-five to thirty rooms.

On the ground floor, large French doors and windows formed a façade on three sides—the front and the wings. This was protected by a red-tiled awning.

The first floor began above the awning. The rooms on this floor were surrounded by an airy veranda, protected by an ornate three-foot iron railing. Next up was a large terrace, half of which was occupied by generous rooms, called barsatis, again with continuous French doors and windows.

The farmhouse was smack in the middle of extensive acreage—Krish estimated the distance of the house from the boundary wall to be about 100 metres on all sides. There was a small outhouse tucked away in a corner next to the rear boundary wall. This was the dwelling for the cook and the housemaid.

The homestead was well guarded. Krish had counted a total of six men, all of whom seemed to be between the ages of twenty and thirty-five. They carried handguns, mostly the local variety called kattas, which were easily available. There were four on guard—two on the outer premises and two who alternatively walked the verandas. The other two were used as reliefs, and rested in the barsatis on the second floor. The cook was middle-aged, and there was one woman in her thirties, who seemed to be the boss of the outfit. Krish barely saw her, except when she stepped out of the house to pass some instructions to the guards. She was always dressed in jeans and a T-shirt. The gates to the house were always shut, and opened only when a truck carrying rations and essential supplies was allowed to enter once in three days.

The instructions to Krish had been precise. Uncovering his G-Shock watch, worn on the left wrist, from its camouflage covering, he looked at the faint glow of the hands on the dial. A minute after midnight. Krish covered the dial face again; the green glow of the hands could be a dead giveaway. It was a starry night. The farmhouse was half a kilometre away from the main road.

All of a sudden, Krish felt movement behind him on the left. The dark silhouette merged with the shadows of the trees noiselessly. Krish smiled. His back-up man had not lost his touch. Looking over his shoulder, Krish nodded as the other man, Shamsher, walked up and stood beside him.

A moment later, they began to tread carefully along the outer side of the wall of the farmhouse, staying safe within its shadows, till they came up to an electricity pole that linked the farmhouse to the main road. The pole had a small metal box, with a large lever on its side, which Krish pulled down to plunge the outer expanse of the farmhouse into darkness. Using his Israeli Ari B' Lilah special forces knife, Krish cut the flimsy straps that attached the box to the pole and threw it into a ditch. The areas surrounding the house would remain in darkness until their task was done.

~

Maymunah sensed, rather than saw, the outer acreage plunge into darkness. She was trying her best to sleep in the stiflingly hot room. Light, which had crept in through the gaps in the locked, shuttered window and between the heavy drapes, had suddenly gone out. She got up from her bed with a start and walked slowly to the window. She parted the drapes ever so lightly to take a look outside.

The past few days had been like a horror movie for Maymunah. Nobody had touched her or any of the other girls, which was a relief. But it was less out of a sense of decency and more out of mortal fear that had been instilled in the guards by their bosses. There had been one incident—one guy, lanky and very young, leched at her all the time. One night, as she entered her room, he crept in silently behind her. Grabbing her, he threw her onto the bed. As she turned in horror to face him, ready to scream, he covered her mouth with his large hand. With his other, he unzipped his trousers, took out his erect penis and masturbated in front of her. His pent-up frustration shone in his expression. He made her watch him while he pleasured himself.

Since then, Maymunah was mortally scared of being alone in her room. She barely slept at night; whatever sleep she could muster was during the day. She cried very often, desperately praying to God to rescue her from the hell she was in.

Peering through the gaps in the shutters, she tried to make sense of what was happening outside. The vast compound was completely dark. The guards had switched on their torch lights and were moving about trying to identify the fault, talking loudly.

~

Meanwhile, Krish and his buddy Shamsher had infiltrated into the compound, having crossed the rear wall of the house where it was least guarded. Once inside, they lay still next to the wall, waiting for the right moment. The guards responsible for the outer premises had, in the meantime, migrated to the front of the farmhouse to identify the cause of the breakdown. The sentries on the first-floor veranda stayed where they were, maintaining an overwatch. The back of the house had a courtyard constructed with paver tiles and, enclosed within, a low walled fence of about 2 feet. A small opening within the wall in the centre led straight to a large door, presumably to the kitchen and pantry. The duo headed for this door.

Sara, the boss of the farmhouse operation, was beginning to worry. Unlike the local staff, she was aware of the problems that had cropped up in the Northeast. Could it be that this place was also being targeted? She asked the two spare guards resting in the barsatis to join the other four. Hurriedly dressing, she left her room to check on the girls, but not before she had tucked in a Glock 43, 9-mm subcompact semi-automatic pistol into her belt. The weapon was packed with a single-stack magazine, with a capacity of 6 rounds, and one round in the chamber. Infallible.

The two spare guards moved down and, with 10 to 15 feet of space between them, began their beat of the perimeter from the rear of the house. But Krish and Shamsher had already crossed the open space between the outer compound wall and the small kitchen wall. They now lay prone safely behind the low wall, a few feet from the kitchen door, which was their chosen point of entry. The odds were nine to two, if you counted the woman in charge, the cook, the maid and the six guards. Not bad.

The first part of their mission was to rescue the girl whose image had been shared on Krish's mobile phone. If the other girls were also saved, that was a bonus. The second part of the mission was to destroy the farmhouse and kill those who perpetrated this despicable trade.

Once the guards patrolling the premises had crossed, Shamsher crawled towards the door and examined the lock. It was a bolt lock, 'tadi-type' latch, which was locked with the help of a keyed padlock. Why would a door be locked from the outside when there were occupants inside? For one reason only, Krish thought—to prevent the occupants from escaping. He watched as Shamsher took out a warded key pick set from his pocket and slowly tried the keys, until one fit. He unlatched the bolt noiselessly and both of them slipped quietly inside the house, allowing their eyes to adjust to the darkness.

In another part of the house, Maymunah heard footsteps, initially on the stairs leading to the first floor where she was being kept, then on the landing and finally outside her door. She quickly hurried to her bed, lay down and pretended to sleep. The key turned once, then the sound of footsteps faded away.

Sara continued her march to the end of the corridor, confirming that the girls were in their rooms. She walked down to the ground floor lobby and stepped out of the main door. Here, she saw the guards returning from their futile attempts to restore power to the house.

'Somebody has cut the power to the house,' said one of the guards, slightly out of breath.

'Fuck! It was deliberate, then. Search the premises. Whoever has sneaked in must be caught,' she said, loud enough for all the guards to hear her. Removing her weapon from her belt, she began to move cautiously around the house in a half-crouch.

The intruders, meanwhile, had already scouted the ground floor, which consisted of a lavish living room, dining hall, kitchen, pantry and a well-stocked bar, adequate for a large party. No sign of the girls, who were probably locked up on the first floor. Krish had no idea which room Maymunah was in. They would have to try each room—a time-consuming exercise. But first, the guards would have to be eliminated. They decided to begin with the pair on the first-floor veranda.

The ground floor had a long corridor and two staircases led up to the first floor. Krish and Shamsher negotiated one of the staircases, silent as cats, and crouched next to the door opening on to the veranda, listening for the sound of footsteps.

The four guards and Sara had, by now, scouted the entire farmhouse and hadn't come across anybody. She began to wonder whether this was all just a figment of her imagination. Deciding to wind up her search and have the problem of the electricity fixed in the morning, she walked to the rear of the house. The lock on the door leading to the kitchen was open. She froze. Feeling fear and a rush of adrenaline, she drew her weapon without even realizing it. Sara beckoned to the guards, two of whom followed her inside the dark house silently, weapons drawn. The other two stayed outside, watching the house.

Krish knew that time was running out. He had picked up the faint sound of footsteps in the corridor below. The woman would have one or two of the guards with her. Three inside and two outside to cut off any escape route. In the house, the odds now were five to two. Manageable. Krish and Shamsher decided to split up.

The group below was moving from one room to another. Krish estimated it would be three minutes before they began to climb the stairs. He nodded to Shamsher, who took up his position outside in a crouch. He found both the guards on the veranda, screening the area in front of them.

One of Shamsher's specialities was a deadly knife-throwing skill. He could throw a knife equally well with both hands. From his belt, he unsheathed two different types of knives. In his left, he held a conventional throwing knife made of a single piece of steel—one half sharpened, and the other portion used to grip and throw the blade. When thrown correctly, it rotated around its axis before hitting the target with its sharpened end. A good thrower could achieve velocities of 100 kilometres per hour and a range up to 50 yards. Shamsher could reach 120 kilometres with a range of 70 yards.

In his right hand, he held a ballistic knife, which had a detachable, spring-loaded blade that could be released by pressing a trigger. It could travel to a distance of 20 feet at 65 kilometres an hour. Shamsher decided to use the ballistic knife on the guard who was on his left and the conventional throwing knife in his left hand on the unsuspecting guard standing to his right. Rising slowly, he raised his left hand to shoulder height. Using his right leg as a pivot, he threw the knife at the guard, aiming for his chest. The blade travelled to its target in less than half a second and punctured the heart. The guard wasn't dead, but would be in a minute, as he bled on the floor of the veranda.

The thump of his falling colleague alerted the other guard. He had begun to turn when Shamsher released the blade of the ballistic knife, aiming it at the guard's throat. It entered his trachea, puncturing the airway to the lungs. The man collapsed—not dead, but incapacitated and trying hard to breathe. He made a move to reach his weapon, but Shamsher quickly retrieved his embedded knife and used it to slit the guard's throat. Turning around, Shamsher retrieved the first knife, took up his position next to the door and waited.

On the other side of the door, Krish waited for the woman in charge and the two guards. The moment they reached the first landing on one flight of stairs, he went down the other, and then, very quietly, began to climb the same stairs taken by his adversaries. He was now behind them.

As he came up on the first floor, he found his targets about 6 feet ahead, in a single file—the woman cautiously leading; the guards behind her, weapons drawn. The woman was now directly in front of the door behind which Shamsher waited. He opened the door in a flash, catching the trio by surprise. Krish then made his move from behind. He elbow-gripped the guard's throat and stabbed him in the back, through his heart. One down, two to go. The second guard, startled by Shamsher's sudden appearance and the noise of his falling colleague behind, turned around half a second late. Krish covered the 2 feet between them in a flash and knifed the man in the throat. The woman, the only one left, half-turned in panic and fired her weapon blindly. The gun went off like a deafening crack of thunder; the bullet grazed Krish's shoulder. Ignoring the sharp sting, he reached out and grabbed Sara's elbow with his left hand, and turned it around towards her. Using his right hand, he twisted her hand holding the weapon, dislodging the pistol from her grip. Then, he shot her dead. The complete sequence did not take more than thirty seconds.

The sound of gunfire created pandemonium in the rooms that lined both sides of the corridor. The girls, scared to death, began to cry and scream, not knowing what was happening outside. Shamsher began to unlock the rooms with the keys taken from the dead caretaker. He gathered the girls in the corridor, trying to calm them down, and led them away from the carnage. Maymunah was among them. As she was being escorted downstairs, her gaze fell on one of the dead men—the young man who had masturbated on her. She could not explain why she felt sadness for him.

Krish picked up the dead woman's pistol and rushed down. He charged through the front doors, just in time to see the other guards sprinting to the house. He shot both of them before they even had a chance to fire a single round.

The girls were now being escorted outside the premises by Shamsher. Krish dragged the bodies inside and piled them up in the ground floor passage. He went to the kitchen and severed the gas cylinder pipe, and lit a fire a few feet away, giving himself just enough time to leave the house, and catch up with his buddy and the girls.

As the cylinders blew up with a tremendous bang and the flames began to engulf the house, Krish looked back and noticed two figures running from the outhouse, screaming in terror.

~

It was just before four in the morning when Gogoi stepped out of his house, dressed in a tracksuit and jogging shoes, for his morning run. Lost in his thoughts, he did not notice the diminutive, hooded figure who walked up from behind.

30

Mihir got the update he had been waiting for from Rehaan within minutes of the rescue. Nothing satisfied him more than a plan executed with no collateral damage, except for the superficial wound on Krish's shoulder. He then spoke to Rehaan, giving careful instructions.

'Are you sure?' asked a surprised Rehaan.

'Yes. At least, that is what I think it could be.'

'I have contacts who can help. I will get to it right away.'

Eager to tell Gogoi of Maymunah's rescue, he rang up the police officer, but got no response. He would call again later. Now, his eyes were on the road leading to the warehouse he planned to visit. Stationing himself across from it, Mihir was concealed from any vehicles passing by. It was getting dark; visibility was low. His gaze never wavered, for it was here that the trap would be sprung.

Night had fallen by the time the Monster, with his team of three men, arrived at the warehouse. The GPS tracker was accurate to about 100 metres and, so, a minor search would have to be mounted to locate the ex-major. The Monster decided to leave his vehicle on the main road, to prevent alerting their prey. The small dot on the Monster's screen was moving very slowly, as if searching for something. The man was wasting his time—the warehouse was empty except for rats and vermin.

The Monster's team began to move cautiously, off track, in the thicket of trees and undergrowth. A single pointsman was in front, followed by two 15 feet behind, with the Monster bringing up the rear. A classic diamond formation, ideal for taking on threats from all directions. Their weapons were JS 9-mm submachine guns.

Maalik was unaware of all this. As it is, he was uninterested in the details of the plan, but the Monster also did not tell him he was planning to call for help. Mihir was beyond the pale; so, the Monster had called in old favours. The result was that the three men in front were amongst the best there were.

Mihir noticed this movement from the moment the vehicle cautiously approached the warehouse. He saw that the four men were carrying submachine guns, their gait indicating a degree of training he had encountered many years ago—so, the Monster had called in reinforcements! Mihir saw him following confidently behind the trio in a diamond formation. These guys were taking no chances.

Using his second cell phone, Mihir sent a missed call and waited. Just then, his mobile buzzed. It was a call forwarded from his original phone—Gogoi calling.

'Hello.'

It wasn't Gogoi.

'Who is this?' asked Mihir.

'This is the SHO of the Bondhuroh Sadar police station.'

Mihir was suddenly wary. 'What are you doing with his phone and how did you get this number?'

'Gogoi is a bachelor with no known relatives. We did not know whom to contact till we found your number in his emergency contact list. May I know who is speaking?'

'I am Mihir, his friend. Why? What's wrong?'

'I have some bad news. Gogoi was shot outside his house in the early hours of the morning today as he stepped out for his jog.'

'Is he okay?' asked Mihir, dreading the answer.

'He was shot from a distance of 20 feet. Apparently, the gunman was waiting for him. He fired thrice—two bullets hit him in the midsection and the third hit him in the head. The assailant left, assuming he was dead. Gogoi was rushed to the hospital by neighbours who heard the firing. Doctors pulled out one bullet that was lodged in his spine. The second one, luckily, only ruptured his small intestine and exited his body from the back. The one fired at his head did the most damage. He barely survived; he is in a coma,' said the SHO, solemnly.

'Thank you for telling me. I will come over as soon as possible.'

'One more thing,' said the SHO. 'The man who shot Gogoi left an odd-looking earring on his body. It is silver-coated and looks like a hideous skull.'

Mihir went still. After a moment, he said, 'Thanks, I will stay in touch.'

All this while, Mihir had not taken his eyes off the group in front, which was now deep on the rough track that led to the warehouse. He crossed the road and followed them on the track, keeping a safe distance, waiting for the right moment to strike.

The thick vegetation and tree cover shielded the warehouse completely from the road. The distance between both was about 300 metres. Unknown to the Monster's group, another team had beaten them to the warehouse and lay in wait. These men belonged to a covert security establishment and had credible inputs that a man they had presumed dead many years ago was likely to visit the site they had now occupied. He was to be taken alive, if possible.

These men, sixteen in number, were well trained in covert and counterinsurgency operations. Each soldier carried with him a Glock-19, which fired a 9x19–mm Parabellum round, and carried a magazine of 17 rounds. Each man carried two extra magazines, other than the one loaded in the pistol.

Six of the men, including their officer, carried an IWI Tavor submachine gun, which fired a similar round as the Glock, with up to 900 rounds a minute. The other ten men were armed with the FN SCAR-L version of assault rifles that had an effective range of 500 metres and fired 600 rounds a minute. Each carried three spare magazines. Their weapons had matching night sights and helmet-mounted displays.

They had another weird contraption—a small robotic vehicle like a miniature Mars Rover, that was moving around the warehouse. The controller was mimicking the movement of a man in search of something. Weirder still was a mobile, Mihir's, strapped on its back, with the location function switched on. The team was deployed in a classic ambush position, with a firing team, a covering team and lookouts. The killing ground was to be in front of the warehouse. The lookouts had already picked up the movement of the Monster's team and had alerted the soldiers.

Three hundred metres away, Mihir's mobile location was being tracked by the Monster. The dot continued to move at a steady pace, would stop in between and begin to move again. Something about the pattern of this movement drew the Monster's attention and made him suspicious. It was too regular and too even-paced. Since the time he had switched on the tracker, the dot had moved twice in a circle. It was beginning to move in the same circuit again. An empty warehouse would not have taken more than five minutes to search. He stopped dead in his tracks and told his men to halt. They got down on their knees in a firing position. He listened intently; it was too quiet. He asked his men to change direction—instead of heading to the warehouse from the north, they decided to come in from the east.

Mihir, who was following the Monster, took cover in the dense undergrowth when the team in front of him stopped. They seemed to have become suspicious. It was quite dark on the track. After five minutes, they got up, changed direction and melted into the thick shrubbery. Mihir lost sight of them for a brief period, but he now knew where they were headed, so he followed suit, staying about 20 yards behind them, khukri drawn, silent as a ghost.

The Monster had knowingly begun to lag behind; he was sure that this was a trap. Physical bravado was not one of his qualities. Survival was important. He had no loyalty to the guys in front—they were cannon fodder. It was important that he lived to fight another day. Mihir was turning out to be an extremely dangerous foe.

This shift by the man in the rear, whom Mihir recognized as the Monster, puzzled him initially. He then realized that the Monster was planning a quick exit. Ignoring the three in front, Mihir continued to stalk the Monster.

The officer commanding the ambush party had been informed by the lookouts that the four had disappeared into the undergrowth. For the lookouts, they were out of sight. Quickly mapping their new location, the officer figured out the exact point at which they would exit the undergrowth and come out in the open ground in front of the warehouse. He redeployed the ambush. As per his calculations, the enemy would break out into the open in about three minutes. His men were ready.

The pointsman among the three men in the Monster's group raised his hand for those following to slow down. They were now nearing the end of the treeline. The first man halted and then stepped out into the open. He was moving cautiously at a crouch, his weapon sweeping an arc in front of him. His other two colleagues followed him at a distance, in similar postures, sweeping the area in a nine o' clock and three o' clock direction. The Monster did not follow. He waited at the edge of the treeline. Mihir was a few yards behind, at a safe distance. The last thing he wanted was to get stuck in a firefight. The stage was set. Everything would depend on the action in front.

Nothing would have pleased the officer more than giving orders to kill the trio who just emerged from the thicket. But there were protocols to be followed. They would be given a chance to surrender. He raised his left hand and closed his fist—a signal to his men. The entire area in front of the warehouse was flooded with searchlights deployed at selected points. The three men froze, like deer caught in the headlights.

The officer shouted his warning to the three to lay down their weapons and surrender. Once in English and then in Hindi. There was a tense silence for ten seconds. Then, understanding dawned on the trio—they would be dead even before they fired the first shot. They quietly dropped their weapons and raised their hands.

The officer leading the operation suddenly grasped that the fourth man—the prize catch—had managed to slip past their net. Cursing under his breath, he ordered his men to begin a search operation to fish him out.

Mihir saw the action unfold from a distance, as the Monster slipped nimbly away into the dense tree cover.

Mihir retraced his steps the way he had come. He had an idea of where the Monster was headed—further east into the trees—where he would use the poor visibility and the dense undergrowth to hit the main road at a safe distance. Mihir assumed he would then call for a fast getaway. The man was armed and dangerous.

Mihir went straight for the road. He stayed within the cover of the jungle and turned east, in the direction that the Monster had taken. The thick shrubbery made it impossible to move at a fast pace. Seeing his adversary disappear into the brush, Mihir estimated that his speed, despite the difficult ground, would be around 3 to 4 kilometres per hour. Assuming that the Monster was moving in a curve, first heading east and then turning north towards the road, the maximum curvature of the path he would take would be 400–500 metres. The time for him to reach the road would be, at most, between seven and nine minutes. Mihir was counting the seconds in his head as he sped towards his target. By the time he reached the road, he was three minutes down and had four minutes left.

The Monster was quite confident about escaping the search party. He was angry at Mihir, because this was the second time he had failed to catch the ex-major, but was sobered up by the fear of punishment from his boss. Where was the Major? The coward must have been hiding behind the soldiers, he thought. If only he would come out in front—the pleasure of killing him would be most satisfying.

Mihir was now moving carefully, on the lookout for the Monster. His adversary knew how to use the ground—he had been on the run for more than a decade. Mihir slowed his speed to a crawl, moving from cover to cover. Any moment now.

The Monster had almost reached the road, but did not break out of the cover. Not just yet. He wasn't too concerned about the car they had left behind—it was just a rental and would lead to a dead end. His gut told him he was still not out of danger. He had the ex-major to reckon with. So, the Monster stood by a tall, twisted tree and listened hard. His weapon was slightly raised, ready to spray the area with bullets.

It was pitch black in the jungle. The Monster was usually cool, even under extreme pressure. But he had to admit, he was scared of the ex-major. It fuelled his anger against the soldier even more.

Was that a glint of metal that caught his eye? Mihir could not tell. It was gone in a flash. Sure that he had spotted something, he concentrated on the source of his distraction, never looking at the spot directly but keeping it in the corner of his gaze. Nothing moved, the visibility barely a few feet. Then he heard it. The whisper of a shuffle; a careful lifting of feet to readjust one's position. The source was barely 10 feet away. Mihir circled around, keeping the source between himself and the road. He was looking at a tall tree with a weirdly twisted trunk. Mihir stopped when the tree was directly between him and the road. There, literally hugging the trunk, stood the shadow of the man he was looking for. Knowing the Monster was armed, Mihir decided to play it differently.

He knelt down slowly, opening his palm and searching the ground beneath his feet with it. He felt a rock large enough to fit his hand. Picking it up in his right hand, with the khukri in his belt, he rose very slowly, then took a step back and threw the rock hard at the centre of the shadow. Then, Mihir broke out of cover and careened headlong into the man at 12 metres per second.

It was devastating for the Monster. He had just begun to turn around at the sound behind him, ready to fire, when the rock hit him. It cracked his lowest rib. He flinched in pain, but that did not stop him from letting loose a volley from his submachine gun. Anticipating this, Mihir had taken a step to the Monster's left, ducking the murderous fire.

Keeping up the momentum, he hit the Monster with the full force of his body on his left side. The impact of Mihir's 90-kg frame crashing into him was such that it lifted the Monster clean off the ground, 4 feet into the air. Mihir held the hot barrel of the submachine gun, ignoring the singeing pain in his palm, and twisted it hard. It broke the Monster's grip on the weapon, which Mihir threw away. He watched as the Monster regained his balance and got up to face his adversary. At 5 foot 6, he was much smaller than the 6-foot-3 Mihir. But that did not stop him from charging at the ex-major, a long knife held in front, screaming in anger.

Mihir waited, then stepped aside as the half-crazed man lunged at him. Mihir gripped his knife hand, turned the elbow and pierced him in the heart with an upward blow. Using the knife like a handle attached to the end of an object, Mihir lifted him off the ground and threw him on his back, keeping the knife embedded deep in the Monster's heart. He twisted it further, as the Monster gurgled and spat blood. He tried to say something, but no sound came as he began to drown in his own gore.

Mihir watched emotionlessly as the piercing stare lost focus and the man's eyes glazed over in death. He took off the Monster's mask; one look at his face and he knew why he was known by that moniker. A moment later, the officer and his team crashed through the undergrowth. They found Mihir standing over the dead man.

'Thought he'd got away,' said the officer.

'Not this time.'

'Pity we couldn't take him alive. Thanks to you, sir, he won't trouble us anymore,' remarked the officer, as he returned Mihir's cell phone.

'I am not a "sir". I was court-martialled.'

'Not to us, sir. You never were,' said the officer, as he watched Mihir melt into the darkness.

31

That very morning, not too far away, a domestic flight landed at the Gopinath Bordoloi International Airport. It carried Maymunah, with Yudhvir escorting her back home. After the dramatic rescue of the girls from the farmhouse, they were discreetly handed to the police.

The farmhouse had been completely gutted in the blaze and fire department authorities, sifting through the wreckage, were puzzled to find seven charred bodies inside. Autopsies would reveal the real cause of death, but that would be much later.

On learning of the fire, the owner did a remarkable job of keeping his emotions under check. He knew the fire was no accident. The girls were missing—so they had been rescued by someone. His profuse gratitude to the authorities who had controlled the fire was matched equally by the hysterical rage he unleashed on his business associate, based at Lal Bangla hundreds of kilometres away, after the fire brigade had left his luxurious premises in Lutyens' Delhi.

Maalik, though polite on the phone, had his own frustrations to deal with. He had faced one defeat after another. To add to his pile of mounting woes, the ticker flashing on a local TV channel during the morning news told the story of a dramatic anti-terror operation that had led to the capture of three militants of a known outfit and the death of a fourth, a terrorist whom the authorities had presumed dead a decade ago. Maalik knew who the dead terrorist was and the man responsible for his death.

Maalik's reaction to the latest setback was stoically epicurean—an apathetic acceptance of defeat, temporary though it may be. But before drowning himself in an orgy of sex and drugs, he set in motion a plan that would relieve his distress. The bastard would have to be lured into his lair, where it would be easy to kill him. For that, he needed bait, sufficiently important to draw his adversary's attention. Drawing satisfaction from that thought, Maalik turned to the two young women who now warmed his bed.

~

As the morning gave way to a sunny afternoon, Mihir met up with Yudhvir in Guwahati. 'She is on her way home,' said Yudhvir, as Mihir shook his hand. 'Pity, someone so young was exposed to the trauma.'

They were seated in a fast-food joint on the road leading to the airport. Mihir was savouring his first meal of the day.

'She's safe, physically. Emotionally, her scars may take a long time to heal,' responded Mihir.

'She kept asking about a boy called Kankan.'

'Her boyfriend, who got her into this shit in the first place,' explained Mihir.

'The boy needs a sound thrashing. He nearly got her killed.'

'You're too late. He was murdered. So were his parents, who I am convinced knew nothing,' Mihir said. 'These guys and these women! Oh yes, there are women too and they are as guilty as the men, involved in some serious human trafficking of minors through a sophisticated network. What you witnessed was just one tentacle of many that are spread far and wide across our nation. Kids are traded like commodities for sex, pornography, begging, child labour, drug peddling. In some cases, they are kidnapped, but many times they are sold by parents who are desperately poor and don't mind selling one child for a few rupees to feed others. Poverty and hunger are evil twins, Yudi. They weaken the most moral hearts.'

'Well, too bad. Time to get back home.'

'No.'

'You want to take them on, all on your own?' asked Yudhvir, looking at his boss. 'You can't change the world, sir. Tell the cops.'

'No,' said Mihir again.

'Why is it so important to you?'

'These are the people who murdered Chris and nearly killed a friend. A decent friend.'

'So, what next?' asked Yudhvir, resignedly.

'I have them riled up enough. I still don't know who the head of the snake is and where he is hiding, though I have spoken to him. So, we wait,' said Mihir, as he took a bite off his hot dog, knowing it would be some time before his next meal. 'Eat up, you will need your strength,' he told Yudhvir.

～

It was late in the evening when Mwhaay walked up to his boss, who was now lounging next to the pool. Maalik's mind was back to its cunning best.

'She's here,' Mwhaay said softly in his ear.

Maalik took a drag of his Cohiba Behike, savouring the taste of one of the most exclusive cigars in the world. 'Just a few thousand of these were ever made. This was gifted by an overseas friend,' he said, as he beckoned for the woman to be brought in.

'Welcome, madam, to my humble abode. I trust you had a pleasant journey?' asked Maalik sarcastically.

'Why am I here?' said Genevieve, walking in.

'What a question. You should have taken him with you while you had the chance. He has caused me much trouble and you should help me put a stop to it.'

'Why should I help you? You had my husband killed, you bastard! You promised not to harm him.'

'Husband, eh? Sad, but then, he shouldn't have meddled in my business. He should have listened to you. He had to pay the price.'

'I would have convinced him eventually. I needed more time. He would have been out of here in a few months. He would have been alive today! I loved him,' said Gene, angrily, as tears welled up in her eyes.

'Well, what's done is done. Will you help us?'

'Fuck you!'

'Somehow, I knew you would say that,' said Maalik, as he slid some photographs across to her. They were images of an older couple, in their fifties, as well as a young man and woman in their twenties. The subjects were unaware that they were being photographed. 'A fresher is warranted once in a while. Don't you agree?'

Gene went pale. 'You bastard! I will kill you if you harm them.' She lunged at Maalik full of rage, but was held back by Mwhaay.

'Hey, who said anything about harming your parents, brother and sister? But then, it would all depend on you.'

'What do you want?' Gene asked, defeat ringing loud in her voice.

'Now, that's more like it. It's simple, actually. Invite him to my home,' said Maalik.

'And why would he come?'

'Because you will convince him to. Remember, you are a hostage.'

~

At the other end of the city, Mihir and Yudhvir were still seated in the restaurant, each with a cup of cappuccino, when Mihir's phone buzzed. It was Rehaan. 'About time,' quipped Mihir.

'Yudi with you?' asked Rehaan.

'Yes.'

'You are going to need him. I have some of the information you had asked for. There are still gaps.'

'Go ahead.'

'It seems that the subject you had asked me to investigate owns a successful ad and modelling agency.'

'I am aware of that and—'

'And she also works in a financial firm,' said Rehaan, cutting Mihir off mid-sentence.

'Why would she work in a financial firm when she owns a successful company of her own?' prompted Mihir.

'Well, as per the Companies Act, each company is required to have at least one woman as a director. A private company is supposed to have at least two directors. This firm has two, including Gene.'

'Nothing out of the ordinary, but something raised your suspicions?'

'Absolutely. After calling friends in the government, I came to know that this firm is under their scanner for the past couple of years for some sort of financial fraud. Remember when I told you about the boss of the HR firm Yudi was tracking? I suspect this is another one of those institutions—false fronts—to launder large sums of ill-gotten cash from the human trafficking business.'

'Who is the other director?' asked Mihir.

'Does the name Abdul Rehman Afzal ring a bell?'

'No. Why would it?'

'Well, since you are in that part of the country and this man is a reputed local politician. He is considered a kingmaker; commands a lot of respect. People call him Maalik.'

'Connect the dots for me, Rehaan, even though I have a fair idea where this is going.'

'I had someone snoop into the firm's premises to search the offices of both directors. He found nothing out of the ordinary except for one photograph, kept in a locked drawer. You can see it on your WhatsApp now.'

'Thanks, Rehaan,' said Mihir.

'One more thing. Chris and Gene were never married. No marriage is registered under their names, at least not in the local registrar's office in his or her hometown.'

After the call, Mihir looked at the snap sent by Rehaan—a group of stylishly attired young girls standing outside a mansion. The girl in the centre drew Mihir's attention. She was recognizable, even though she was much younger then. Standing next to her was a man he did not recognize. Mihir googled the name of the politician Rehaan had given him. It was the same man. The pieces of the jigsaw were coming together.

'I knew you would call back,' said Rehaan once Mihir did so. 'The man's house is called Lal Bangla. I have pinged the location to you. Also, my contact from Kochi just called. Gene has disappeared.'

'Thanks. And stop gloating, you bum,' said Mihir sportingly to his old colleague.

'So, now what?' asked Yudhvir.

'Wait for the curtains to rise for the final act.'

32

The call Mihir had been waiting for came at 5.37 p.m. The sun had dipped just below the horizon, bathing the sky above in a fading orange glow. Its light was not enough to reach the east, where the moon had risen above the hills—a silver sliver in a cool nautical twilight.

'Mihir,' the voice said, sounding exhausted and scared.

'Gene?' he asked. He needed to confirm it, even though he knew who it was.

'Yes. It's me.'

'Where are you?'

'In a house. I am being held by …'

Midway through her sentence, her voice was seemingly choked into silence.

'I think that's enough,' came a voice from the background. Mihir recognized it instantly—the voice that had spoken to him earlier. The phone was snatched away from Gene and Maalik came on the line.

'We speak again; though I would have preferred not to have had this conversation at all. I wished you dead.'

'Yes, and you spared no effort in ensuring your plans bore fruit. They failed, just like the male floozy you sent to kill me,' said Mihir.

'Look at the video I have sent you,' said Maalik, ignoring his words.

Mihir opened the video he had just received—it had been shot using a mobile camera. The visuals were of a cell of some sort, with a bed, and a wash basin and toilet beside it. Gene was seated in the centre of the miserable room; her hands and feet tied to an iron chair. The front of her blouse was ripped open, exposing her breasts. Behind her stood a short man, with a blade in his right hand. Then the camera zoomed in for a closer shot of Gene, just as the man standing behind her placed the blade across her throat, as if to cut it. Mihir recognized the blade instantly—it belonged to Chris. He was looking at the man who had murdered him. Mihir cursed under his breath.

'I don't have to tell you that the throat only comes in the end. I believe breasts make a fine pouch for keeping tobacco moist. But, before I do that, I will savour the body they are attached to, to my heart's content,' said Maalik, venomously.

Mihir remained silent.

'Cat got your tongue? I was hoping to hear something like "don't you dare touch her or I will kill you".'

Becoming serious again, Maalik continued, 'Your silence shows the hopeless situation that you and your woman friend here find yourselves in.'

'What do you want?' Mihir asked slowly.

'You, Major sahab! You! Be there at the university main gate by 6.30 p.m. You will be picked up. Time you enjoyed my hospitality. Come alone, unarmed. I may then consider releasing your friend.'

The line went dead.

'What will you do now?' asked Yudhvir, who couldn't help but overhear.

'Do as he says,' said Mihir, deep in thought.

'I know what I have to do. He doesn't know I am here. We have a chance.'

'I am banking on it.'

~

The SUV arrived at 6.30 on the dot—the rear door opened and Mihir was beckoned inside. He was then blindfolded and handcuffed, his hands behind his back. The barrel of a weapon, most probably a pistol, was shoved painfully into the back of his neck.

Yudhvir, now on Mihir's bike, stood across the highway and watched the SUV head back the way it had come. He followed at a safe distance.

It was dark by the time they reached the junction where the highway met the unmetalled road to Lal Bangla. The vehicle turned on to the narrow path and began to climb gradually. Yudhvir stopped short of the turn, allowing for some distance. He looked up at the sky—a quarter moon had risen high over the eastern horizon; its cool white light shone across a clear, cloudless sky, illuminating the narrow track very clearly, but not quite intensely enough to penetrate the thick canopy that covered the path like an arched roof.

Yudhvir then began to move cautiously on the narrow road, headlights switched off, the bike in low rev. He knew that the vehicle he had been following was heading to the same house that Rehaan had indicated. The road wound around the hilly terrain for nearly 15 kilometres before reaching the politician's mansion.

Three kilometres short of his destination, Yudhvir decided to ditch the bike and move on foot. He dropped it in the shadow of a large tree and began to move uphill on a direct path to the house where Mihir had been taken.

The vehicle had stopped at the main gate. Mihir couldn't figure out much through his blindfold, but from the sounds of footsteps, voices and the time taken, he knew that mandatory security checks were being carried out by the guards on the left of the main gate. Once inside, the vehicle continued its movement. Mihir surmised that they were now on a paved road. Five minutes later, they halted. Mihir was led by his arm into the main lounge, where his blindfold was removed. The handcuffs, however, remained. His eyes, hurt by the bright light, narrowed.

'Ah! So, finally, we meet in person,' said a voice behind him. Mihir turned around and saw a short, portly man observing him keenly.

'This short meeting isn't going to end too well for you,' said Maalik. 'I wanted to look into the eyes of the man who has been the cause of so much trouble and see the fear of death in them.'

'You had said you would consider releasing Gene if you had me.'

'I've changed my mind. Maybe I won't release her after all,' said Maalik.

Then, addressing his goons, he said, 'Take him below to his woman friend. Let them share their last moments together. I am sure they have much to talk about.'

Then, looking at Mihir, he added, 'I would have finished you both, but I am expecting guests. We can't inconvenience them.'

Mihir was blindfolded again and taken through a maze of corridors. It seemed to be a large establishment. He could hear servants' voices and scurrying feet, paying little attention to a handcuffed and blindfolded man. He could smell food being cooked as he went past the kitchen, before being pushed down a flight of steps that led to a dim corridor. Here, the air was dank and reeked of filth. A door was opened, he was pushed inside, and it slammed shut behind him.

'Is it you?' a weak voice called out. Gene, he recognized.

Still blinded by the coarse scarf tied over his eyes, Mihir turned in the direction of the voice and walked towards it. A few steps later, his shins scraped against the side of the cot. A hand touched him.

'It's me,' he said, without feeling.

'Thank God.'

Mihir sat down on the ground. As he lowered himself to his knees, he moved his hands first under and then forward of his buttocks. Leaning on his back, he folded his legs and slid his hands out from underneath to bring them in front of him. He reached up and took the blindfold off, rubbed his eyes and allowed them to adjust to the darkness. Reaching inside his belt, he took out a paper clip from a crevice, opened it up, then pushed it inside the lock. He felt the ridged bar slide back to unlock the handcuffs.

Mihir reached out and helped Gene get up. She was still groggy and unclothed above the waist. He retrieved her ripped blouse that had been thrown next to her cot and handed it over. 'Thank you for coming,' she said, embarrassed.

'Did they harm you?'

'No.'

'They never meant to. You were just the bait.'

'When did you know?' she asked after a minute.

'When I read your nickname in a diary, in a list where it didn't belong. "Kid". Isn't that what Chris called you lovingly, because of your age difference?'

'I didn't mean for him to die. It was a horrible mistake. I am so sorry. I loved him. It was a matter of only a couple of months.'

'But he died. Why did you do it, Gene?'

She started to cry. Mihir couldn't figure out if it was genuine or an act. He didn't care. Nothing could justify his friend's death.

'Do you know a fear that claws at your heart, day and night? A numbing dread? A bottomless pit in your gut? You think sleep might help, but it lurks in your mind, ready to pounce when you wake up. It wears you down to the bone. The fear of being shamed in front of family and friends; the fall from grace as a celebrity; the media; the endless trolling. What choice did I have?'

'How did it begin?' he asked, tonelessly.

'I had made quite a name as a model within a couple of years of being in the industry. Fashion houses were lining up to sign me. There were film offers, as well. I was signed up for one such venture. We arrived for a shoot in the Northeast. The cast was invited to a party in this house. Drugs and alcohol flowed freely. I resisted initially, but quickly became the odd one out. In a moment of weakness, I gave in. What harm could a little bit of fun do?'

'And?'

'I didn't know how long the revelry went on. But when I woke up, I was in a king-sized bed, completely naked, with three strangers, two men and a woman. Shocked and still groggy, I dressed quickly and stumbled out. Over the next few days, we finished our work and left for home. Months later, when I had almost forgotten about that night, I received a short video by email, sent by an unknown person, with a number mentioned under the sender's address. I opened it and my world crashed around me.'

She paused, trying to look at Mihir in the darkness.

'Are you familiar with the term ménage à quatre?'

She continued without waiting for an answer.

'That was the caption of the video. I didn't have to look up the meaning; the video made sure of that. It would have put any porn flick to shame. I was humiliated and scared like never before. What I had done under the influence of drugs and booze that night in bed with complete strangers was now evident. I had no control, but who would believe me? This video would have ruined me, my reputation. Feeling trapped, I rang the number in the email. There was no answer. I tried it many times. I knew I was being left to sweat. Life took on a whole new meaning. I was terrified of finding the clip uploaded on some seedy porn site or on social media.'

'Why did you not go to the police?' asked Mihir, beginning to feel an ounce of sympathy.

'I was terrified. I did not tell anybody. It was unthinkable. Just when I thought I would go out of my mind, I received a call from that number. The caller gave specific instructions. As long as I did what they wanted, there would be no problem.'

'So, they helped you establish a modelling agency and an advertising firm, which was actually a front to traffic gullible girls for commercial sexual exploitation.'

'Oh, it was much more than that. The girls would come to me from various parts of the country. They were then auctioned off to the highest bidder, from anywhere in the world. It was all done online. The girls were bought for obscene amounts. Then we would arrange transportation to the chosen destination.'

'And the cash flow from these proceeds would be routed to the financial firms that were merely fronts for money laundering. You were a director in one of them,' he finished for her.

'I was trapped many times over,' she said sadly. 'Chris had no idea when we fell in love. I looked at him as a knight in shining armour; that he would save me from these monsters.'

'What happened?'

'A few months into our relationship, he proposed. I was so excited and happy. But before we began our new life together, I wanted to tell him everything. I should have known though, that these bastards would have other ideas. They threatened to kill Chris if I even thought about marriage or telling him the truth. They couldn't risk their venture. But I knew the army would protect him. I went ahead and told him everything.'

'What did he say?'

'He was quite upset. He didn't speak to me for days. He felt cheated. I understood and, fearful of hurting him more, I decided to end our relationship. But you knew Chris,' she said, remembering him with a smile. 'He would have none of it. He was thinking of an exit strategy. He was fine with the video; he knew it wasn't my fault. He could live with that and the embarrassment, and he felt that people would move on and forget all about it. But he wanted me to come clean about the other business to the authorities and help them stop this racket. He thought the punishment would lessen if I became an informer. He was quite sure of it.'

'I think so too.'

'I dithered. He coaxed me, but I was scared. He then started investigating by himself. He asked me for help, but I knew very little. I hadn't a clue about how it all worked. Nevertheless, he managed to piece together a lot of information, using local contacts whom he knew from his earlier tenure here. The bosses knew he was getting too close. I was told to stop him at any cost. I begged him and promised to do whatever he said, even if that meant going to the police.'

'But they still went ahead and killed him.'

'They couldn't trust me. I think they just lost patience and lured him into a trap. These people are very powerful, Mihir.'

She fell silent, lost in thought.

'So, us being followed from the time we landed in Guwahati was also part of the plan?' Mihir asked. 'And it was you who planted the diary in the hut when you insisted on sleeping in there one last time?'

'Yes, it was a way for them to keep tabs, so I wasn't tempted to spill the beans. The whole plan began to unravel when you gave us the slip and stayed back to find Chris's murderer. And I am glad you did. As for the diary, yes, I stole it from Chris, to stop him from going any further. But when they killed him, I wanted revenge. That was the only way I could point you in their direction. Though the numbers made no sense to me, I realized they would to you. So, I left the diary in a place where you would find it,' Gene explained.

'Why not just give it to me?'

'It would have aroused your suspicions about me. Chris never talked about working with me.'

'And what about the diary I got in the graveyard, the one with your nickname in it?'

'I had no idea it existed. I was hoping you would take these people down without my name surfacing anywhere. But that was Chris's integrity—I think he sent it out to you after he discovered the one I took had gone missing. I desperately wanted you to kill those responsible, hoping that would also free me from their clutches.'

Just then, there were a series of light taps on the door. Mihir recognized them, so he rose and waited for the door to open. He could hear the lock being picked before the door swung open.

'That wasn't too difficult, was it?' said Yudhvir. The weak light from the corridor illuminated the inside of the cell. He saw Gene on the cot and Mihir standing next to it.

'About time,' said Mihir, looking at the forlorn figure on the cot. 'Are you coming with us? We don't have the whole day.'

'What will you do?' she asked.

'You can't just walk away from it all, Gene. You know how this will end.'

33

It was close to midnight and Mihir could still hear sounds emanating from the party. Yudhvir guided him and Gene to a flight of that stairs that led straight out into the open through a small trapdoor, barely enough to crawl through.

'Is this where you came from?' whispered Mihir.

'Yes, I found a small gap in between the wall and the ground while I was looking for a way in. I stumbled upon this door, more by mistake than design. I heard voices and recognized yours.'

'Good. We put Gene in a safe place and then get back to finish the job.'

'Lead on, sir,' said Yudhvir, aware of Mihir's incredible ability to innovate under tough conditions. Their training would take care of the rest.

When Mihir explained the plan, it seemed hare-brained, but his ideas were often audacious enough to work.

Yudhvir escorted Gene deep into the woods that surrounded the mansion, found a safe spot and told her to wait till he came back for her. He circled back to Mihir, who led him to the same cell they had just left. The younger man lay down on the cot and Mihir took his place on the floor. They waited.

It was nearly three in the morning when Maalik's men came for Mihir and Gene. The two who entered the cell did not expect any resistance, especially from a half-starved, exhausted woman and a handcuffed man. Had they noticed that the cell door was unlocked, they might have been saved some agony. The encounter was swift and brutal, lasting less than thirty seconds. In the end, the two guards were dead, their weapons now in the able hands of two former army men.

Mihir and Yudhvir quickly crossed the length of the corridor, went up the flight of stairs and then reached a large arched doorway that opened onto a huge quadrangle with a swimming pool. As they crept up quietly to the archway, they could hear music and loud conversation. Mihir peeked and saw at least four guards, armed with automatics, around the pool. Their boss, floating on a pool lounger, was in deep conversation with two men and a woman. Mihir had seen one of the men, who had a ponytail, and the woman outside the warehouse where he had rescued the women and children from the reefers. The other man was the one from the video of Gene's kidnapping—the one with Chris's knife.

To get to Maalik, they would have to cross the 20-foot-wide veranda and negotiate 10 feet of open space, before they made it to the pool. They would be dead even before they had a chance to cover half the distance. He signalled for them to withdraw; they retraced their steps back through the corridor in the basement, past the cells and out of the small trapdoor, into the open.

'We need to cut the power to the house. There are too many to take down in one go,' said the boss.

'I know where the main switch is,' said Yudhvir.

Meanwhile, Maalik, running low on patience, looked over Mwhaay's shoulders towards the archway, behind which, not a moment ago, Mihir had been taking cover.

'What's taking them so long?' he asked impatiently to no one in particular. The ponytailed guy, who was called Bonnet, then volunteered to go get the prisoners.

Mihir and Yudhvir had made good their exit from the rear of the house and were now moving towards the guardhouse at the front gate. They kept low in the undergrowth as the lawns surrounding the house and the outer perimeter were covered with night-enabled closed-circuit cameras, which were constantly monitored. The main electrical switch was in the guardhouse.

Inside the mansion, there was some commotion as Bonnet returned hastily, sweating, out of breath, scared. He described the scene that had greeted him in the cell.

Hearing the panicked speech, Maalik flopped from his lounger and paddled awkwardly to the edge of the pool. He then lifted himself out of the water and hurried to the cell as fast as his pudgy legs could carry him. His men lay dead, packed together on the narrow cot inside. What horrified and angered him was that they had been scalped—their severed hides lay on top of their faces like some macabre veil.

Maalik walked back through the corridor, head bent, seething with anger and fear. 'Get him and the woman to me, alive. I will make them pay for this,' he screamed at Mwhaay and Bonnet. 'Wake up the men. I want everyone out searching for them. Remember, I want them alive.'

The guardhouse was manned by two at the gate and one inside, who monitored the CCTV cameras. The main switch and the circuits that controlled the lights to the property were located in a small room that abutted the main one, kept secure by a locked steel door. All three guards were armed with automatic weapons. There was no way they could be taken out silently.

Mihir thought the two bodies in the cell would have been discovered by now. This was confirmed by the sudden flurry of activity in the house—all lights had come on and the guards were out in strength. The men on the perimeter and the gate had been alerted, and orders to mount a search were being barked back and forth.

Mihir knew that Afzal, or 'Maalik', would hide behind his men till he and Gene were found. He was quite sure they did not know about Yudhvir. That was an advantage. Getting to Maalik would involve cutting through his inner ring of four guards. Before that, Mihir would have to tackle most of the men that were now roaming the grounds. Too much blood. At the end of it, these men were just hired hands—unlike the ones they had scalped inside the cell, who presumably were part of his core team. Mihir was sure most had families to feed. He decided he would let them live; he only wanted the two at the top.

The guards at the gate were standing together, looking inside at the heightened activity. The man in the hut was still looking at the CCTV feed. So, the three were taken by surprise when the attack developed from outside the perimeter. The guard monitoring the cameras was knocked unconscious by Yudhvir, while Mihir kept watch on the pair at the gate, 30 feet away. Yudhvir took the keys lying on the table, opened the steel door and killed the lights to the estate. The black shroud forced everyone into silence; the only illumination was a quarter moon peeking through thick cloud cover. Yudhvir then cut up the wires, smashed the circuit boards and threw away the power switches. It was now impossible to get the lights back on, at least for a few hours.

The pair guarding the main gate rushed towards the hut to get the lights back on, but stumbled headlong into Mihir and Yudhvir. The encounter was short and swift, and Mihir was satisfied—they were merely unconscious, not dead.

Yudhvir's next move was to gain access to the house, fish out Maalik and take him down. He must be holed up somewhere secure. But to get inside would require a diversion to draw the guards away from the mansion's main entrance. He headed out into the trees that lined the perimeter wall. Using them as cover, he began to fire short bursts of automatic fire, making sure no one was hurt. The guards ducked instinctively and dived for the ground. They began to crawl towards the direction of the flashes. The guards let loose a murderous volley, but one with no fire discipline.

Yudhvir had, by now, moved out of harm's way. Mihir used the diversion to sprint across the front lawns, a weapon from one of the guards at the gate in his hands, to enter the house by the front door. But before entering, he punctured the tyres of both SUVs standing outside. There would be no fast getaways.

Inside the mansion, it was pitch black and quiet as a tomb. No effort had been made to switch on emergency lights, which Mihir realized was a deliberate ploy—the darker the house, the more difficult it would be to find them.

As Mihir's eyes adjusted to the darkness, his vision was aided by the meagre light from the night sky, reflecting off the water in the pool. There was no one on the ground floor. Maalik's four bodyguards and his three lieutenants had disappeared deep into the house. Yudhvir came up behind him, in a crouch, weapon drawn. Both stood still, ears straining to pick up a sound.

Mihir reckoned they would have taken up positions on the first floor, with their boss safe in a room above. It is always advantageous to dominate from a higher floor—you can observe and fire better. It would be foolish to try the stairs; the only way up was to bypass them.

The ex-army men took up supporting tactical positions in the open courtyard to scout for an alternate route. All the windows on the first floor opened out into the courtyard, providing a view of the swimming pool from each room. Then, there was a wide veranda with seating arrangements, where Mihir had first met Maalik. The roof was a sloping, red-tiled affair, which Mihir noticed was connected to the outer walls of the first floor. Luckily, the roof of the veranda was level with the first-floor windows. It was possible to scale up to the roof and enter the first floor through one of the windows.

The duo climbed up a rainwater drainpipe. They quickly shuffled to the end of the roof and, using the support of the wall, Mihir carefully stepped out with his left foot on to the narrow parapet, using his right foot as an anchor and arms spread out for balance; his automatic slung loosely across his shoulders.

With his left hand, he tried prying open the window. Mihir realized that it was a sliding window latch that was operated from inside the room. There was no chance of opening it. He then manoeuvred himself carefully, placing both feet on the narrow parapet. He observed that further ahead, the third window was slightly ajar—just enough to pry open with his fingers. He signalled for Yudhvir and stepped into the room.

Inside, he could make out the shape of the furniture. It was a living room. A door in one corner presumably led to a bedroom. Crossing quietly, they stood at the door, listening for any sounds. By now, the din outside had quietened down. Apparently, a search was being mounted. Mihir hoped he could finish the job before Gene was found.

But there was nothing to go off on—no sound, not even a whisper. He opened the door very quietly. Kneeling down, he looked through the gap between the door and the frame. It looked like a long corridor with rooms on both sides. Mihir saw the end of the corridor to his right and a flight of stairs leading down. Towards his left, the corridor ended within a few feet, with a wall and window in its centre.

The two stepped out quietly into the corridor. Kneeling, nerves taut, weapons ready, they covered either side of the corridor. Still no one. They advanced in a crouch, ready to support each other in case of a firefight in the confined space. Yudhvir, who was leading, signalled Mihir to stop with a raised fist. In that split-second, Mihir heard a shuffle, as if someone was getting ready to charge out from one of the rooms.

How could they know? Then it dawned on him—the CCTV cameras were possibly being monitored remotely, from inside one of the rooms. They hadn't been disabled completely. The ex-soldiers had been led into an ambush. Mihir turned towards the sound, ready, as Yudhvir continued to cover him, without taking his eyes off the end of the corridor where he had seen something.

Two figures rushed out from the door together—a momentary lapse of judgement; a fatal one. They should have staggered their move.

The two figures, Bonnet and Silki, realized that the doorway was too narrow, which slowed them down a little. That was enough for Mihir. Bonnet came out slightly off balance, charging and screaming. He lunged at Mihir, aiming for the heart, a long knife flashing in his right hand. Mihir sidestepped the charge, but not before the sharp edge of the blade scraped his left shoulder, tearing his T-shirt. Silki, meanwhile, followed a couple of steps behind, pistol in hand, ready to fire.

Yudhvir, who was in a crouch three steps ahead of Mihir, pivoted on his left knee. Staying low, he shot Silki in the head; her brains splattered on the wall behind her. The sound of gunfire was sharp and loud in the passage. One shot, one target. Yudhvir had turned back to his original direction even before the woman had flopped to the ground, dead. Hearing the screaming and the firing, one of the guards rushed up the stairs to the landing, stopped, knelt in a firing position and poked his head around the corner, looking for a target. Yudhvir turned around just in time to see the head poking around the wall and took just a second to shoot the man in the head. The guard dropped down with a thud and rolled down the stairs. Yudhvir waited. There was no further movement from the stairs.

Mihir, meanwhile, had pivoted on his right foot and was now facing Bonnet, who found himself staring at the wall. The ex-major fired a burst of three rounds at the man's midsection, completely shredding it. Three down. The odds had evened out considerably. The corridor fell into a deathly silence, the acrid smell of gunpowder was everywhere.

Still no sign of Maalik and Mwhaay, the snake, who would face his death for killing Chris. Mihir reckoned that both may have escaped from the front entrance, as they had been monitoring the cameras and had time to escape. But the vehicles were useless. They must be on foot. Not difficult to intercept them.

There was only one direction in which they could have travelled—the main highway. Any other direction would take them deep into the reserve forest, which was not a good idea at night.

To chase them, Mihir and Yudhvir would have to go through the men still prowling the compound, as well as the three positioned on the stairway. Mihir nodded to his younger colleague.

'We are not interested in hurting you,' Yudhvir announced. 'It is your boss and Mwhaay we want. We are giving you and your buddies three minutes to clear out. Go back to your families and no harm will come to you. But if you don't listen to us, we will have no choice but to kill you.'

Mihir began to examine the first floor, room by room. At first, there was no reaction to Yudhvir's announcement. Then, suddenly, came the sound of footsteps scampering down the stairs and running out. Yudhvir and Mihir followed at a crouch, weapons ready to fire. But it was unnecessary. The men had dropped their weapons and were making their way out of the main gate. They would be no more trouble.

As Yudhvir began to move past the main gate to look for the fugitives, Mihir stopped him. 'Why delay? Let's go get them; they couldn't have gone far,' said Yudhvir.

'Where do you think Afzal would feel the safest? Running across the forest, or somewhere in the house—safely locked up in one of the numerous rooms, till it is safe enough to venture out? He would want us to think he has escaped from here; wait for things to calm down and then resurface.'

'But where in the house? We have looked for him everywhere.'

'We have,' said Mihir. 'But not everywhere.'

'The basement where you were kept,' said Yudhvir, after a moment of reflection.

'Yes. Dark, dank, putrid. The dirty underbelly of his opulent mansion. Who would think of going there? That's what he wants us to think. Clever.'

'Why has he not called the cops?'

'Because the cops would have more questions than answers, especially if they come across the stuff in the basement.'

'Yes, that peculiar stench from the basement was possibly that of a meth lab.'

'And the other cells are packed with women, completely doped out with drugs. His play arena.'

'Can you get the mains back on?' asked Mihir.

'Yes, give me a few minutes.'

Yudhvir rushed behind the guard hut, reconnected a few wires and pushed a lever up. The lights came on with full intensity. He and Mihir re-entered the house, retracing the steps the latter had taken blindfolded, till they reached the stairs that led down to the basement. They waited, crouched, weapons at shoulder height, eyes scanning the dark corridor. The only light came from the kitchen behind them. If Maalik was hiding in one of the cells, Mwhaay would be in the corridor guarding it, hidden in the dark part of the passage. Mihir stopped and quietly told Yudhvir what to do next.

Down in the dungeon, Mwhaay felt, rather than saw, movement at the top. There were two of them; he had thought the ex-major was alone. The Snake had been very impressed—this guy was far better than anyone he had encountered, even compared to the officer he had killed. He hadn't taken the bait and had come back. He deserved respect and so Mwhaay was being extra cautious.

He listened hard—no movement, no shuffling of feet, no breathing. Then, Mwhaay heard a faint creak behind him. Somebody was opening the trap door. He had been outflanked.

In that instant, Mwhaay took his chance and rushed out in the direction of the kitchen, climbing the stairs two at a time, firing his automatic in short bursts, hoping to keep his opponent's head down till he reached the top of the stairs.

Mihir had expected that. Had he turned towards Yudhvir, The Snake would have stood no chance, since the steps to the trap door were too steep and his angle of fire would have been too high. Mihir was waiting for him, having taken cover behind the wall of the archway that connected the pantry to the landing.

The moment Mwhaay reached the landing, Mihir stepped out and, with his left hand, pushed the barrel away. Using his right hand, he hit the man's forehead with the base of his palm. Mwhaay was expecting an attack, but the speed and the ferocity took him by surprise. He landed on his back, immobilized for a brief second. Mihir took the weapon from Mwhaay's grasp and threw it to one side.

The Snake quickly recovered, staggering a little as he got back to his feet. He took out Chris's dagger, shifted his weight on his front foot, and levelled it to Mihir's midsection.

'Recognize this? It was a pleasure to kill your friend. And now, I am going to carve you up with his knife,' he hissed.

Mihir waited for the attack—he knew his opponent was fast, but for the knife to work, he would need momentum. He leaned a little on his back foot, like the pulling back of a bowstring before its release.

A second later, Mwhaay uncoiled and catapulted himself at his opponent, the knife aimed at Mihir's throat. But the force lifted him clean off his feet, so he lost his balance, which was an essential part of any attack.

Mihir, who was waiting for the move, shifted his body weight on his left leg, leaned on it and lashed out with his right leg at the man's solar plexus. The Snake was fast, but Mihir was faster—his kick connected before the dagger's tip could get anywhere near his throat. Two hundred pounds of momentum was packed into 100 square centimetres—the surface area of a foot. The result was catastrophic for Mwhaay. The ferocity of the kick lifted him off the floor of the pantry and propelled him back down the stairs. Mihir heard the body landing with a crack—neck broken on impact. He was dead in an instant.

Mihir walked down the stairs to find Yudhvir holding Maalik by the scruff of his neck. Mwhaay was lying at their feet, his neck bent at a grotesque angle. Maalik, who had instilled fear in his opponents, now peed in his pants after watching the Snake's fate at the ex-major's hands.

He stared in fear as Mihir bent down and picked up Chris's knife. He grabbed Maalik by his collar and lifted him off his feet. Pointing the knife at his throat, Mihir looked him in the eye, his face barely inches away.

'Maalik' no more, Afzal started begging for mercy.

'You shouldn't have killed my friend. You do not deserve mercy,' Mihir said coldly, plunging the knife into his throat very slowly, twisting it by 90 degrees. Blood gushed out in spurts from Afzal's throat, and he began to sputter and choke, the metallic taste of blood in his mouth. Mihir stared into his eyes till there was no life left in them. He then dropped the dead man on the floor and walked up the stairs. Yudhvir followed.

Dawn was breaking as they stepped out into the open. It would be a glorious, sunny day, with not a cloud in the sky. The dark veil that had been cast on the Sol had finally been lifted.

Epilogue

It had been a long time since the Basumatary family had known happiness. They now got together to celebrate Rongali or Bohag Bihu, in the middle of April, heralding the arrival of spring. It had been a month since Maymunah had returned to her parents; now, her kidnapping was a distant nightmare, and she felt loved and secure.

The previous week, ASI Gogoi had awoken from his coma. He had found a grateful Ranjan Basumatary, his wife and children standing next to his bed, welcoming him back.

Later, Gogoi watched the news on the television in his hospital room. It had been a week, but the channels were still covering the fire that had mysteriously engulfed the mansion of the well-known politician, Abdul Rehman Afzal. The leader was found dead in the rubble, along with his bodyguards, who were burnt beyond recognition. When the cops reached the site, they found young girls, under the influence of drugs, roaming the premises for no apparent reason. Party loyalists were already terming it a conspiracy to malign the image of their martyred leader. The tamasha had begun.

Turning to his side table, Gogoi read the get-well card he had received that morning. It contained an open invitation to Gurugram. 'It would be an honour to host you,' the card read. It was signed 'M'.

Gogoi closed his eyes and smiled. He promised himself he would undertake that journey, for he hadn't ever been to that part of the country. But before that, he still had some unfinished business—he had to find those responsible for murdering Kankan's parents. He owed it to the boy's sister, the only surviving member of a once-happy family.

~

In Gurugram, Tuhin Khanna's office and residential premises had been raided the day the tip-off was received from Rehaan. The top cop in charge of the investigation spoke to him later, as a gesture of gratitude and respect. What had been unearthed was far bigger than even Rehaan's initial assessment. Tuhin's arrest—the first and definitely not the last—led to many more across the country. A massive racket involving powerful people had been unearthed. The culprits were being brought to justice.

'I am glad Chris got closure. The bastards have paid for his murder,' said Lt Col Sumer Singh, after Mihir had briefly narrated the events leading to the deaths of Mwhaay and Afzal.

'But not in the manner he would have preferred. Chris was always a stickler for rules. He would have gone to the authorities with the evidence,' Sumer added.

'Somehow, it would have all got buried for no one to find. The man was too powerful to be touched,' said Colonel Randhawa. 'We would have kept pursuing the matter endlessly. And it just becomes a file to be handed over from one officer to another. Other, more urgent matters take over.'

'One more thing,' said Mihir. 'When I had visited the scene where Chris and his source were murdered, I noticed a group of huts about 6 kilometres away, near some low hills towards the west.'

'Connected with the murder?' questioned Randy.

'No, but the huts afford an excellent vantage point from where the entire area could be monitored. My guess is the Snake used that as a hideout. Don't be surprised if you find a cache of ammunition and communication gear stored there, supplied by our adversaries from across the border to keep the pot boiling. It is worth a look.'

'Thanks, I know where I am headed next,' said Sumer, promising to stay in touch.

~

A week after the killing of Afzal, the retired Colonel Thomas Zachariah, recipient of the Sena Medal for gallantry, received a letter from an unknown source.

Dear Col. Zachariah,

I trust this letter finds you in the best of health and spirits. The loss of your son can never be compensated and the gaping hole he has left behind in your life cannot even be fathomed. But I sincerely hope you will draw some comfort from the fact that Chris sacrificed his life for his motherland, which he loved above all else and had sworn to protect.

I am proud to return to you a family heirloom. I was fortunate enough to come by this, which I am sure will proudly adorn your home, until the baton is passed on to the next generation of soldiers in your illustrious family.

With profound regards,
Yours sincerely,
Mihir.

Col. Zachariah read the letter to his wife, as well as Chris's younger brother, Jacob, his wife and their two adorable sons, as they sat in the living room over evening tea.

The colonel then got up slowly and took the Fairburn-Sykes to the mantelpiece, where it would stay till, as the writer had suggested, it would be passed on to the next soldier of the Zachariah bloodline.

Turning back, he gazed worriedly upon his daughter-in-law Gene, who was seated in a corner, staring vacantly outside the window.

Since her abrupt return from her trip to the Northeast, the local cops had visited her a number of times to question her about her job in the financial firm and her modelling agency. Both had closed down. The cops gave up after some time. She had been arrested but was out on bail. Investigation would continue despite her fragile state of mind for which a professional assessment was underway. Col Zachariah had also assured the authorities complete cooperation.

The colonel worried about Gene's health—she was pregnant with Chris's child. She had changed; her face hauntingly vacant. She was prone to bouts of crying and spent all her time at home—silent, not speaking to anyone. The colonel knew she loved Chris deeply and her grief was immeasurable. But, given time, she would heal. Maybe the baby would bring Chris back into her life and she would be happy once again.

About the Author

A former third-generation army officer with more than thirty-one years in uniform, Sachin Warty commanded a 230-year-old, storied armoured regiment.

After hanging up his spurs, he took inspiration from his grand-uncle, Dr A.W. Warty, and decided to keep the literary tradition alive with *Black Sol*, the first book in the Mihir thriller series. This book is set in India's beautiful and scenic Northeast, where the author had his last army assignment.

Besides being a writer, he is a keen artist who won several awards for his art as a child. His favourite mediums are watercolour, charcoal and pencil sketches. He lives with his wife and sons in Gurugram, India.

HarperCollins *Publishers* India

At HarperCollins India, we believe in telling the best stories and finding the widest readership for our books in every format possible. We started publishing in 1992; a great deal has changed since then, but what has remained constant is the passion with which our authors write their books, the love with which readers receive them, and the sheer joy and excitement that we as publishers feel in being a part of the publishing process.

Over the years, we've had the pleasure of publishing some of the finest writing from the subcontinent and around the world, including several award-winning titles and some of the biggest bestsellers in India's publishing history. But nothing has meant more to us than the fact that millions of people have read the books we published, and that somewhere, a book of ours might have made a difference.

As we look to the future, we go back to that one word— a word which has been a driving force for us all these years.

Read.